# The
# Art *of* Hearing
# Heartbeats

*a novel*

## Jan-Philipp Sendker

Translated from the German
by Kevin Wiliarty

OTHER PRESS
New York

Originally published in German as *Das Herzenhören* in 2002 by Karl Blessing Verlag, a division of Verlagsgruppe Random House GmbH, Munich, Germany. Published in English by agreement with Verlagsgruppe Random House GmbH.

Translation copyright © 2006 Kevin Wiliarty

Excerpt from "And how long?" from *Extravagaria* by Pablo Neruda, translated by Alastair Reid. Translation copyright © 1974 by Alastair Reid. Reprinted by permission of Farrar, Straus and Giroux, LLC.

Production Editor: Yvonne E. Cárdenas
Book design: Cassandra J. Pappas
This book was set in 12.3 pt Van Dijck by Alpha Design & Composition of Pittsfield, NH.

30 29 28 27 26 25

Library of Congress Cataloging-in-Publication Data

Sendker, Jan-Philipp.
  [Herzenhören. English]
  The art of hearing heartbeats : a novel / Jan-Philipp Sendker ; translated from the German by Kevin Wiliarty.
    p. cm.
  ISBN 978-1-59051-463-4 (trade pbk.) — ISBN 978-1-59051-464-1 (ebook)
1. Missing persons—Fiction.  2. Americans—Burma—Fiction.
3. Family secrets—Fiction.  4. Burma—Fiction.  I. Wiliarty, Kevin.  II. Title.

PT2721.E54H4713 2012
833'.92—dc23

                                        2011030638

*The*
Art *of* Hearing
Heartbeats

*For Anna, Florentine, and Jonathan*

*And in memory of Vivian Wong (1969–2000)*

Part One

# Chapter 1

THE OLD MAN'S eyes struck me first. They rested deep in their sockets, and he seemed unable to take them off me. Granted, everyone in the teahouse was staring at me more or less unabashedly, but he was the most brazen. As if I were some exotic creature he'd never seen before.

Trying to ignore him, I glanced around the teahouse, a mere wooden shack with a few tables and chairs standing right on the dry, dusty earth. Against the far wall a glass display case exhibited pastries and rice cakes on which dozens of flies had settled. Next to it, on a gas burner, water for the tea was boiling in a sooty kettle. In one corner, orange-colored sodas were stacked in wooden crates. I had never been in such a wretched hovel. It was scorching hot. The sweat ran down my temples and my neck. My jeans clung to my skin. I was sitting, getting my bearings, when all at once the old man stood up and approached me.

"A thousand pardons, young lady, for addressing you so directly," he said, sitting down at my table. "It is most impolite, I know, especially since we are unacquainted, or at least since you do not know me, not even in passing. My name is U Ba, and I have already heard a great deal about you, though I admit that this fact in no way excuses my forward behavior. I expect you find it awkward to be addressed by a strange man in a teahouse in a strange city in a strange land. I am exceedingly sensitive to your situation, but I wish—or should I be more frank and say I need—to ask you a question. I have waited so long for this opportunity that I cannot sit there watching you in silence now that you are here.

"I have waited four years, to be precise, and I have spent many an afternoon pacing back and forth out there on the dusty main street where the bus drops off the few tourists who stray into our city. Occasionally, on the rare days when a plane was arriving from the capital and when I could manage it, I would go to our little airport to keep futile watch for you.

"It took you long enough.

"Not that I wish to reproach you. Please, do not misunderstand me. But I am an old man and have no idea how many years remain for me. The people of our country age quickly and die young. The end of my life must be drawing near, and I have a story yet to tell, a story meant for you.

"You smile. You think I have lost my mind, that I am a bit mad, or at least rather eccentric? You have every right.

But please, please, do not turn away from me. Do not let my outward appearance mislead you.

"I see in your eyes that I am testing your patience. Please, indulge me. There is no one waiting for you, am I right? You have come alone, as I expected you would. Spare me just a few minutes of your time. Sit here with me just another little while, Julia.

"You are astonished? Your lovely brown eyes grow larger still, and for the first time you are really looking at me. You must be shaken. You must be asking yourself how on earth I know your name when we have never met before, and this is your first visit to our country. You wonder whether I have seen a label somewhere, on your jacket or on your little knapsack. The answer is no. I know your name even as I know the day and hour of your birth. I know all about little Jule who loved nothing better than to listen to her father tell her a story. I could even tell you her favorite one here and now: 'The Tale of the Prince, the Princess, and the Crocodile.'

"Julia Win. Born August 28, 1968, in New York City. American mother. Burmese father. Your family name is a part of my story, has been a part of my life since I was born. In the past four years I have not passed a single day without thinking of you. I will explain everything in due course, but let me first ask you my question: Do you believe in love?

"You laugh. How beautiful you are. I am serious. Do you believe in love, Julia?

"Of course I am not referring to those outbursts of passion that drive us to do and say things we will later regret, that delude us into thinking we cannot live without a certain person, that set us quivering with anxiety at the mere possibility we might ever lose that person—a feeling that impoverishes rather than enriches us because we long to possess what we cannot, to hold on to what we cannot.

"No. I speak of a love that brings sight to the blind. Of a love stronger than fear. I speak of a love that breathes meaning into life, that defies the natural laws of deterioration, that causes us to flourish, that knows no bounds. I speak of the triumph of the human spirit over selfishness and death.

"You shake your head. You do not believe in any such thing. You do not know what I am talking about. I am not surprised. Just wait. You will understand what I mean once I tell you the story I have borne in my heart for you these past four years. I require only a bit of your patience. The hour is late, and you are surely weary from your long journey. If you like, we could meet again tomorrow at the same time, at this table, in this teahouse. This is where I met your father, by the way, and, as a matter of fact, he sat right there on your stool and took up his tale while I sat exactly where I am now, astonished—I will admit—disbelieving, even confused. I had never before heard anyone tell a story like that. Can words sprout wings? Can they glide like butterflies through the air? Can they captivate us, carry us off into another world? Can they open the last secret chambers of our souls? I do not know whether words alone can accomplish these things, but, Julia, your father had a voice on that day such as a person hears maybe only once in a lifetime.

"Though his voice was low, there was not a person in this teahouse who was not moved to tears by the mere sound of it. His sentences soon took the shape of a story, and out of that story a life emerged, revealing its power and its magic. The things I heard that day left me as firm a believer as your father.

"'I am not a religious man, and love, U Ba, is the only force I truly believe in.' Those were your father's words."

U Ba stood up. He brought his open palms together in front of his chest, bowed ever so slightly, and left the teahouse in a few quick, light steps.

I watched until he disappeared into the bustle of the street.

No, I wanted to call after him. Do I believe in love? What a question. As if love were a religion you might believe in or not. No, I wanted to tell the old man, there isn't any force more powerful than fear. There is no triumph over death. No.

I sat hunched and slouching on my low stool, feeling that I could still hear his voice. It was tranquil and melodious, not unlike my father's.

Sit here with me just another little while, Julia, Julia, Julia . . .

Do you believe in love, in love . . .
Your father's words, your father's . . .

M y head ached; I was exhausted. As if I'd woken from a relentless and sleepless nightmare. Flies were buzzing all around me, landing on my hair, my forehead, and my hands. I didn't have the strength to drive them off. In front of me sat three dry pastries. The table was covered with sticky brown sugar.

I tried to sip my tea. It was cold, and my hand was shaking. Why had I listened to that stranger for so long? I could have asked him to stop. I could have left. But something had held me back. Just when I was about to turn away, he had said: Julia, Julia Win. I could never have imagined that the sound of my full name would unsettle me so. How did he know it? Did he in fact know my father? When had he seen him last? Could he know whether my father was still alive, where he might be hiding?

# Chapter 2

THE WAITER DIDN'T want my money.

"U Ba's friends are our guests," he said, bowing.

Still, I took a kyat bill out of my pants pocket. It was worn and filthy. Repulsed, I stuck it under the plate. The waiter cleared the table but ignored the money. I pointed to it. He smiled.

Was it too little? Too dirty? I set a larger, cleaner bill on the table. He bowed, smiled again, and left it, too, untouched.

Outside it was even hotter. The heat paralyzed me. I stood in front of the teahouse unable to take a single step. The sun burned on my skin, and the dazzling light stung my eyes. I put on my baseball cap and pulled it low over my face.

The street was full of people, yet all was oddly quiet. There were hardly any motorized vehicles to speak of. People were walking or riding bicycles. Parked at one intersection were three horse-drawn carriages and an oxcart. The few cars on the road were old Japanese pickups, dented and rusty, crammed with woven baskets and sacks to which young men clung for dear life.

The street was lined with low, single-story wooden shops with corrugated tin roofs, where vendors offered everything from rice, peanuts, flour, and shampoo to Coca-Cola and beer. There was no order—at least none I could discern.

Every second shop seemed to be a teahouse with patrons out front crouching on tiny wooden stools. Around their heads they wore red and green towels. In place of pants, the men wore what looked like wraparound skirts.

In front of me a couple of women had smeared yellow paste on their cheeks, brows, and noses and were smoking long dark-green cigarillos. They were all slender without seeming gaunt and moved with the same elegance and lightness I had always admired in my father.

And the way they stared at me, looking me square in the face and in the eye and smiling. I couldn't make heads or tails of those smiles. How threatening a little laugh can seem.

Others greeted me with a nod. What, did they know me? Had all of them, like U Ba, been expecting my arrival? I tried not to look at them. I walked down the main street as quickly as possible, my eyes fixed on some imaginary point in the distance.

I was homesick for New York, for the din and the traffic. For the unapproachable faces of pedestrians who took no interest in one another. I wanted to be back where I knew how to move and how to behave.

The road forked after about a hundred yards. I had forgotten where my hotel was. All I could see were the oversized bougainvilleas, taller even than the shacks they hid. The parched fields, the dusty sidewalks, the potholes deep enough to swallow basketballs. Wherever I turned everything looked strange and sinister.

"Miss Win, Miss Win," someone called.

Hardly daring to turn around, I glanced back over my shoulder. There stood a young man who reminded me of the bellhop at the hotel. Or of the skycap at the airport in Rangoon, or of the cabdriver. Or perhaps the waiter at the teahouse.

"Are you looking for something, Miss Win? Can I help you?"

"No, thank you," I started, not wishing to depend on this stranger. "Yes . . . my hotel," I said, desiring above all some place to hide, if only within the hotel room I had checked into that morning.

"Up the hill, here, to the right. Not five minutes away," he explained.

"Thank you."

"I hope you enjoy your time in our city. Welcome to Kalaw," he said, and stood, smiling, as I turned back around.

I n the hotel I walked silently and quickly past the smiling desk clerk, climbed the massive wooden staircase to the second floor, and sank down onto my bed.

The trip from New York to Rangoon had taken more than seventy-two hours. Then I had spent a whole night and half of the next day in a ramshackle bus crammed with people who stank, people wearing nothing but grimy skirts, threadbare T-shirts, and shabby plastic sandals. With chickens and squealing piglets. A twenty-hour journey on roads that bore little resemblance to streets. Dried-up river beds, if you ask me. All just to get from the capital to this remote little mountain village.

I must have slept. The sun disappeared; night fell. A semi-darkness filled the room. My suitcase lay unopened on the other bed. I looked around, my eyes wandering back and forth as if I needed to remind myself where I was. An old wooden fan hung from the ceiling high above me. The room was big, and the Spartan furnishings gave it a monastic air. Beside the door a plain cupboard, by the window a table and chair, between the beds a little nightstand. The whitewashed walls were unadorned, without pictures or mirrors. The old wooden floorboards were worn smooth. The sole luxury was a tiny Korean refrigerator. It didn't work. Cool evening air wafted through the open windows.

In the twilight, at a few hours' remove, my encounter with the old man seemed even more absurd and mysterious than it had by the full light of day. The memory of it was blurred and indistinct. Spectral images drifted through my mind, images I could not interpret, images that made no sense. I tried to remember. He wore a white shirt yellowed with age, a green longyi, and rubber flip-flops. He had white, thick, closely cropped hair. His face was creased with wrinkles. I couldn't tell how old he was. Sixty, maybe seventy. On his lips yet another smile whose import I could not divine. Was it sneering, derisive? Compassionate? What did he want from me?

Money. What else. He hadn't asked for any, but those remarks about his teeth and shirt were clear enough. I knew what he was getting at. He could have learned my name from the hotel. He was probably in cahoots with the front desk. A con man who wanted to whet my curiosity, to make an impression before offering me his services as a fortune-teller. No, no—an astrologer. I wasn't buying it. He was wasting his time.

Had he said anything to suggest he had actually known my father? My father supposedly said to him: "I'm not a religious man, and love, U Ba, love is the only force I truly believe in." My father would never even have thought such a thing, let alone have spoken it out loud. Least of all to a stranger. Or was I kidding myself? Wasn't it more likely a ridiculous presumption on my part to imagine I understood my father's thoughts or feelings? How well had I really known him? Would the father I thought I knew have disappeared, just like that, without leaving even a note? Would he have abandoned his wife, his son, and his daughter without explanation, without ever sending word?

His trail evaporates in Bangkok, the police say. He might have been robbed and murdered in Thailand.

Or was he the victim of an accident on the Gulf of Siam? Was he hoping to enjoy two weeks of peace and quiet, for a change? Maybe he went to the coast and drowned there while swimming. That's our family's version, the official one at least.

The homicide squad suspected him of leading a double life. They refused to accept my mother's assertion that she knew nothing about his first twenty years. They considered the very notion so preposterous that at first they suspected her of having played some part in his disappearance, either as his accomplice or as the perpetrator. Only when it became clear that there were no high-stakes life-insurance policies involved, that no one would profit financially from his purported death, did they shake off every shadow of suspicion. There very well could have been some side of my father lurking behind the mystery of those first, long-lost twenty years, a side that we, his family, had never seen.

# Chapter 3

MY LAST MEMORY of him is already four years old.

It was the morning after I'd graduated from law school. We had celebrated my graduation the previous evening, and I did not feel like going home that night. For some reason, I wanted to start the day within the safety of my childhood rituals. To feel that sense of security. Just once more.

Perhaps I'd had a premonition.

My father woke me early, standing at the foot of my bed wearing his old-fashioned gray overcoat and a brown Borsalino. As a little girl I used to watch him going off to work dressed like that. Every morning I would stand at the window waving good-bye, crying sometimes because I didn't want him to leave. Even years later, when his chauffeur would wait for him and he had only to take three steps across the sidewalk to get into the limo, he always wore the coat and the hat. In all that time he never varied his ward-robe; he just bought new coats and hats at regular intervals, the hats exclusively Borsalinos. He owned six of them: two black, two brown, and two navy. When he could no longer find the overcoats, even at the most conservative haber-dashers in New York, he started having them tailor-made.

The Borsalino was his talisman. He had bought that Italian hat to wear to his first job interview. He got the job. Back then the hat had been clear evidence of his good style and taste. Over the years, though, it had come to seem old-fashioned, then eccentric, until finally he looked like an extra from a fifties film. As a teenager I had been embar-rassed by my father's choice of clothes. He looked so com-pletely out of step, and he would greet my friends' mothers with a bow. The other kids giggled when he picked me up at school. He never wore sneakers, jeans, or sweatshirts. He despised the casual American style of dress, which he said pandered to the lower human instincts, one of which was craving comfort.

My father stood by my bed and whispered my name. He said he had an appointment in Boston and didn't know exactly when he would be back. Probably not for a couple of days, which was odd because his appointment calendar ran as reliably as his wristwatch. Besides, he flew to Bos-ton all the time and never stayed overnight. But somehow I had been too tired to take notice. He kissed me on the forehead and said, "I love you, little one. Never forget that, you hear?"

I nodded groggily. "I love you, too."

I rolled over, pressed my face into the pillow, and went back to sleep. I haven't seen him since.

T he first indication that something wasn't right came just after ten that morning. I had slept in and was coming into the kitchen. My mother was waiting to have breakfast with me. She was sitting in the solarium with a cup of coffee, leafing through *Vogue*. We were both still in our bathrobes. There were warm cinnamon rolls on the table along with fresh bagels. I was sitting at my old place, my back against the wall, feet on the edge of the chair, arms wrapped tightly around my knees, sipping orange juice and telling my mother about my summer plans when the phone rang. Susan, my father's secretary, wanted to know if he was sick. His ten o'clock appointment—by no means a trivial one—was wondering where he was. No one had said anything about Boston.

Something must have come up on short notice, both women agreed. He hadn't managed to call, was stuck at the moment in some meeting, and would surely check in within the next couple of hours.

My mother and I finished breakfast. I felt a bit anxious, but she was so calm that I let it go. After breakfast we went together for a facial, then through Central Park to Berg-dorf Goodman. It was one of those warm early-summer days when New York is its freshest. The park smelled of cut grass, people were lying in the sun on the Sheep Meadow, and a couple of young guys, shirts off, were tossing around a Frisbee. Two older men went Rollerblading hand in hand in front of us.

My mother nudged me along. At Bergdorf Goodman she bought me a yellow floral summer dress, and afterward we very predictably went to have tea at the Plaza.

I didn't care much for that particular hotel. Its faux French-Renaissance style was a bit too fanciful for me, too kitschy, but I had long ago recognized the futility of trying to have tea with my mother anyplace else. She adored the lobby with the gilded plaster on the high ceilings and walls, the columns so elaborate and ornate—as if made of icing. She basked in the waiters' pretentious bearing, the way the French maître d' saluted her (*"Bonjour*, Madame Win"). We sat between two palms by a small buffet of cakes, sweets, and ice cream. Two wandering violinists played Viennese waltzes. My mother ordered caviar blinis and two glasses of champagne.

"Is there something else to celebrate?" I asked.

"Your graduation, my dear."

We sampled our blinis. They were too salty, the champagne too warm. My mother signaled to the waiter.

"Let it go, Mom," I protested. "Everything's fine."

"Hardly," she said to me in a mild tone, as if I knew nothing about such things.

She chastised the waiter, who took back our order amid profuse apologies. Her voice could sound so cool and sharp.

There was a time I had feared it. Today I found it merely unpleasant.

She looked at me. "You would have eaten them, wouldn't you?"

I nodded.

"Your father, too. In a lot of ways you're quite like each other."

"How do you mean?" I asked. It didn't sound like a compliment.

"Is it your humility," she asked, "your passivity, or your fear of conflict? Or is it arrogance?"

"What does arrogance have to do with it?"

"Neither of you is ever willing to deal with waiters," she said. I couldn't understand the rage smoldering in her voice. It had no connection to lukewarm champagne and salty blinis. "They're not worth the trouble. I call that arrogance."

"It's just that it's not that important to me," I said. That was only half true. I found it embarrassing to complain about anything, whether at a restaurant, a hotel, or a shop. Still, such things mattered more to me than I let on. They would rankle, and after the fact I was often annoyed with myself for having been a pushover. With my father it was different. His silence in such situations was genuine. To him it truly did not matter. He smiled whenever anyone cut in front of him in line. He never counted his change. My mother counted every cent. I envied his composure. My mother couldn't figure him out. She was strict with herself and others alike—my father only with himself.

"How can it not matter to you whether or not you get what you've paid for? I can't fathom it."

"Can't we just let it go?" I asked, more pleading than demanding. "Aren't you worried about Dad?"

"No. Should I be?"

Looking back, I wonder if my mother's equanimity wasn't an act. Neither of us said a single word about the broken appointment. She never checked back with his office to see if he'd called in. Why was she so sure that nothing untoward had befallen him? Did she just not care? Or had she been suspecting for years that it would eventually come to this? Her apparent lightheartedness that day smacked of the relief—even happiness—a person might feel when a long-foreseen and inevitable catastrophe has finally come to pass.

I nfluential Wall Street Lawyer Disappears Without Trace," the *New York Times* reported a few days after my father's disappearance. For the next several days the papers were full of speculation. Was it murder, a client out for vengeance? A dramatic kidnapping? Was there some Hollywood connection? Everything the police uncovered in the first two weeks only made the case more mysterious. Early in the morning on the day of his disappearance, my father had indeed driven to JFK, but instead of flying to Boston he had gone to Los Angeles. He had bought the ticket at the airport, and he didn't check any bags. From Los Angeles he flew first class to Hong Kong on United Airlines Flight 888.

One flight attendant remembered him because he didn't drink any champagne, and instead of a newspaper he read a volume of Pablo Neruda's poetry. The flight attendant described my father as very calm and exceptionally polite. He didn't eat much and barely slept, didn't watch any movies, and spent most of his time reading.

My father apparently then spent one night in Hong Kong at the Peninsula hotel, room 218, ordered curry chicken and mineral water from room service, and, according to the staff, never left his room. The next day he boarded Cathay Pacific Flight 615 to Bangkok, where he spent a night at the Mandarin Oriental. He made no attempt to cover his tracks. He stayed in the same hotels he always used on business trips and paid all his bills by credit card, as if he knew that this would be his journey's end, at least for the investigators. Four weeks later a construction worker found his passport in the vicinity of the Bangkok airport.

A number of circumstances suggested he had never left Thailand. The police went over all the passenger lists for flights out of Bangkok. His name failed to show up anywhere. On occasion the detectives speculated that he had acquired a false passport in Thailand, then flown elsewhere under an assumed name. Several Thai Airways flight attendants claimed to have seen him: one on a flight to London, another en route to Paris, and still a third on a plane to Phnom Penh. Not one of these leads panned out.

According to the immigration authorities, my father came from Burma to the United States on a student visa in

1942. He studied law in New York and became an American citizen in 1959. He listed Rangoon, the capital of the former British colony, as his place of birth. Inquiries by the FBI and by the American embassy in Rangoon led nowhere. Win is a common surname in Burma, and no one seemed to have any knowledge of my father's family.

# Chapter 4

AND SO THERE must be in life something like a catastrophic turning point, when the world as we know it ceases to exist. A moment that transforms us into a different person from one heartbeat to the next. The moment when a lover confesses that there's someone else and that he's leaving. Or the day we bury a father or mother or best friend. Or the moment when the doctor informs us of a malignant brain tumor.

Or are such moments merely the dramatic conclusions of lengthier processes, conclusions we could have foreseen if we had only read the portents rather than disregarding them?

And if these turning points are real, are we aware of them as they happen, or do we recognize the discontinuity only much later, in hindsight?

These are questions that had never interested me before and to which I had no answers. My father's disappearance, at any rate, was nothing of the kind. I loved my father, I missed him, but my life over the past four years wouldn't have played out any differently, it wouldn't have altered a single important decision, if he had still been with us. At least that's what I used to think.

About a week ago, just after eight, when I came home from the office, the doorman called me back out of the elevator. It was pouring outside. My shoes were wet. I was freezing and couldn't wait to get to my apartment.

"What is it?" I asked impatiently.

"Package," he said.

I glanced out the huge glass windows of the lobby into the street. The taillights of the cars glistened on the wet asphalt. I was dying for a hot shower and a cup of tea. The doorman handed me a bag containing a brown package about the size of a shoebox. I tucked it under my arm and rode up to my studio on the thirty-fifth floor. My father had bought it for me before I graduated from law school.

I checked my answering machine: two messages. On the table was a stack of bills and junk mail. There was a lingering smell of cleaning chemicals, so I opened the balcony door. It was still raining, and the clouds hung so low that I could barely make out the opposite bank of the East River. Below me traffic was backing up on Second Avenue and the Queensboro Bridge.

After my shower I took the package out of its bag. I instantly recognized my mother's handwriting. Occasionally she sent me greeting cards or newspaper clippings that she thought I would be—or at least ought to be—interested in. She despised answering machines, and that was her way of leaving a message. It had been a long time, though, since she'd sent me a package. Inside I found a stack of old photos, documents, and papers belonging to my father, along with a few lines from her:

Julia

I discovered this box while straightening out the attic. It had fallen behind the old Chinese dresser. Maybe you're interested in these things. I've included the last picture of the four us. I don't need any of it anymore. Call me.

Yours,
Judith

I spread the little stack out on the table. On the very top was the family portrait taken the day I graduated. I'm standing arm-in-arm between my parents, beaming. My brother is standing behind me, his hands on my shoulders. My mother is smiling proudly into the camera. My father is grinning, too. The perfect happy family. How photographs can lie. There was nothing to indicate that this would be the last picture of all of us together or, worse still, that one of us had long been plotting to disappear. My mother had also included two expired passports, my father's American naturalization certificate, and a couple of old appointment calendars, chock-full of tiny notations. Boston. Washington.

Los Angeles. Miami. London. Hong Kong. Paris. There were years when my father circled the globe multiple times. He had worked his way up to partner, one of eight in his firm, and as a lawyer he had specialized early in the entertainment industry. He advised Hollywood studios on film contracts, takeovers, and mergers. He also counted some of the biggest stars among his clients.

I never really understood why he was such a professional success. He worked a lot but never exuded an air of personal ambition. He was not vain, and he never tried to capitalize on the fame of his clients. His name never turned up in the gossip columns. He never attended parties, not even the opulent charity balls that my mother and her friends organized. The need to fit in somewhere, so typical of immigrants, seemed utterly alien to him. He was a loner and the antithesis of most people's image of the celebrity lawyer. Maybe that was the very quality that inspired trust and made him such a coveted negotiator: his calm and composure, his lack of pretense, his absent, always somewhat innocent manner. But he had other ways, too, which sometimes made his business associates and his few friends uneasy. For example, his memory was too good, and he was an uncanny judge of character. A cursory glance sufficed for him to memorize almost anything; he cited memos and letters from years back, verbatim. At the beginning of a conversation he would close his eyes and concentrate on a person's voice as if losing himself in a song, whereupon he seemed to know exactly what frame of mind people were in, how confident they were, whether they were telling the truth or bluffing. Supposedly it was something one could learn, but who had taught him, when, and where, he wouldn't reveal, no matter how I pleaded. Not once in my life had I managed to deceive him.

The oldest calendar enclosed was from 1960. I flipped through it—nothing but business appointments, unfamiliar names, places, and times. In the middle of it all was a note in my father's hand:

> *How much does a man live, after all?*
> *Does he live a thousand days, or only one?*
> *For a week, or for several centuries?*
> *How long does a man spend dying?*
> *What does it mean to say "for ever"?*
> —Pablo Neruda

Then, at the very back, a thin blue airmail envelope, folded neatly into a small rectangle. I took it out and unfolded it. It was addressed to:

> Mi Mi
> 38 Circular Road
> Kalaw, Shan State
> Burma

I hesitated. Did this unassuming blue onionskin hold the key to my father? I took the letter and walked over to the stove. I could burn it. The flames would transform the thin paper to ashes in a matter of seconds. I turned on the burner, heard the gas hissing, the automatic ignition clicking, the flame. I held the envelope close to the fire. One move and the family would have its peace. I can't remember how long I stood in front of the stove; I only know that I suddenly started to cry. Tears streamed down my cheeks. I didn't know why I was crying, but the tears just kept coming, harder and faster, until at some point I found myself back on my bed, bawling and sobbing like a little girl.

The clock on my nightstand read 5:20 when I woke. I could still feel the grief in my bones. For the space of a few breaths I couldn't remember the reason and hoped that it had all been a dream. At the table I unfolded the letter very gently, as if it might pop like a soap bubble in my hands.

April 24, 1955
New York

My beloved Mi Mi,

Five thousand eight hundred and sixty-four days have passed since last I heard the beating of your heart. Do you realize how many hours that is? How many minutes? Do you know how impoverished a bird is that cannot sing, a flower that cannot blossom? How wretched a fish out of water?

It is difficult to write to you, Mi Mi. I have written you so many letters that I have never sent. What could I tell you that you don't already know? As if we needed ink and paper, letters and words, in order to communicate. You have been with me through each of the 140,736 hours—yes, it has already been that many—and you will be with me until we meet again. (Forgive me for stating the obvious just this one time.) When the time comes, I will return. How flat and empty the most beautiful words can sound. How dull and dreary life must be for those who need words, who need to touch, see, or hear one another in order to be close. Who need to prove their love, or even just to confirm it in order to be sure of it. I sense that these lines, too, will never find their way to you. You have long since understood anything I might write, and so these letters are in truth directed to myself, meager attempts to still my desire.

I read it a second time and a third, folded it and tucked it back into its envelope. I looked at the time. It was Saturday morning, just after seven. The rain had stopped, the clouds had given way to a deep blue sky under which Manhattan was slowly waking. The sun rose across the East River. It was going to be a cold and beautiful day.

I grabbed a piece of paper in order to make a few notes, to analyze the situation, to come up with a strategy, just as I would have done at the office. But the paper remained blank; I had already passed the point of no return. The decision had been made for me, though I could not have said by whom.

I knew the number for United Airlines by heart. The next flight to Rangoon would be leaving on Sunday and traveling via Hong Kong, then Bangkok. I would have to get a visa there to continue on Wednesday with Thai Air to Burma.

"And the return flight?"

I thought for a moment.

"Leave it open."

Then I called my mother.

# Chapter 5

MY MOTHER WAS already having coffee and reading the *Times* when I got there.

"I'm going out of town tomorrow." My voice sounded even more cowardly than I had feared. "To Burma."

"Don't be ridiculous," she said without looking up from her paper.

It was with sentences like this that she had been able to silence me all my life. I took a sip of mineral water and looked at my mother. She had had her gray hair colored dark blond and cut short again. Short hair made her look younger, but also more severe. Her sharp nose had grown more prominent over the years. Her upper lip had almost disappeared, and the corners of her mouth, tending ever downward, gave her face an embittered air. Her blue eyes had lost the glint I remembered from my childhood. Was it age, or was it the look of a woman who hadn't been loved—at least not in the way she needed or wanted to be? Had she known about Mi Mi and hidden it from her children? She took a sip of coffee; I could not interpret her expression.

"How long will you be gone?"

"I don't know."

"And your job?"

"I don't know."

"You're risking your career."

She was right. I didn't know who Mi Mi was, where she was, what role she had played in my father's life, or whether she was even still alive. I had a name and an old address from some village whose precise location was unclear to me. I'm not the kind of person to act impetuously. I trust my intellect more than my instincts.

Still.

"What do you expect to find over there?" she asked.

"The truth," I answered. It was supposed to be a statement, but it sounded more like a question.

"Whose truth? His truth? Your truth? I can tell you mine here and now in three sentences. If you care to hear it." She sounded tired and empty.

"I'd like to know what's happened to my father."

"What does it matter now?"

"Maybe he's still alive."

"So what if he is. Don't you think he would have gotten in touch if he had wanted anything more to do with us?"

She could see that I was taken aback and added: "Or is it that you want to play detective?"

I shook my head and looked at her.

"What do you want to know?"

"The truth."

Slowly she put down the paper and looked at me for a long time. "Your father left me long before the day he disappeared. He betrayed me. Not once and not twice. He betrayed me every hour, every day of the thirty-five years we were married. Not with any lover who accompanied him secretly on his travels or with whom he spent the evenings when he was supposedly working late. I don't know whether he ever had an affair. It doesn't matter. He made false promises. He promised himself to me. He became a Catholic for my sake. He repeated the priest's words at the wedding: 'In good times and in bad.' He didn't mean it. His faith was a sham, and his love for me was a sham. He never gave himself to me, Julia, not even in good times." She paused.

"Do you think I never asked him about his past? Do you really think I didn't give a damn about the first twenty years of his life? The first time I asked him he consoled me, gave me that soft, knowing look that I hadn't yet learned to resist, and promised that one day he would tell me everything. That was before we got married, and I believed him, trusted him. Later I pestered him. I wept and wailed and threatened divorce. I told him I'd move out and come back only when he stopped keeping secrets from me. He would say that he loved me, why wasn't that enough? How can anyone truthfully claim to love someone when they're not prepared to share everything with that person, including their past?

"After you were born I found an old letter in one of his books. He had written it shortly before our wedding. It was a love letter to a woman in Burma. He wanted to explain it to me, but I didn't want to hear anything about it. It's odd, Julia, but a confession, a disclosure, is worthless when it comes at the wrong moment. If it's too early, it overwhelms us. We're not ready for it and can't yet appreciate it. If it's too late, the opportunity is lost. The mistrust and the disappointment are already too great; the door is already closed. In either case, the very thing that ought to foster intimacy just creates distance. For me, it was too late. I had no more interest in tales. They would not have brought us closer together; they would only have deepened the wounds. I told him I would leave him if I ever found another letter like that, no matter how old it was, and that he would never see me or his children again. I never found anything else, though I went through his things thoroughly every couple of weeks."

She paused, drained a glass of water, and stared at me. I tried to take her hand, but she pulled it away and shook her head. For that, too, it was too late.

"How could I defend myself? How could I make him pay for what he was doing to me? I decided to keep secrets of my own. I shared less and less with him, kept my thoughts and feelings to myself. He never asked. As far as he was concerned, if I wanted to tell him something, to share something with him, I would do it. And so we went on living in parallel worlds until the morning he disappeared."

She stood up and got another glass of water, walked around the kitchen for a while, sat down again. I remained silent.

"I was young, not even twenty-two, and very naïve when we met. It was at a friend's birthday party. I saw him coming through the door, tall and lean, with his full lips, a mouth that seemed always to smile slightly. He was good-looking, and women adored him, whether their attention was welcome or not. Maybe he didn't even realize it. Any one of my girlfriends would have been happy to get him. His strong nose, high forehead, and those narrow cheeks gave his face an ascetic look that attracted everybody. His black, round glasses emphasized his beautiful eyes. There was an ease to his movements, an elegance in his face and voice, an aura that impressed even my parents. He would have made the perfect son-in-law for them—educated, intelligent, flaw-less manners, self-confident without a trace of arrogance—if only he had been white. Even on their deathbeds they never forgave me for marrying a 'colored man.' It was the first and last time that I truly rebelled against them.

"As you know," she said, "that's not the kind of person I am. I stepped out of line just once, and I've been paying for it the rest of my life."

She told me my father didn't want to marry her.

"At first he said that we didn't know enough about one another, that we ought to wait until we knew one another better. Later he claimed we were too young, that we ought to take our time. Shortly before the wedding he warned me that he couldn't love me the way I perhaps expected or needed him to.

"But I wouldn't listen to him. I wouldn't believe him. His reluctance, his hesitation, only strengthened my resolve. I wanted him, him and no other. During the first few months I suspected him of having a wife in Burma, but he said that he wasn't married. That was all he would tell me about those years in his native country. And at that point it didn't really interest me, anyway. I was convinced that in the long run he wouldn't be able to resist me and my love. Burma was far away.

"I was the one who fell asleep and woke up next to him," she said. "I wanted to conquer him. Was it my bruised vanity? Or the well-behaved child from a respectable family rebelling against her parents? What better protest against my father's world than to marry a dark-skinned man. I don't know. I still don't know.

"I've tried for many years to find an answer to these questions. Without success. Maybe it was a combination of reasons. By the time I realized that I couldn't change your father the way I had hoped, it was already too late. At first we stayed together for your sake and your brother's. Later, we lacked the courage to separate. At least I did. As for your father, I can't really say what motivated him.

"Go to Burma if that's what you want," she said, exhausted. "When you get back I won't ask you a thing, and

I don't want you to tell me anything, either. Whatever you find there, it's no longer of any interest to me."

I left the next morning. The limousine to the airport was waiting right outside my building. It was a cold, clear morning. The taxi driver's breath smoked in the frigid air as he walked back and forth in front of the car. The doorman carried my bags to the car and loaded them into the trunk. I didn't feel well. I was scared, anxious, and sad. I never realized how unhappy my mother had been in her marriage. I thought of a sentence my mother had said to me the day before: "Your father left me long before the day he disappeared." And how about me, I thought. How long ago had my father left me?

# Chapter 6

EVEN THOUGH I could hardly move from weariness and exhaustion, I lay awake for a long time and then slept poorly. The questions gave me no rest. Several times during the night I woke with a start, sat up in my bed, and looked at the little travel alarm next to me. 2:30. 3:10. 3:40.

Come morning, I didn't feel any better. I was wide awake from one moment to the next. I had a headache and my heart was pounding as hard as if someone were pressing on my chest. I knew that feeling from New York, from the eve of important conferences or negotiations.

A light breeze drifted through the open window, and the morning chill crept slowly under my covers. A fresh, exotic fragrance that I couldn't place filled the room.

It was light now. I stood up and went to the window. The sky was dark blue, cloudless. The sun still lingered somewhere behind the mountains. On the lawn in front of the hotel were the trees, flowers, and blossoming bushes of a fairy tale—colors wilder and fiercer than anything I had ever seen. Even the corn poppies seemed redder than red.

There was no hot water for the shower.

The walls and ceiling of the breakfast room were paneled in dark wood, nearly black. One table by the window was set for breakfast. I was the only guest in the hotel.

The waiter approached with a deep bow. I had the choice of tea or coffee and fried or scrambled eggs. He had never heard of cornflakes. There was neither sausage nor cheese.

"Fried or scrambled eggs?" he repeated.

"Scrambled," I said. "Coffee."

I watched him disappear through a swinging door at the other end of the large room. He stepped so lightly that I couldn't hear his footfalls, and so it seemed to me he must be floating through the room a few inches above the floor.

I was alone. The silence made me uncomfortable. I felt that the empty tables and chairs had eyes that were focused on me, that tracked my every move and breath. I was not accustomed to this kind of quiet. How long could it take to make coffee? To scramble eggs? Why were there no voices or sounds from the kitchen? The place oppressed me. I found it increasingly eerie and wondered if it was possible to turn up the silence in the same way one could turn up the volume. As if in response to my question, the stillness intensified with each passing moment until it hurt my ears and became unbearable. I cleared my throat and tapped my plate with my knife just so I might hear something.

I stood, walked to the door that led into the garden, opened it, and stepped out. It was windy. Never before had the rustling of a tree, the buzzing of a bee, the chirping of a grasshopper sounded so soothing.

When breakfast finally arrived, the coffee was lukewarm, the scrambled eggs burnt. The waiter stood in the corner smiling and nodding while I ate the burnt eggs, drank the lukewarm coffee, and nodded and smiled back. I ordered a second cup of coffee and flipped through my travel guide. Kalaw warranted barely a page.

> Situated on the western edge of the Shan Plateau, a popular mountain retreat among the British. Today a quiet, peaceful town with plenty of residual colonial atmosphere. Elevation 4,300 feet, pleasantly cool, an ideal spot for hiking in pine and bamboo forests, impressive views of the mountains and valleys of the Shan Province.
>
> Population: a unique mixture of Shan, Burmese, various mountain tribes, Burmese and Indian Muslims, and Nepalese (Gurkhas who once served in the British army), many of whom attended missionary schools. Until the 1970s American missionaries taught in the schools. Many of the older residents especially still speak English today.

Three pagodas and the market were highlighted as points of interest. There was apparently a Burmese, a

Chinese, and a Nepalese restaurant, a movie theater, and several teahouses. An Englishman had designed my Tudor-style hotel. Even in colonial times it had been the leading establishment in the area. There were, in addition, a number of small hotels and guesthouses "to satisfy the most modest needs."

After breakfast I went into the garden and sat on a wooden bench under a pine tree. No trace of the morning's chill remained. With the sun had come the heat. A heavy, sweet fragrance floated in the air.

Where to begin my search? My sole point of reference was the address on the thin blue envelope:

> 38 Circular Road
> Kalaw, Shan State
> Burma

That was nearly forty years ago.

I desperately needed a vehicle and a local who knew his way around. What else?

In my notebook I made a list:

Hire car and driver
Find tour guide
Track down phone book
Buy local map
Find address
Question neighbors and/or police

Ask police about father
Check with mayor and/or local residency office
Maybe try to find other Americans or Brits
Show father's picture in teahouses, hotels, and restaurants
Check all hotels, clubs, etc.


That was how I always got ready for conferences and ne-gotiations with clients—making lists, systematic research. This was familiar and reassuring.

The hotel recommended a driver who could double as a tour guide. He was on the road at the moment with two Danish tourists but would be available in the coming days. He was supposed to arrive at the hotel around eight that evening. It made sense to wait for him, even though it meant putting off the search until the next day. Besides, it couldn't hurt to ask U Ba about the address, even if he was a fraud. He had spent his whole life in Kalaw, by the looks of it.

It was just past noon, and I decided to go for a run. After the long trip my body was dying for some exercise. True, it was warm, but the dry mountain air and the wind made the heat bearable. I was in good shape and would run several miles through Central Park even on the hottest and muggi-est summer evenings.

The physical exertion did me good. It freed me. I stopped caring about the stares. I didn't need to avoid them because I was too busy concentrating on my legs. I felt as if I could run away from everything strange and sinister, as if I could watch and observe, without myself being watched. I ran down into the village, along the main road, past a mosque and a pagoda, circling the market in a wide arc, overtaking oxcarts and horse-drawn carriages and several young monks. Only now that I was running did I notice how slowly and unhurriedly the local people dawdled along, for all they were light-footed. Now I was ready to take them on. I could set my own pace. I didn't need to conform to their tempo.

After a shower I lay down and rested on the bed. I felt better. On the way to the teahouse, though, the weariness hit my legs. I felt every step. I was nervous and excited, wondering what lay in store. I'm not one of those people who likes surprises. What was U Ba going to tell me, and how much of it could I believe? I was planning to ask him detailed questions. If he got tangled up in contradictions I would be out of there in a flash.


U Ba was already there. He stood up, bowed, and took my hands. His skin was soft, his palms pleasantly warm. He ordered two glasses of tea and a couple of pastries. After a moment he closed his eyes, drew a deep breath, and started again on his tale.

# Chapter 7

DECEMBER IN KALAW is a cold month. The sky is blue and cloudless. The sun wanders from one side of the horizon to the other, but no longer climbs high enough to generate any real warmth. The air is clear and fresh, and only the most sensitive people can still detect any trace of the heavy, sweet scent of the tropical rainy season, when the clouds hang low over the village and the valley, and the water falls unchecked from the skies as if to slake a parched world's thirst. The rainy season is hot and steamy. The market reeks of rotting meat, while heavy black flies settle on the entrails and skulls of sheep and cattle. The earth itself seems to perspire. Worms and insects crawl out of its pores. Innocent rills turn to rushing torrents that devour careless piglets, lambs, or children, only to disgorge them, lifeless, in the valley below.

But December promises the people of Kalaw a respite from all this. December promises cold nights and mercifully cool days. December, thought Mya Mya, is a hypocrite.

She was sitting on a wooden stool in front of her house, looking out over the fields and the valley to the hilltops in the distance. The air was so clear that she felt she was looking through a spyglass to the ends of the earth. She did not trust the weather. Although she could not remember ever in her life having seen a cloud in a December sky, she would not rule out the possibility of a sudden downpour. Or of a typhoon, even if not a single one in living memory had found its way from the Bay of Bengal into the mountains around Kalaw. It was not impossible. As long as there were typhoons anywhere, one might well devastate Mya Mya's native soil. Or the earth might quake. Even, or perhaps especially, on a day like today, when nothing foreshadowed catastrophe. Complacency was treacherous, confidence a luxury that Mya Mya could not afford. That much she knew at the bottom of her heart. For her there would be neither peace nor rest. Not in this world. Not in her life.

She had learned her lesson seventeen years ago on that scorching hot day in August, playing down by the river, she and her twin brother, when he slipped on the slick stones. When he lost his balance and flailed his arms about, helpless, like a fly under an inverted glass. When he fell into the waters that swept him away. On his journey. The everlasting one. She had stood on the bank, unable to help. She had watched his face emerge from the waters once again, one last time.

A priest would have called it God's will, a test of faith that the Lord, in his infinite wisdom, had set for the family. The Lord moves in mysterious ways.

The Buddhist monks made sense of the tragedy by referring to the boy's previous lives. He must have done something dreadful in one of these lives for which his present death was the consequence.

The day after the accident, the local astrologer offered his own explanation: The children had gone north to play, and they ought not to have done that, not with their birth date, not on that Saturday in August. It was no wonder they got into trouble. If only he, the astrologer, had been consulted earlier, he might have warned them. Life was that simple, that complicated.

Some part of her had died with her brother, but there had been no funeral ceremony for it. Her family hadn't even noticed it was gone. Her parents were farmers busy with the harvest, with sowing, and with four other children. It was difficult enough just putting rice and a few vegetables on the table every evening.

Mya Mya, the half-dead, was alone. In the years that followed she worked hard to bring order into a world off-kilter. Every afternoon she went to the water to sit in the place where she had seen her brother for the last time, to wait for him to resurface. The river took his body as plunder and never returned it. At night before sleep she would tell him about her day, knowing he could hear her. She slept on his side of their shared straw mat, under his blanket, and years later she still had the scent of him in her nose.

She refused to help her mother with the washing down at the river. Indeed, she avoided water altogether and bathed only in the company of her parents. As if she could drown in a bucket. She wore certain clothes on certain days, refused until she was fifteen to speak on Saturdays, and always fasted on Sundays. She wove herself an intricate web of rituals and dwelt entirely therein.

Rituals offered security. Since her brother's death, the family was no longer consulting the astrologer just once a year. They saw him almost weekly. They crouched beside him. They hung on his every word. They followed his instructions, desperate to be protected from any of the world's harm. Even more than her parents, Mya Mya took the astrologer's words to heart. Having herself been born on a Thursday, she had to watch out especially for Saturdays, a day on which misfortune loomed, particularly in April, August, and December. In order never to take any chances, she refused to leave the house on a Saturday, until once, in April of all months, when a blanket next to the cooking pit in the kitchen caught fire. The flames were ravenous. In a few minutes they had not only devoured the wooden shack but also robbed Mya Mya of the last shred of confidence she had that any place in the world could be safe for her.

~~~~~

Now, recalling these things, she felt a chill. The fire crackled in the kitchen, and she got to her feet. A thin layer of ice, delicate and brittle, covered the water in the bucket before her. She kicked it and watched the tiny fragments of broken ice disappear into the water.

She took a deep breath, held her belly with both hands, and looked down at her body. She was a beautiful young woman, even if she had never felt that way and no one had ever told her so. She wore her long black hair in a braid that reached nearly to her hips. Her dark, big, almost round eyes and full lips gave her face a sensual expression. She had long, thin fingers and muscular but slender arms and legs. Her belly was round and thick and big—so big that it seemed foreign to her, even after months. There was a kick, a knock, and she knew: Here they come again.

They'd started yesterday evening, an hour apart. Now they were coming every couple of minutes. Waves breaking against a fortification, always more and higher and stronger. She tried to get a purchase on something, an arm, a branch, a stone. There was nothing. She didn't want the child, not today, not on a Saturday in December.

Her neighbor, who had already brought four children into the world, thought it was an easy birth, especially for a first child. Mya Mya herself couldn't remember; she had lived for hours in another world, one in which her hands and legs no longer obeyed her, in which her body was no longer her own. She was nothing now but a giant wound. She saw fat black rain clouds, and a butterfly settled on her forehead. She saw her brother in the tide. One very last time. A thought sailed by, like a chicken feather carried aloft on the wind. Her child. On that Saturday. A sign? Her brother reborn?

She heard a baby cry. Not whimpering, but defiant and angry. A boy, someone said. Mya Mya opened her eyes and looked for her brother. No, not this ugly, shriveled, blood-smeared thing. This helpless bundle with its distorted head and face.

Mya Mya had no idea what a child needed. She came to motherhood empty-handed. Any love she had possessed was gone, had long since been washed away, on a scorching-hot day in August.

# Chapter 8

NO ONE COULD say that Mya Mya hadn't tried during those first days of her son's life. She did whatever the neighbor told her. She laid him on her plump, full breast and fed him with her milk. She rocked him to sleep or carried him about when he was restless. She wrapped him close to her body when she went to buy things in the village. She lay awake nights between her husband and her child, listening to hear the little one breathe, following the infant's short, quick breaths and wishing that she would feel something. Feel something when her child nursed, when it grasped her finger with its dimpled little hand. She wished that something would come to fill the emptiness inside her. Anything.

She turned to the side and pressed him to her, an embrace somewhere between fainting and violence. She pressed more firmly and two big brown eyes looked at her, astonished. Mya Mya felt nothing. Mother and son were like magnets that repelled each other. Press as she might, they would never touch.

It might have been just a matter of time. She might have had a chance after all, and the instinct to provide might have developed into a feeling of affection, and the feeling of affection into the miracle of love—if it hadn't been for the incident with the chickens.

It happened on a Saturday, two weeks to the day after the birth. Just after sunrise Mya Mya walked out into the yard to fetch wood for the fire in the kitchen. It was a cold morning, and she hurried along. Looking for brushwood and a few stout logs, she went behind the house. The dead chicken lay right in front of the woodpile. She had nearly stepped on it. She found the second one right around twelve o'clock, the hour of the birth, the third and the fourth shortly thereafter, and the rooster in the afternoon. Her husband looked at the dead animals but could find nothing. Just the evening before, they had been strutting about the house, clucking feistily, and there was no indication that a dog or cat, much less a tiger, had gotten hold of them. For Mya Mya there was no doubt. The cadavers confirmed her worst fears. They were the sudden downpour—no, worse—the typhoon in December, the earthquake she had always dreaded and secretly desired: A curse lay upon her son. He was a harbinger of misfortune. The astrologer had prophesied it. She ought never to have borne a child on a Saturday, not in December.

Even the fact that in the ensuing days more than a dozen of the neighbors' chickens died the same mysterious death could not console Mya Mya. On the contrary, it only confirmed the worst. She knew now that this was but the beginning and that the misfortune the boy brought would not be confined to her own family.

Now she lay awake nights, fearing the next catastrophe. She knew it was only a matter of time. Every cough, every gasp, every sigh sounded like thunder on the horizon. Hardly daring to move, she strained her ears every time the child stirred. As if his very breaths were the footfalls of calamity's stealthy approach.

A week later her milk failed. Her breasts hung slack against her body, like two deflated balloons. A friend of the neighbor, a woman who had just had a child of her own, took over the nursing. Mya Mya rejoiced in every hour that her son was out of the house. She wanted to talk with her husband. It couldn't go on like this. They had to do something.

# Chapter 9

KHIN MAUNG RECKONED that his wife was over-stating the problem. Of course he, too, believed in the power of the stars. Everyone knows that the day, the hour, even the minute of one's birth can determine the course of one's life—there was little doubt about that. And there were niceties one did well to observe, days on which one ought to remain inactive, rituals one needed to follow in order to avert catastrophes. There, too, Khin Maung was in agreement with his wife. No one was enthusiastic about a Saturday birth in December, of course not. Everyone knew that the stars did not smile upon these children, that they faced a difficult life, that their souls seldom sprouted wings. Every family knew an uncle or an aunt or at least a neighbor or a friend of a neighbor who knew someone who had a relative who had been born on one of those inauspicious days and who slunk through life like a beaten dog, who remained small and stunted like a shade plant. His son would not have it easy, Khin Maung had no illusions about that, but to jump to the conclusion that he was cursed, that was going a bit too far (even if the incident with the chickens did worry him, although of course he would never admit it to his wife). When Mya Mya suggested they consult the astrologer, Khin Maung readily assented, and not only because he was the kind of person who didn't like to say no. He also hoped that the old man might console his wife with his wisdom or, should the stars confirm her fears, that he might advise them on how to minimize, if not exactly to forestall, the calamity that threatened their child.

The astrologer lived in an unassuming wooden shack on the edge of the village. Nothing betrayed the esteem that he enjoyed in the community. Not a house was built in the area without his first being asked whether the site was well situated or whether the day of the groundbreaking stood under a favorable star. Prior to any wedding, the prospective couple or their parents would come to him to ascertain whether the horoscopes of the bride and groom were suitably matched. The astrologer would ask the stars about the best dates to go on a hunt or to undertake a journey to the capital. Over the years his auguries had proven themselves so accurate that people started coming from remote corners of the province. His reputation was so good that supposedly—no one knew for certain, but there were persistent rumors—even many of the English who lived in

Kalaw and who publicly ridiculed Burmese astrology as superstition regularly sought him out.

The old man sat cross-legged in the middle of his tiny room. A head as round as the full moon, thought Khin Maung. Eyes, nose, and mouth were equally shapely, and only the two large, protruding ears disturbed the image of a perfectly proportioned face. No one knew how old he was. Even the eldest in the village claimed to have no memory of him as a young man, and so everyone imagined that he had been born well over eighty years ago. He never spoke of it himself, though. His countenance and his mindful spirit seemed to defy the ravages of aging. Since time immemorial his voice had been gentle and quiet, his hearing and vision those of a twenty-year-old. The years had creased his face, but the skin did not hang slack from his body the way an old man's usually did.

Khin Maung and Mya Mya bowed and hesitated on the threshold. Mya Mya had sat across from him so frequently since her childhood that she had long ago ceased to count the visits, but still she felt something in her knees and stomach every time. Not familiarity, only reverence. Even awe.

It was Khin Maung's first visit, and his respect was mingled with curiosity. His parents had always visited the astrologer alone, and even concerning his marriage to Mya Mya it was they who had asked the astrologer whether they had found the right bride for their son.

Khin Maung glanced around before bowing a second time. The floor and walls were dark teak. Dust motes danced in the beams of light that fell through the two open windows. The sun drew two rectangles on the floor. They gleamed on the wood worn smooth by the years. This radiance had a power to make Khin Maung tremble. Then he caught sight of a glistening golden Buddha carved in wood. Never in his entire life had Khin Maung seen one so beautiful. He sank to one knee and bowed until his forehead grazed the floor. In front of the Buddha were two flower arrangements and a plate full of offerings. Someone had lovingly stacked four oranges into a pyramid. Beside them lay two bananas, a papaya, and several portions of tea artfully arranged into a small mound. The walls were covered with white papers crammed full of tiny numbers and letters. Smoldering sticks of incense stood in little sand-filled vases in each of the four corners of the room.

The old man nodded. Khin Maung and Mya Mya knelt down on two straw mats in front of him. Mya Mya heard and felt nothing but the wild beating of her heart. It was up to Khin Maung to do the talking, to ask the questions; she had made that unmistakably clear to him ahead of time. They had been married for hardly a year, but she knew too well her husband's passivity. He was a quiet individual who might say no more than a few sentences all evening. She had never seen him cross, angry, or agitated. Even joy and satisfaction were barely perceptible in him. A smile flitting across his face was all he would reveal of his emotions.

He was no slouch. On the contrary, he was one of the most industrious farmers in the village, and often he would be cultivating his field at the crack of dawn, long before the others. But life seemed to him a tranquil river whose course, by and large, was predetermined. Any attempt to alter it significantly was doomed to failure. Khin Maung was hardworking without ambition, curious without posing questions, happy without radiating joy.

"Venerable master," Mya Mya heard her husband say in a quiet voice after a long pause, "we have come to ask your advice."

The old man nodded.

"Our son was born on Saturday three weeks ago, and we wish to know if calamity threatens him."

The old one took up chalk and a little slate and asked for the exact date and hour of the birth.

"December third, eleven-forty a.m.," said Khin Maung.

The astrologer wrote the numbers in little boxes and began to calculate. He added further numbers and signs, struck out others, and drew several full and half circles on various lines, as if he were writing the life in musical notation.

After several minutes he set the slate aside, looked up, and gazed at Mya Mya and Khin Maung. Any trace of a smile had left his face.

"The child will bring sorrow on his parents," he said. "Great sorrow."

Mya Mya felt herself sinking into a morass. Something was dragging her down, and there was no one to help her, nothing to hold on to. Not a hand. Not a branch. She heard the old man's voice and her husband's, but she no longer followed what was being said. Their voices sounded muffled and very distant—as if in another room, in some other life. Great sorrow. Great sorrow.

"What kind of sorrow?" asked Khin Maung.

"Various kinds, especially medical," said the old one.

He took up the slate and resumed his scribbling and reckoning.

"In his head," he said at last.

"Where in his head?" asked Khin Maung, word by word, enunciating as if constructing each letter out of individual parts. In retrospect he would be astonished by his own utterly uncharacteristic bout of persistent curiosity.

The old one looked at the slate, which revealed to him all the secrets of the universe. It was the book of life and death, the book of love. He could have told the parents what else he saw, the exceptional capacities this child would develop, the magic and power latent in this individual, and the gift of love. But he knew that Mya Mya was not listening and that Khin Maung would not understand. So he said: "In his eyes."


Mya Mya had not registered this part of the conversation, and afterward, too, on the way home, while her husband fell into a stream of talk the like of which she had never heard from him, she stumbled on, uncomprehending. The words buzzed through her head like flies. Great sorrow.

In the ensuing months Khin Maung tried several times to explain to his wife that the astrologer had indeed spoken of sorrow, even of great sorrow, but primarily medical sorrow, and that there had been no talk of a curse or of a harbinger of calamity. She would not listen. He saw it in her eyes. He saw it in the way she treated their son, taking hold of him without touching him, looking at him without seeing him.

Tin Win's life had not spanned twenty-one days when, at least from his mother's perspective, its whole course had been decided. Lived. Forfeited. Now it was just a question of her getting through the rest of it gracefully.

It would prove too much.

# Chapter 10

NOW THAT THE stars had spoken and her child's fate was determined, Mya Mya slept more soundly. She knew what to expect. She felt right at home with strokes of fate and ill fortune. Happiness and joy made her nervous, strange and unfamiliar as they were. She needn't plague herself with false hopes. There were no illusions gnawing at her soul, no dreams making her fancy run wild. That calmed her.

So now, in the days and weeks after the visit to the astrologer, it was Khin Maung who lay awake beside his sleeping wife and child while the most hideous thoughts wrought their mischief in his mind. Perhaps the old man had made a mistake? Was there really such a thing as a fate we could not escape? If we were not the masters of our lives, then who was? He had no wish to listen to the stars.

"Mya Mya. Mya Mya," he said, sitting up in bed that first night. His wife lay sleeping next to him.

"Mya Mya." It sounded like an incantation.

She opened her eyes.

There was a full moon, a cloudless night, and in the sickly light that fell through the window from outside he saw the outline of her face, the movements of her eyes, the slender nose. He thought how beautiful she was and that it had never occurred to him before. He had married her because his parents had selected her for him. Love will come later, they had assured him, and he had believed them—for one because he always did whatever they told him, and then also because he had only very vague notions about love. He considered it a gift, a boon bestowed on some and not on others. No one was entitled to it.

"Mya Mya, we have to, we ought to, we must not . . ." There was so much he wanted to say to her.

"I know, Khin Maung," she said, sitting up. "I know."

She crept to him, took his head in her arms, and pressed it to her bosom. A rare gesture for Mya Mya, for whom tenderness was a luxury as profligate as hot water in the morning or a smile when parting. It was something for dreamers or for people with an excess of time, power, and emotions. She did not belong to either category.

Mya Mya thought she knew what was going on inside her husband, and she pitied him. By his heartbeat, by the convulsions of his body, by the way he wrapped his arms around her, she sensed that he would need time. He still believed they could protect themselves, that there might still be a chance to alter what could no longer be altered.

Khin Maung lay in her arms and talked. Not loudly, not to her. She couldn't understand a word he said. He was talking to himself, swiftly and without pause. His whispering sounded demanding, defiant, almost threatening, then pleading, beseeching, doubtful, a stream of talk that would not run dry. It was as if he were sitting at someone's deathbed and only his voice could keep the patient alive.

He wanted to fight for his son. Every life held promise, he told himself, and in his son's case, he, Khin Maung, would explore every possibility to realize that promise. If it must happen without his wife's help, then so be it.

That's what he wanted to tell her, first thing in the morning, even before breakfast. Then he fell asleep.

But the opportunity for a discussion never materialized, either before breakfast or in the evening after the day's work.

The following night he recalled every detail of their visit to the astrologer. The house appeared before his eyes, blurry at first, then clearer and clearer, like a landscape when the fog lifts. He saw the room, the candles, the sticks of incense, the slate that revealed the mysteries of life. The great book of love. He heard the old man's pronouncements, let them amble through his mind, slowly, word by word. There had been no talk of a curse. He would speak with his wife. Early tomorrow morning. The opportunity never presented itself.

So passed the nights. And the days. If Khin Maung had been a different person, he would not have waited for an opportunity; he would have looked for one and seized it. But that was not in his nature. He would have had to transcend limitations, his own limitations, and he was no hero. He could allow himself only the thoughts, and it was not long before his strength was spent. The doubts returned, and with his resistance broken, they fell on him like rats and vultures on carrion. The stars had it right. On a Saturday in December. Great sorrow in various respects. It could hardly have been plainer.

On the heels of the chicken incident, a great-aunt passed away—eight weeks to the day after the birth of the boy. She had been, admittedly, quite old and sick and had not left her hut in years, and for a brief moment Khin Maung had wanted to point these things out to his wife. A brief moment—then he also saw the sign and could not contradict his wife.

And so he withdrew from the life of his son, consoling himself with the thought that the boy would, after all, be only the first of many children that he, Khin Maung, would have with Mya Mya, and that not all of them would come into the world on a Saturday in December, April, or August. He leased out his field and took work as a gardener and caddy at the golf course of the English. That work paid better than farming and also allowed him to avoid his own house even in the dry season, when farmers had little work to do in the field. Golf was a year-round pursuit.

Mya Mya buried herself in her housekeeping. The family lived in a small hut of wood and mud behind a grand two-story villa belonging to a distant uncle of Khin Maung. It stood on a hilltop above the village, and like most of the houses of the colonial lords in Kalaw, it was built in a Tudor style. The town was especially popular during the dry season. When temperatures in the capital, Rangoon, and in Mandalay topped a hundred degrees, Kalaw, with an elevation of more than four thousand feet, offered relief from the heat of the flats and the delta. There were English nationals who stayed in the country after their retirement and who relocated to one of the mountain resorts such as Kalaw. An English officer had built himself this villa as a place to retire, but then tragically had not returned from a tiger hunt undertaken just two weeks after his release from His Majesty's service.

The man's widow had sold the house to Khin Maung's uncle, who had won respect and a handsome fortune as a rice baron in Rangoon. He was one of the few who had managed to establish himself in a market dominated by an Indian minority, and he was one of the richest Burmese in the country. The villa had no practical value to him. In the six years he had owned it he had never yet seen it. Instead it was a token of his wealth, a status symbol the mere mention of which was calculated to impress his business associates in the capital. It was Mya Mya and Khin Maung's responsibility to look after the property and to maintain it as if the master of the house might arrive at any moment. Since the birth of her son, Mya Mya had dedicated all her energy to this task. She polished the wooden floors every day, as if the point were to transform them into mirrors. She dusted the shelves in the morning, and in the evening she dusted them again, though not a visible speck of dust had settled on them in the intervening twelve hours. She washed the windows every week and trimmed the lawn with a pair of scissors, which was more thorough than using the lawn mower. She kept the effusive bougainvilleas in check and tended the flower beds passionately.

Mya Mya saw the two policemen coming up the hill. She was standing by the kitchen scrubbing carrots. It was one of those cold, clear December days, and Mya Mya was in a hurry. She had taken too much time polishing the floors on the second story and was worried now that she would no longer finish the kitchen that afternoon, and if the master should arrive tomorrow, he would not find his estate in immaculate condition, and then all the work of the previous years would have been for nothing because he would think that Mya Mya had not been maintaining his property. One day of disarray can count for more than a thousand days of order, she thought, looking into the valley.

Coming up the hill, the officers in their crisp blue uniforms had not followed the road used by oxcarts and the occasional car. Instead they had taken the narrow footpath that wound in tight serpentines first through the pine wood and then among the fields up to the hilltop. Mya Mya saw the men approaching, saw their faces, and felt her panic mounting. It was Tin Win's sixth birthday, and she had always been firmly convinced that especially on the anniversaries of his birth she had to be ready for just about any kind of catastrophe.

Within the space of two breaths dread had taken hold of her, of her soul, of her mind, of her body. Her stomach and intestines contracted as if wrung by giant hands. Tighter and tighter. She gasped for breath. She heard herself whimpering. She heard herself pleading. She heard herself begging. Let it not be true.

The men opened the gate, stepped into the yard, and closed the gate behind them. Slowly they walked over to Mya Mya. She sensed the reluctance in their movements. Each step was like a kick to her body. The younger of the two kept his head lowered. The older one looked her in the eye. She knew him from brief encounters in the village. Their eyes met, and for the duration of a heartbeat Mya Mya was able to read his gaze. That sufficed. She knew everything, and the dread, the monster that had been devouring her, disappeared as quickly as it had come. She knew that a terrible calamity had befallen her, that no one would ever be able to unmake it, that nothing in her life would ever be as it had been, that this was happening for the third time now, and that she did not have the strength to bear it.

The policemen stood in front of her, the younger one still not daring to lift his head.

"Your husband's had an accident," the older one said.

"I know," said Mya Mya.

"He's dead."

Mya Mya said nothing. She did not sit down. She did not cry. She did not break out in lamentation. She said nothing.

She heard the men saying something about an accident, about a golf ball apparently driven off course by the wind. Right in the temple. Dead on the spot. The Englishman will take over the funeral expenses. A small compensation. No acknowledgment of any guilt. A gesture of sympathy. Nothing more. Mya Mya nodded.

When the officers had left she turned around and looked for her son. He sat alone behind the house, playing. Next to him lay a great pile of pinecones. He was trying to throw them into a hole he had dug a few yards away. Most of them far overshot their target.

Mya Mya wanted to call to him, to tell him of his father's death. But why? Presumably he already knew about it. He was, after all, the one who had brought on the calamity, and Mya Mya noticed how for the first time she was admitting that she blamed him for it. It was not merely the inauspicious arrangement of the stars; it was Tin Win, that inconspicuous boy with his black hair, those enigmatic eyes so inscrutable that she never knew whether he was really looking at her. She could read nothing in them. It was he who had brought on the misfortune, he who had wrought the havoc. He created it the way other children built caves or played hide-and-seek.

Mya Mya wanted somehow to leave it all behind. She wanted never to see that child again.

Over the course of the next thirty-six hours she operated the way a person does who has only one goal in mind, a goal that drives her, a goal she serves above all else. She played the mourning widow, received neighbors and friends, organized the burial for the next day, stood before her husband's open grave, and watched the wooden casket vanish into the earth.

The next morning she packed her few belongings—a couple of blouses and longyis, a second pair of sandals, a comb, a hair clip—in an old bag for golf balls her husband had once brought home from the club. Tin Win stood mute beside his mother, watching.

"I have to go away for a few days," she said without looking up.

Her son said nothing.

She left the house. Her son ran after her. She turned around, and he stood still.

"You can't come," she said.

"When are you coming back?" he asked.

"Soon," she said.

Mya Mya turned away and walked to the garden gate. She heard his light steps behind her. She turned around.

"Didn't you hear what I told you?" she said loudly and in a sharp tone.

Her son nodded.

"You stay here." She pointed to the sawn-off stump of a pine tree. "You can sit there and wait for me."

Tin Win ran to the old tree stump and clambered onto it. From there he had a good view of the path leading to their house. Mya Mya set off again, opening and closing the garden gate without turning around. Walking quickly, she took the road into the village below.

Tin Win watched her go. He saw her walk through the fields and into the wood. This was a good spot. From here he would be able to see his mother coming even from a long way off.

# Chapter 11

TIN WIN WAITED.

He waited the rest of that day and night. He squatted on the flat tree stump, feeling neither hunger nor thirst, nor even the cold that settled over the mountains and valleys in the evening. It passed over him without touching him, like a bird over a clearing.

He waited the next day. He watched it get dark and then watched as the fence and the bushes and the fields re-emerged out of darkness. He gazed into the distance, where the trees stood on the edge of perception. That's where his mother would be coming from, and with her red jacket he would recognize her even from afar, and he would scramble down the tree stump, climb over the fence, and run to her. He would cry out loudly with joy, and she would kneel down and wrap him in her arms and press him to her. Very firmly.

That's how he often pictured the scene to himself—when playing alone and dreaming—even though Mother and Father never actually bent down to pick him up, not even when he stood in front of them, hugging their legs. He sensed their reluctance even to touch him. It was his fault; there was no doubt about that. It was a punishment, a just one, only he didn't know what for, and he hoped that whatever the crime, the period of atonement would soon be over. This hope was more fervent than ever now that they had laid his cold, stiff father in a casket of wood and buried him deep in a hole. His longing for his mother and her love compelled him to tough it out on that tree stump, to wait patiently for the red dot on the horizon.

On the third day a neighbor brought him water and a bowl of rice with vegetables and asked whether he wouldn't prefer to wait at her house. He shook his head vehemently. As if going there might cause him to miss his mother. He didn't touch the food. He wanted to save it for her, to share with her when she returned hungry from the long journey.

On the fourth day he sipped at the water.

On the fifth day Su Kyi came, the neighbor's sister, bringing a pot of tea and more rice and bananas. Preoccupied with his mother, he ate none of that, either. It couldn't be much longer. Soon, she had said.

On the sixth day he could no longer make out the individual trees. The forest was blurred, as if he had water in his eyes. It looked like a cloth, waving in the wind, mottled with tiny red dots. These came nearer to him and got larger, but they weren't jackets; they were red balls hurtling violently in his direction. They whistled past him left and right and over his head, so close that he felt their draft. Still others flew straight at him, only to lose their momentum in the last few yards and crash into the ground just inches in front of him.

On the seventh day he squatted stiff and motionless at his post. When Su Kyi saw him she thought he had died. He was cold and white as the hoarfrost that covered the grass in front of the house on many an especially cold January day. His face was sunken, his body like an empty shell, a lifeless cocoon. Only when she got closer could she see that he was breathing, that under his shirt his lean chest was fluttering, like a fish from the market gasping for breath in her kitchen.

Tin Win neither heard nor saw the woman. The world around him was veiled in a milky white fog into which he was slowly but surely vanishing. His heart was pounding. There was still life enough in him, but his hope had faded, and that made him resemble a corpse.

He felt two hands touching him, lifting him up, hugging him and carrying him away.

It was Su Kyi looking after him. A vigorous older woman with a deep voice and a laugh over which the trials of life had passed without a trace. Her only child had died at birth. Her husband had died later the following year of malaria. After his death she had been forced to sell the hut they had finished building only a short time earlier. Since then she

had been living with relatives, more tolerated than welcome. To her family she seemed a crotchety, somewhat un-
nerving old woman with eccentric views on life and death.
In contrast to everyone else, she read no deeper meaning
into the misfortunes fate had dealt her. Nor did she believe
that unfavorable arrangements of the stars had occasioned
her loved ones' deaths. Instead these losses merely showed
that fortune was capricious, a fact one must accept if one
was going to love life. And love life she did. She did not have
much use for predestination. Happiness might find a home
in every individual. She never dared say so out loud, but
everyone knew of her convictions, and they made her into
Tin Win's first ally.

Over the years she had frequently observed her neighbors' son and been astonished at his fair skin, like the light
brown of fallen pine needles or eucalyptus leaves. He was
so much fairer than his parents. She had watched the child
grow into a tall, almost gangly boy, shy like one of the owls
she heard calling so often but never spied, a boy she never
saw in the company of other children.

She had met him once in the woods. She was on her way
into town, and he was sitting under a pine tree watching a
small green caterpillar crawl across his hand.

"Tin Win, what are you doing here in the wood?" she
asked.

"I'm playing," he said without looking up.

"Why all alone?"

"I'm not alone."

"Where are your friends?"

"All around. Don't you see them?"

Su Kyi looked around. She didn't see anyone.

"No," she said.

"The beetles and the caterpillars and the butterflies are my friends. And the trees. They are my best friends."

"The trees?" she asked, surprised.

"They never run away. They're always there, and they tell such beautiful stories. Don't you have any friends?"

"Of course I do," she said, and added after a pause: "My sister, for example."

"No, real friends."

"No trees or animals, if that's what you mean."

He raised his head, and the sight of him frightened her. Had she never really looked at him before, or was it the light in the wood that so altered his face? It seemed hewn of stone, so well proportioned and at the same time so terrifyingly lifeless. Then their eyes met, and he looked at her, much too sternly and seriously for a child, and she was frightened a second time, because she sensed that he knew far too much about life for a boy his age. Seconds later a smile—wistful and tender like none she had ever seen—swept over that stony face. It was that smile that had stuck with her. So deep was the impression it made that it had taken her days to get over it. She saw it at night when she closed her eyes and in the morning when she woke.

"Is it true that caterpillars turn into butterflies?" he asked suddenly, just as she was about to go.

"Yes, that's right."

"And what do we turn into?"

Su Kyi stood still and reflected.

"I don't know."

Neither spoke.

"Have you ever seen animals cry?" he asked.

"No," she answered.

"And trees and flowers?"

"No."

"I have. They cry without tears."

"Then how do you know they're crying?"

"Because they look sad. If you look closely, you'll see it."

He stood up and showed her the caterpillar on his hand.
"Is she crying?" he asked.

Su Kyi considered the creature awhile.

"No," she ultimately decided.

"Right," he said. "But you were guessing."

"How do you know that?"

He smiled again and said nothing, as if the answer was too obvious.

I n the weeks following his mother's disappearance, Su Kyi looked after Tin Win, caring for him and restoring him to good health. When the first month had passed without any word from his family in Rangoon and Mandalay, she moved in with him and promised to care for him and to keep his uncle's house in order until his mother's return. Tin Win did not object. Instead, he withdrew further, so that even the vigor and optimism of a woman like Su Kyi could not reach him. His mood fluctuated from day to day, sometimes from one hour to the next. He would go for days without uttering a word, spending most of his time alone in the garden or the nearby wood. On days like that, in the evening, when they sat at the fire in the kitchen eating their portions of rice, he would keep his head down and say nothing. When Su Kyi asked him about the games he had played in the wood, he would gaze at her through transparent eyes.

Nights were an entirely different story. In his sleep he would crawl over to her and cuddle into her round, soft body. Sometimes he would put his arm around her and squeeze so hard that it woke her up.

On other days he would take her along into the garden and the wood, reporting to her whatever his friends the trees told him. He had given each one a name. Or he would come to her with a handful of beetles, snails, or the most wonderful butterflies that had landed on his hands and flew off only when he stretched his arm high into the air. Animals were not afraid of him.

In the evening, before going to sleep, he would ask Su Kyi to tell him a bedtime story. He would lie motionless until the end, then say: "Sing another one." And Su Kyi would laugh and say: "But I'm not singing at all."

And Tin Win would answer: "But you are. It sounds like a song. Please, another one."

Su Kyi would tell another and another, and she would keep on talking until he had fallen asleep.

She suspected that her words only ever reached him in that way, encoded, that he lived in a world closed to her, one she must approach gingerly and respectfully. She had experienced so much sorrow of her own, so much of life, that she knew better than to press for access to his places of refuge. She had witnessed herself how individuals became prisoners of these strongholds, of their loneliness, confined therein until their dying day. She hoped that Tin Win would learn what she had learned over the years: that there are wounds time does not heal, though it can reduce them to a manageable size.

# Chapter 12

SU KYI COULD not remember the first time she noticed it. Was it on that morning standing in front of the house? Tin Win had been by the fence. She'd called to him, and he'd looked around, turning his head this way and that, as if looking for her. Or perhaps it was a few days later, at dinner, as they squatted on a wooden beam by the kitchen, eating their rice. She had pointed out a bird sitting a few yards in front of them on the lawn.

"Where?" he asked.

"There, beside the stone."

"Oh," he said, nodding in the wrong direction.

He always seemed to follow the same routes in the yard, in the house, or in the adjacent meadows and fields, and he often stumbled over sticks or stones when he deviated from his accustomed paths. When she offered him a bowl or cup he would reach out and feel the space between them for a split second that seemed to her to last forever. He squinted slightly whenever he focused on anything more than a few yards away. As if he were peering through the thick mist that drifted through the valley on so many mornings.

Indeed, Tin Win himself did not know when it had started. Hadn't the mountains and clouds on the horizon always been somewhat unclear?

The condition seemed to worsen after his mother disappeared. At some point he could no longer see the woods from the yard; the clean, dark lines of individual trees ran together and blurred into a distant brown-green sea. A gray mist slowly enveloped the teacher at school. He heard the voice plainly enough, as if they were sitting side by side, but he could no longer make out the visual image—no better than the trees or the fields or the house or Su Kyi from more than a few arms' lengths away.

So Tin Win simply no longer oriented himself to objects and their details. Instead he lived in a world that now consisted primarily of colors. Green meant the wood, red meant the house, blue the sky, brown the earth, purple the bougainvillea, and black the fence around the yard. Nor were colors themselves entirely reliable. They, too, faded away, until eventually a milky white cloth settled over him, obscuring everything outside a radius of a few yards. Thus the world vanished before his eyes, dying like a spent fire that gives neither warmth nor light.

Tin Win privately had to confess that it did not particularly bother him. He had no fear of the everlasting darkness—or of whatever might replace the pictures his eyes had once seen. Even if he had been born blind, he told himself, he would not have missed out on much. Nor could he imagine he would miss much now should his blindness become complete, as indeed came to pass. Upon his waking and opening his eyes three days after his tenth birthday, the mist had entirely engulfed the world.

Tin Win lay still in his bed that morning, breathing quietly. In and out. He closed his eyes and opened them again. Nothing. He looked up to where until recently the ceiling had been and saw nothing but a white hole. He sat up and turned his head this way and that. Where was the wooden wall with the rusty nails? The window? The old table where he kept the tiger bone his father had found in the woods all those years ago? Everywhere he looked was a featureless white vault with neither foreground nor background. Without limit. As if he was looking upon infinity.

Next to him, he knew, lay Su Kyi. She was sleeping but would soon stir. He could hear it in her breath.

Outside it was already light—the birdsong told him that. He rose cautiously, feeling with his toes for the edge of the straw mat. He felt Su Kyi's legs and stepped over them, then stood in the room and considered briefly where the kitchen ought to be. He took a few steps and found the door without collision. He walked into the kitchen, around the fire pit, past the cupboard with the tin bowls, and out into the courtyard. He had not stumbled once nor even stretched out his hands to feel his way. Outside the door he paused, sensing the sun on his face, bemused by the confidence with which he moved about in this mist, in this no-man's-land.

Except that he'd forgotten about the wooden stool. His face hit the hard earth, and the pain in his shin made him cry out briefly. Something tore up his face, which was now a mess of saliva mixed with blood.

He lay still and unmoving. Something crept along his cheek, over his nose, and onto his forehead before disappearing into his hair. It was too quick to be a caterpillar. An ant perhaps? A beetle? He didn't know and he started to cry, softly, without tears. Like the animals. He didn't want anyone ever to see him crying again.

He groped with his hand across the ground, noted the irregularities, reached with his fingers through the little dips and rises as if exploring uncharted terrain. How rough the ground was, how ridden with stones and ruts. How had he failed to notice them before? He rolled a twig between his thumb and forefinger and felt as though he could see it. Would that image, and all the visual impressions in his memory, eventually fade? Or in the future would he see the world only through a window of recollection and imagination?

He listened hard. The ground was humming, singing softly, barely audibly.

S u Kyi lifted him up.
"The stool was right in front of you," she said. It was an observation, not an accusation.

She fetched water and a cloth. He rinsed out his mouth, and she washed his face. Her heavy breathing betrayed how frightened she had been.

"Does it hurt much?" she asked.

He nodded. He had the sour taste of blood in his saliva.

"Come into the kitchen," she said, standing up and leading the way.

Tin Win sat unmoving, uncertain of the direction. A few seconds later, Su Kyi came back out of the house.

"What's keeping you?"

Her wail carried all the way down to the town, and for years afterward the people of Kalaw would talk about how deeply it had frightened everyone who heard it.

The doctor in the little hospital at the end of the main street was nonplussed. Blindness, at this age, without any trauma, just like that. He had never known of anything like it. He could only speculate. It could hardly be a brain tumor, since the patient exhibited neither dizziness nor headaches. Perhaps some neural or genetic disorder. Without knowing the precise cause, he could not prescribe any therapy. There was no remedy. The best one could hope for was that his eyesight would return as mysteriously as it had failed.

# Chapter 13

IN THOSE FIRST months Tin Win struggled to reclaim his world—the house, the yard, the nearby fields. He sat for hours in the yard, at the fence, on the stump of the pine tree, under the avocado tree, and before the poppies, trying to discover whether each place, each tree had its own unique fragrance, like a person. Did the garden behind the house smell different than it used to?

He paced out his pathways, calculating distances and drafting mental maps that incorporated everything his feet and hands touched, every bush, every tree, every stone. He wanted to preserve them. They would replace his eyes. With their help he would impose order on the opaque fog enshrouding him.

It didn't work.

The next day nothing would be where he remembered it. As if someone had rearranged the furniture overnight.

Nothing in this world had a fixed place. Everything was in motion.

The doctor had assured Su Kyi that the other senses would eventually compensate for the loss of eyesight. Blind individuals learn to rely on their ears, their noses, and their hands, and in that way, after a phase of acclimation and re-adjustment, they learn to renavigate their environment.

For Tin Win the case seemed to be precisely the opposite. He tripped over stones he had known for years. He collided with trees and branches upon which he had previously clambered. Even in the house he ran into doorjambs and walls. Twice he would have stepped into the fire pit had Su Kyi's timely cries not spared him.

A few weeks later, on his first venture back into town, he was nearly run down by a car. He stood at the roadside, listening to the sound of the approaching motor. He heard voices and footsteps, the snorting of a horse. He heard birds and chickens and an ox defecating, and none of it made any sense or gave him any indication of which way to go. His ears were of less use to him than his nose, which could at least smell a fire, or his hands, which could alert him to obstacles. Not a day passed without torn knees, dark bruises, bumps on the head, or scrapes on his hands and elbows.

It was especially hard at school with the nuns and the padre from Italy. Although they now allowed him to sit in the front row, and although they frequently inquired whether he was following the lessons, he understood less and less of what they said. In their presence he felt lonelier than ever. He heard their voices and felt their breath but couldn't see them. They stood beside him, an arm's length or a hand's breadth distance, yet they were out of reach, miles away.

The proximity of other children was even more intolerable. Their voices unnerved him and their laughter still rang in his ears when he lay in bed at night. While they ran about in the courtyard next to the church, romping and frolicking, he would sit on a bench under the cherry tree as if tied to it, and with every step he heard, every cry, every expression of joy, however insignificant, he felt the bonds tightening.

Su Kyi was unsure whether the world had truly melted away before his eyes or Tin Win had somehow buried himself far from it. And if he was so inclined, how far would he go? Would his ears, too, eventually cease to function? His nose? Would his delicate, slender fingers cease to feel, degenerating into numb, useless appendages? He was strong, much stronger than he himself knew or his lean body betrayed. She had come to understand that over the years. And he no doubt had the power to withdraw to the very ends of the earth. The boy could will his own heart to stop beating if he wished it, just as his eyes had ceased to see. In the deepest core of her soul she sensed that he would one day end his life in just that way and no other.

# Chapter 14

U BA FELL silent.

How long had he been talking? Three hours? Four? Five? I hadn't taken my eyes off him, and I now suddenly noticed that everyone else had left. The tables were empty. The room was quiet. There was no sound at all but the soft snoring of a man sitting behind the glass pastry display. His breath hissed and rolled like steam rising from a teakettle. Two candles burned on the table between U Ba and myself. I realized I was shivering. The rest of the room was dark.

"You don't believe me, Julia?"

"I don't believe in fairy tales."

"This is a fairy tale?"

"If you knew me as well as you claim to, it would come as no surprise that I don't believe in magic. Or supernatural powers. Or even in God. Least of all in stars or constellations. People who abandon a child because of some alignment of the stars at his birth? They must be sick."

I took a deep breath. Something had set me off. I tried to calm myself. I didn't want him to see I was angry.

"You have traveled far and wide, Julia, while I have seldom left our village. And when I did, my road took me no farther than to our little provincial capital, a day's journey in a horse-drawn cart. My last excursion was many years ago, but you have seen the world. Who am I to contradict you?"

His humility angered me even more.

"If you say it is so," he continued, "then I will gladly believe that there are no fathers or mothers in your world who cannot love their children, for whatever reasons. Perhaps only stupid, uneducated people behave that way, a further proof of our backwardness, for which I can only beg for your continued forbearance."

"Of course I didn't mean that. But for us it's not about the stars."

He looked at me and fell silent.

"I didn't come six thousand miles to hear tales. Where is my father?"

"Please have a bit more patience. This is your father's story."

"So you say. Where's your evidence? If at any time in his life my father had been blind, don't you think that we, his family, would have heard about it? He would have told us."

"You are certain."

He knew I was not.

I told him I had no use for introspection and navel-gazing. I was probably one of the few New Yorkers who had never been to a therapist. I was not the type to go looking for the causes of all my problems in my childhood, and I had no respect for those who did. I reiterated that I could not believe my father had been blind at any time in his life, but the longer I talked, the less I was addressing myself to U Ba. He listened and nodded. It seemed as if he understood exactly what I meant and agreed with me. When I was done, he wanted to know what that was, a therapist.

He took a sip of his tea.

"I fear, Julia, that I must excuse myself for now. I am no longer accustomed to speaking at such great length. I often spend entire days in silence. At my age there is not much left to say. I know that you would like to ask me about Mi Mi, the woman to whom your father wrote. You would like to know who and where she is, and what role she plays in your father's life and thereby—perhaps—in yours." He stood up and bowed. "I'll see you to the street."

We went to the door. I was a full head taller than he was, but U Ba did not seem small. On the contrary, I was too big. His quick, easy strides left me feeling clumsy and stiff.

"You will find the way to your hotel?"

I nodded.

"If you wish, I can collect you there tomorrow after breakfast and show you my home. We would be undisturbed there. I could show you a few photographs."

He departed with a bow.

I had turned to walk down the street when I suddenly heard his voice again, behind me. He was whispering. "And your father, Julia, he is here—very near. Do you see him?"

I spun around, but U Ba had disappeared into the darkness.

# Chapter 15

BACK IN MY hotel I lay on the bed. I am four or five years old again. My father is sitting on the edge of my bed. The room is painted a light pink. A mobile hangs from the high ceiling—striped bees, black and white. Beside my bed two cases filled with books, puzzles, and games. Across the room a baby carriage in which three dolls lie sleeping. My bed is full of stuffed animals: Hopsy, the yellow rabbit, who brings me chocolate eggs once a year. Dodo, the giraffe, whose long neck I somehow envy. Arika, the chimpanzee who I know, when no one else is around, can walk. Two Dalmatians, a cat, an elephant, three bears, and Winnie-the-Pooh.

Dolores, my favorite doll, is lying in my arms with her scraggly black hair. She's missing one hand. My brother cut it off to get even with me for something. It's warm, a mild summer's evening in New York. My father has opened the window, and from outside a light breeze blows into the room, setting the bees dancing overhead.

My father has black hair, dark eyes, cinnamon skin, and a prominent nose on which his thick glasses rest. They are round, with black frames; years later I would discover a picture of Gandhi and marvel at the resemblance.

He leans over me, smiles, and takes a deep breath. I hear his voice, a voice that is more than a voice. It sounds like a musical instrument, a violin, a harp. He was never, ever loud. I never heard him yell. His voice could carry and comfort me. It could protect me and put me to sleep. And when it woke me, I woke with a smile. It could calm me like nothing and no one else in the world, even today.

Take the day I lost my balance on my new bicycle in Central Park and cracked my head on a rock. Blood poured from two gaping cuts as if from open faucets. An ambulance took me to the hospital on Seventieth Street. A paramedic bandaged me up, but the blood was leaking through the gauze onto my face and down my neck. I remember the sirens, my mother's worried expression, and a young doctor with bushy eyebrows. He stitched the cuts, but still the bleeding wouldn't stop.

Next thing I knew, my father was by my side. I'd heard his voice from the waiting room. He took my hand, stroked my hair, and told me a story. Not a minute had passed before the red stream from my head stopped. As if his voice had settled gently on my wounds, covering and stanching them.

These stories my father told seldom had happy endings. My mother hated them. Cruel and brutal, she said. Aren't all fairy tales that way? my father asked. Yes, my mother conceded, but yours are confused and bizarre and without any moral and completely unsuitable for children.

But how I loved them—precisely because they were so peculiar, so completely different from any other stories or fables I had heard or read. They were all Burmese, these stories he told, and gave me a rare glimpse into his old life and mysterious past. Maybe that's why they fascinated me so.

"The Tale of the Prince, the Princess, and the Crocodile" was my favorite. My father told and retold it until I knew every sentence, every word, every pause, every inflection by heart.

Once upon a time there was a beautiful princess. The princess lived on the bank of a great river. She lived with her mother and her father, the queen and the king, in an old palace. It had thick, high walls behind which everything was cold and dark and quiet. She had neither brothers nor sisters and was very lonely at court. Her parents spoke nary a word with their daughter. Her servants only ever said "Yes, Your Majesty" or "No, Your Majesty." In the whole palace there was no one to talk to or play with. She was terribly bored, and filled with longing. With time she came to be a lonesome and sad princess indeed, who could not even recall the last time she laughed. At times she wondered if she had forgotten how. Then she would look into a mirror and try to smile. She twisted her face into a grimace. It was not even funny. When she grew altogether too sad to bear it, she would walk down to the river. There she would sit in the shade of a fig tree, listening to the rushing current and hearkening to the birds and the cicadas. She loved the thousands of little stars the sunlight sprinkled on the waves. Then her spirits would rise a little, and she would dream of a friend who might make her laugh.

On the opposite bank of the same river lived a king notorious throughout his realm for his severity. Not one of his subjects ever dared to be idle or to daydream. The farmers toiled stalwartly in their fields; the craftsmen labored unswervingly in their workshops. And so that he might know whether all his subjects were truly hard at work, the king dispatched his inspectors throughout the land. Anyone found sitting down on the job caught ten swift strokes of the bamboo cane. Nor was the king's son in any way exempt. The prince had to study from morning till night, day after day. The king summoned to his court the most revered scholars in the whole country to instruct him. He intended to make of his son the cleverest prince that ever there was.

But one day the young prince managed to slip away from the palace. He leapt up on his charger and rode down to the river, where he beheld the princess sitting on the opposite shore. She had tucked yellow blossoms into her long black hair. He had never seen a more beautiful girl and was immediately consumed by a single desire: to get across that river.

Now, there was neither bridge nor ferry to cross that torrent. Indeed, the two kings, harboring great enmity for each other, had forbidden their subjects to set foot in each other's realms. Anyone who disregarded the ban paid with his life. Moreover, the river swarmed with crocodiles just waiting for a fisherman or farmer to venture in.

The prince first thought to swim across, but hardly was the water up to his knees when there came the crocodiles, wide mouths agape. The prince reached the bank only just in time. If he could not speak with the princess, though, he could at least watch her.

Henceforth he returned secretly to the river every day, where he settled himself on a rock and gazed, full of longing, across to the princess. So weeks passed and months until finally, one day, one of the crocodiles swam up to him.

"I have been watching you for a long time, my dear prince," it said. "I know how unhappy you are, and I have taken pity on you. I would like to help you."

"But how can you help me?" inquired the prince, astonished.

"Climb onto my back, and I will carry you to the opposite bank."

The prince looked warily at the crocodile.

"It's a trick," he said. "You crocodiles are voracious and ravenous. You have never yet let a person out of the water alive."

"Not all crocodiles are alike," replied the crocodile. "Trust me."

The prince hesitated.

"Trust me," the crocodile said again.

The prince had no choice. If he wanted to reach the beautiful princess, he would have to trust the crocodile. He climbed up on its back, and it brought him, as promised, to the opposite bank.

The princess could not believe her eyes when the prince was suddenly standing before her. She herself had often observed the prince and secretly hoped he would eventually find his way across. The prince was embarrassed and did not know what to say. He stuttered, muddling every sentence, and soon the two could not help laughing. And the princess laughed as she had not laughed in a long, long time. When the hour came for the prince to leave, she grew very sad and implored him to stay.

"I cannot," said he. "Great will be my father's wrath if he learns I have been with you. He would be sure to lock me up, and I would never again be able to come to the river alone. But I promise you I'll return."

The kindly crocodile carried the prince back across the river.

The next day the princess waited, again full of longing. She had all but given up hope when she caught sight of the prince on his white steed. The crocodile was there, too, offering its faithful services. From that day on, the prince and the princess met every day.

The other crocodiles were furious. One day, in the middle of the river, they barred the crocodile and the prince's way. "Give him to us, give him to us!" they cried, stretching their mouths wide and snapping at the prince.

"Leave us in peace," the great crocodile roared, swimming down the river as fast as it could. But after only a short while it was surrounded by the others. "Crawl into my mouth," the crocodile cried to its human friend. "You will be safe there." It opened its mouth as wide as it could, and the prince scrambled in. Not for one moment did the other animals let those two out of sight. Wherever they swam, the others followed, waiting and waiting. The prince would eventually have to emerge, after all. But the kindly crocodile was patient, and after several hours the others finally gave up and swam away. The crocodile crawled back to the bank and opened its mouth. The prince did not move. The crocodile shook itself and cried: "My friend, my friend, run ashore, run, as fast as you can."

Still the prince did not move.

Then the princess, too, called from the opposite shore: "My dear prince, please, come out."

But it was no use, for the prince was dead. He had suffocated in his friend's mouth.

When the princess realized what had happened, she, too, sank to the ground, and perished of a broken heart.

The two kings decided independently not to bury their children but to burn them on the riverbank. As chance would have it, the two ceremonies fell on the same day, at the same hour. The kings cursed and threatened one another, each blaming the other for the death of his child.

It was not long before the flames were roaring and the two corpses were ablaze. All at once the fires began to smolder. It was a windless day, and two great, mighty columns of smoke climbed straight up to heaven. And suddenly it grew quite still. The fires ceased their crackling, burning on without a sound. The river ceased its chortling and gurgling. Even the kings fell silent.

Then the animals began to sing. First the crocodiles.

But crocodiles can't sing, I object at this point every evening.

Sure they can, answers my father very quietly. Crocodiles sing, if only you let them. You just have to be quiet to hear them.

And elephants, too?

Elephants, too.

And who sang next?

The snakes and the lizards. The dogs sang, then the cats, the lions, and the leopards. The elephants joined in, the horses and the apes. And of course the birds. The animals sang in chorus, more beautifully, in fact, than they had ever sung before, and suddenly, no one knew why, the two columns of smoke drifted slowly toward each other. The louder and clearer the animals' song, the closer the columns drew, until at last they embraced each other and became one, as only lovers can.

I close my eyes and hear my animals and think: my father's right. They can. They hum me quietly to sleep.

My mother didn't like this story because it didn't have a happy ending. My father thought that it did so have a happy ending. So vast was the gulf between them.

I myself was never sure.

Part Two

# Chapter 1

THE NIGHTTIME QUIET was torture. I lay in my hotel bed, craving familiar noises. Car horns. Fire sirens. Rap music or voices from a television in the next apartment. The elevator bell. Nothing. Not even a creak on the stairs or the footsteps of other guests in the hallway.

Some time later, I heard U Ba's voice. Like an invisible intruder it wandered through the room speaking to me from the desk and the cupboard, then sounding as if it came from the bed next to mine. I couldn't get his story out of my mind. I thought about Tin Win. Even with a few hours' distance I couldn't see my father in him. But how much did that matter? What do we know about our parents, and what do they know about us? And if we don't even know the individuals who have accompanied us since birth—we not them and they not us—then what do we know about anyone at all? Don't I have to imagine, from that perspective, that anyone is capable of anything, even the most heinous crime? On what or whom, on which truths, can one ultimately depend? Are there individuals I can trust unconditionally? Can there ever be such a person?

Not even sleep released me. I dreamt of this Tin Win. He had fallen down, stricken blind, and lay crying on the ground before me. I wanted to pick him up, so I bent over him, but—despite his small size—he was impossibly heavy. I took his hands and pulled. I wrapped my arms around his child's body, but I might as well have tried to lift an iron bull. I knelt beside him as if beside the wounded victim of a car wreck, bleeding on the side of the road. I spoke words of comfort to him, assuring him that help was on the way. He begged me not to go, not to leave him alone. Suddenly my father was standing next to us. He picked the boy up and whispered something in his ear. Finally in my father's arms Tin Win was consoled. He put his head on my father's shoulder, sobbing, and fell asleep. The two of them turned from me and walked away.

The air was warm when I woke and smelled vaguely sweet, like fresh cotton candy. Outside I could hear insects buzzing and two men talking under my window. My calves ached when I stood, but I felt much better than the day before. The long sleep had done me good. The hot morning made the cold shower bearable. Even the coffee tasted better and was hotter than it had been the day before. I felt my purpose returned and for a moment even felt ready to begin my search for Mi Mi, but something held me back. U Ba's story. It had cast a spell over me.

I sat unmoving before the hotel and watched an old man trim the lawn with long shears. Corn poppies ran riot in their beds amid freesias, gladioli, bright yellow orchids. Over these, arched branches laden with hundreds of red, white, and pink hibiscus blossoms. In the middle of the lawn stood a pear tree; white blossoms lay strewn about the grass beneath its branches. A bit farther off stood two palms and an avocado tree heavy with fruit. There were beans and peas, radishes, carrots, strawberries, raspberries.

U Ba came for me just after ten. I watched him approach from a long way off. He walked along the street, greeted a cyclist, and turned into the hotel entrance. To ease his movement he lifted his longyi a bit with both hands, like a woman in a long dress stepping over a puddle. He met me with a smile and a conspiratorial wink, as if we had known each other for many years and had not parted on a bad note the day before.

"Good morning, Julia. You enjoyed your nightly repose?" he asked.

I smiled at his archaic way of putting things.

"Ah, how beautifully radiant your eyes. Exactly like your father's! The full lips and the white teeth you also get from him. Forgive me for repeating myself. It's not my simple-mindedness but your beauty that causes me to repeat myself."

His compliment embarrassed me. We walked into the street and turned onto a trail that led down to the river. The plants on the edge of the path flourished and blossomed as obscenely as in the hotel garden. Our way was lined with date palms, mango trees, and tall green plants laden with small yellow bananas. The warm air smelled of fresh jasmine and ripe fruit.

By the river several women were standing up to their knees in the water, washing clothes, singing at their work. They laid the wrung-out shirts and longyis on the rocks in the sun to dry. A few of them greeted U Ba and watched me inquisitively. We crossed over a little wooden bridge, climbed an embankment on the other side of the river, and hiked along a steep footpath. The women's singing followed us up to the summit.

The view of the valley and the peaks in the distance set me on edge somehow. Something about the postcard scenery wasn't right. The slopes were sprinkled only sparsely with young pines. Between the trees was brown, burnt grass.

"There was a time you would have seen nothing but dense pine forests from this spot," said U Ba, as if reading my mind. "In the seventies the Japanese came and cleared the trees."

I wanted to ask why they had allowed it and whether no one had resisted, but decided instead to hold my tongue.

We plodded on past old, dilapidated English manor houses and dingy, windowless shacks whose lopsided walls were woven of dried leaves and grass. When finally we stopped it was in front of one of the few wooden houses. It was of nearly black teak and stood on stilts almost five feet off the ground, with a corrugated tin roof and a narrow porch. A pig was rooting around beneath it. Chickens ran loose in the yard.

U Ba led me up the porch steps and into a large room with four unglazed windows. The furniture looked like hand-me-downs from an earlier, colonial time. Coil springs rose through the seat of a brown leather armchair set beside two threadbare couches, a coffee table, and a dark cupboard. An oil painting of the Tower of London hung on the wall above the chair.

"Make yourself at home. I'll fix some tea," said U Ba, disappearing.

I was about to sit down when I heard a strange droning. A small swarm of bees flew right across the room from one of the windows to the open cupboard and back. Only then did I see their nest hanging on the top shelf, larger than a football. I retreated cautiously into the other corner of the room, took a seat, and held still.

"I hope you're not afraid of bees," asked U Ba when he returned with a pot of tea and two cups.

"Only wasps," I lied.

"My bees cannot sting."

"You mean they haven't stung anyone yet."

"Is there a difference?"

"What do you do with the honey?"

"What honey?"

"From the bees."

U Ba looked at me. "I wouldn't touch it. It belongs to the bees."

I followed the flight of the bees with a wary glance. Was he serious? "Then why not have the nest removed?"

He laughed. "Why should I drive them off? They do me no harm. On the contrary, I feel honored they have chosen my home. We have lived together peacefully for five years. We Burmese believe they bring good fortune."

"Is it true?"

"One year after the bees moved in, your father returned. Now you are sitting across from me."

He smiled again and poured the tea.

"Where were we obliged to interrupt our story? Tin Win had become blind, and Su Kyi was trying to find help, correct?"

And so he resumed his tale.

# Chapter 2

RAIN CLATTERED ON the corrugated tin roof as if the house were collapsing under a hail of stones. Tin Win had retreated into the rearmost corner of the kitchen. He did not like these downpours. The drumming of the water on the roof was too loud, and the vehemence with which it tore from the sky made him nervous. He heard Su Kyi's voice, but the rain swallowed even her words.

"Where on earth are you?" she called yet again, poking her head through the kitchen door. "Come on now, let's get going. It'll stop soon enough."

Su Kyi was right, as she almost always was when it came to the weather. She claimed to feel the storms and tropical showers in her gut and above all in her ears, which would first warm, then tickle, and finally itch terribly just before the first drops fell. Tin Win had long ago ceased to doubt her forecasts. Not two minutes later they were standing in front of the house, the rain having stopped, the only sound water dripping from the roof and from the leaves and racing in a wild torrent through the ditch across the yard.

Su Kyi took his hand. The ground was slick; muck oozed between his toes at every step. It was still early, not much after seven. The sun broke through the clouds and shined pleasantly on his face, though it would soon burn his skin and raise white clouds of vapor from the ground, sweating the earth itself. They trudged through the mud past huts ringing with the sounds of the morning: children crying, dogs barking, the clatter of tin pots.

She wanted to take him to the monastery in town where a monk named U May was abbot. She had known him for a long time and believed he would be able to help. U May was perhaps the only person whom Su Kyi trusted, whom she sensed was a kindred spirit. If not for him, she would not have survived the deaths of her daughter and husband. U May himself was already old, probably over eighty. She didn't know for sure. Since going blind a few years earlier, he had been teaching a small class of local children every morning. Su Kyi was hoping he would be able to take Tin Win under his wing, too, to coax him out of the darkness that beleaguered him, to teach him what he had taught her: that life is interwoven with suffering. That in every life, without exception, illnesses are unavoidable. That we will age, and that we cannot elude death. These are the laws and conditions of human existence, U May had explained to her. Laws that apply to everyone, everywhere in the world, regardless of how dramatically times might change. There is no power that can release a person from pain or from the sadness one might feel as a result of that insight—unless it be that person himself. And in spite of it all, U May had told her again and again, life is a gift that none might disdain. Life, U May told her, is a gift full of riddles in which suffering and happiness are inextricably intertwined. Any attempt to have one without the other was simply bound to fail.

The monastery itself was surrounded by a high stone wall just off the main street, behind which half a dozen little white pagodas were festooned with colored streamers and tiny golden bells. As a safeguard against flooding, the monastery stood on pilings a good ten feet off the ground. Over the years a number of outbuildings had grown up around the main building. In the middle of it all a four-cornered tower jutted upward, narrowing in seven tiers to a single golden pinnacle visible far and wide. The walls were pine, browned by the sun, and each roof was shingled with blackish wooden shake. Across from the entrance, a massive wooden Buddha nearly as high as the ceiling sat cloaked in semidarkness and overlaid with gold leaf. At its feet stood tables crowded with offerings: tea, flowers, bananas, mangos, and oranges. On the wall behind the Buddha hung shelves with dozens of smaller Buddhas, shimmering gold, many draped in yellow robes, others holding parasols of red, white, or gold paper. Of course, Tin Win saw none of this.

~~~

He and Su Kyi walked hand in hand across the wide courtyard to the central staircase, passing two monks who swept the damp earth with twig brooms. Dark red monks' robes hung drying on a line. The air around the buildings crackled with burning wood and smelled of smoke.

U May sat cross-legged and motionless on a dais at the end of the hall, gaunt hands folded in his lap. A pot of tea, a small cup, and a plate of roasted seeds sat on a low table before him. His head was clean shaven. His lidded eyes sat deep in their sockets. His cheeks were lean but not sunken. Su Kyi was mildly taken aback every time she saw him. His features seemed so frank and naked to her. He was slender but not emaciated, wrinkled but not shriveled. His face was obviously the mirror of his soul. Not a trace of excess baggage.

Su Kyi could not help but recall the first time she had seen him. He had come in on the train from the capital, and he was standing in front of the station. That was more than twenty-five years ago. She had been on her way to the market. He was barefoot, and he smiled at her. His face had touched her even then. He asked her for directions. Out of curiosity she accompanied him all the way to the monastery. During that walk they fell into conversation, and so began their friendship. In the years that followed U May occasionally told her about his childhood, his youth, and the life he had led before becoming a monk. It wasn't much to go on, just some scraps of stories that Su Kyi collected and out of which a contradictory picture slowly emerged.

He came from a wealthy family that owned several rice mills in Rangoon and that belonged to the Indian minority who had come to Burma after the English annexation of the delta in 1852. His father was a patriarch, authoritarian and hot-tempered, feared in the family for his violent outbursts of rage. His children avoided him, and his wife withdrew into illnesses that not even the British doctors in Rangoon could diagnose. After the birth of their third child, the father, weary of his perennially ailing wife, shipped her and the two younger children off to relatives in Calcutta. The medical care was superior there, he said. As the oldest son, U May was intended to one day carry on the family business and so was forced to stay with his father, who would soon have forgotten the rest of the family had not letters arrived from Calcutta every few months describing the mother's remarkable recovery and announcing her impending return—a prospect that never failed to fill U May with indescribable joy. Over the years, however, the letters came less frequently, until U May realized he had seen the last of his mother and siblings there on the wharf in Rangoon harbor where, as a seven-year-old, he had stood gazing after the ship to India.

And so the domestic servants and nannies raised him— especially the cook and the gardener, whose company he'd sought since learning to walk. U May was a quiet, even reticent child whose particular talent appeared to consist in divining the expectations of others and in doing everything in his power to fulfill them.

Back then he loved best to play in the garden. In the rearmost corner of the property, the gardener laid out a plot for him that U May tended with assiduous devotion. His father, when he learned of it, had each plant uprooted and the soil turned over. Garden work was for servants. Or girls.

U May accepted this without a word, just as he accepted and followed all of his father's instructions until the day—he wasn't even twenty—when his father announced U May's engagement to the daughter of a shipping magnate. The match would benefit both businesses and families. Shortly thereafter the father learned of his son's relationship with Ma Mu, the cook's daughter. The episode in itself would not particularly have troubled him; this kind of thing happened. It would even have been possible to find a solution for the sixteen-year-old girl's pregnancy. But his son's assertion that he loved the girl was ridiculous and inexcusable. Indeed, the father's unsuppressed laughter filled the house for several minutes when he heard of it. Years later the gardener still swore that hundreds of blossoms withered at the sound.

U May explained very simply to his father that under no circumstances was he prepared to wed the bride who had been selected for him. Later the same day his father packed the cook and her daughter off to a business partner in Bombay, refusing to give his son any information concerning their whereabouts. U May left the house in search of them. In the years that followed, he traveled ceaselessly throughout the British colonies in Southeast Asia. Once he thought he saw Ma Mu or at least heard her voice. It was in Bombay Harbor just before boarding a steamer to Rangoon. He felt as if someone had called his name, but when he turned he saw only unfamiliar faces and at some distance on the dock a cluster of men gesticulating excitedly. A child had fallen into the water.

Each month that passed without any trace of Ma Mu or her mother left U May more desperate and furious. It was a vague, ill-defined fury he felt. It had neither name nor face and was directed largely at himself. He took to drinking, frequented the brothels between Calcutta and Singapore, and earned more in a month in the opium trade than his father made in a year, only to lose it again in illegal gambling. On a passage from Colombo to Rangoon he made the acquaintance of an odd and loquacious Bombay rice merchant who told him one evening on deck of his former Burmese cook and of the tragic death of her daughter and the daughter's little boy. They had fallen into the harbor and drowned when the young woman tried to follow a man who was boarding a passenger ship. According to eyewitnesses she had mistakenly taken him for an acquaintance from Rangoon. The cook's meals had subsequently become inedible, leaving the rice baron no choice but to dismiss her.

U May never told Su Kyi, or anyone, what he went through that night. When the ship reached Rangoon, he left his baggage on board and went from the harbor directly to the Shwegyin monastery at the foot of the Shwedagon Pagoda. He spent a few years there before journeying to Sikkim, Nepal, and Tibet, seeking tutelage in the teachings of the Buddha from several famous monks. He lived for more than twenty years in a small monastery in Indian Darjeeling until deciding to leave for Kalaw, Ma Mu's birthplace. The young lovers had dreamt of Kalaw during their trysts in the cellar, in the rambling garden, and in the servants' quarters. They planned to flee there with their child. Afterward, when he was wandering ceaselessly from place to place, U May never dared visit. Now he felt the time was ripe. He was over fifty, and Kalaw was where he wanted to die.

Standing before U May now, Tin Win held Su Kyi's hand. He followed her across the room and they both knelt down. Tin Win let go of her, and they leaned over until their hands and foreheads brushed the floor.

The old man listened attentively while Su Kyi related Tin Win's story. Occasionally he rocked a little with his upper body and repeated isolated words. When she had finished, he said nothing for a long time. At last he turned to Tin Win, who had crouched mute beside Su Kyi the entire time.

U May spoke slowly and in short sentences. He described the life of the monks, who knew neither home nor property aside from robe and thabeik, a bowl they carried when gathering alms. He explained how the novices walked the streets every morning, just after sunrise, how they stood silently in front of a house or paused in front of a doorway, accepting with gratitude whatever offerings they were given. He described how, with the help of a younger monk, he instructed his pupils in reading, writing, and arithmetic. In essence, however, his principal aim was to pass on the lesson life had taught him: that a person's greatest treasure is the wisdom in his own heart.

Tin Win knelt motionless before the old man, listening intently. It was not the words or sentences as such that transfixed him. It was the voice. A gentle and melodic intoning, subtle and well-tempered like the soft ringing of bells of the monastery tower, bells that needed only a breeze to set them singing. It was a voice that reminded Tin Win of birds at dawn, of Su Kyi's quiet and even breathing as she lay sleeping next to him. He did not merely hear the voice; he felt it on his skin like two hands. He wanted nothing more than to entrust the weight of his body to that voice. The weight of his soul. Something happened then for the first time that would happen ever more frequently in the future: Tin Win saw the sounds—saw them as smoke rising from a fire into the air and spreading throughout the room, wafting back and forth in gentle waves, moved as if by an unseen hand, curling and dancing and slowly dissipating.

On the way home neither Tin Win nor Su Kyi spoke a single word. He held her hand. It was warm and soft.

~~~~~

Tin Win was agitated on the way to the monastery before sunrise the next morning. He would be spending
the next few weeks with the monks. He would be given a
robe and would be going out with the other boys to collect
alms in the vicinity. The thought of it made him queasy,
and his dread deepened with every step. How would he
find his way in the town when he could barely walk a few
yards—even on familiar terrain—without stumbling? He
asked Su Kyi to just let him be, to leave him in peace. He
preferred to stay home on his sleeping mat or on the stool
in the kitchen corner, the only two places he felt at all safe,
or at least unthreatened.

There was no talking her out of it. Tin Win followed
her reluctantly, dragging his feet all the way down into the
town. Su Kyi felt as if she were leading some stubborn animal. All at once the sound of children singing in the monastery stopped them in their tracks. The voices calmed Tin
Win. As if someone were stroking his face and his belly,
soothing him. He stood frozen, listening. The soft rustling
of leaves intermingled with the voices. It was more than a
simple rustling, though. Tin Win realized that leaves, like
human voices, each had their own characteristic timbre.
Just as with colors, there were shades of rustling. He heard
thin twigs rubbing together and leaves brushing against
one another. He heard individual leaves dropping lightly to
the ground in front of him. Even as they drifted through the

air, he noticed that no two leaves sounded alike. He heard buzzing and blowing, chirping and cheeping, rushing and rumbling. A daunting realization was creeping up on him. Might there be, parallel to the world of shapes and colors, an entire world of voices and sounds, of noises and tones? A hidden realm of the senses, all around us but usually inaccessible to us? A world perhaps even more exhilarating and mysterious than the visible world?

Many years later, in New York, when he sat for the first time in a concert hall and the orchestra began to play, he would remember this very moment yet again. He was nearly drunk with happiness when he heard in the background the quiet drumbeats that opened the piece, and then the violins joining in, the violas and the cellos, the oboes and the flutes. Each raised its voice just as the leaves on that summer morning in Kalaw. Each instrument independently at first, and then in a chorus that so overwhelmed his senses he broke into a sweat and lost his breath.

Su Kyi nudged him along toward the monastery and through the music; he staggered along at her side like a drunk. A few moments later it all left him as quickly as it had come. He heard his own footsteps and Su Kyi's labored breathing, the choir and the crowing roosters—but nothing more. Still, he had savored the first taste of a life so intense that it hurt. Indeed, it was sometimes unbearable.

# Chapter 3

DAY WAS JUST breaking when they arrived at the monastery. U May sat meditating in the hall, surrounded by older monks. A young monk sat on a stool below the kitchen, breaking dry branches. Round and round him two dogs circled and frisked. A dozen novices in their red robes, heads freshly shaven, stood in a row beside the staircase. They greeted Tin Win and gave Su Kyi one of the dark red robes for him. She draped it around his slender body. She had shaved his head the night before, and when she saw him standing there amid the other monks she realized again that he was tall for his age and a beautiful boy. The back of his head was distinctive. He had a slim neck, a prominent nose, not too long, and teeth as white as the blossoms of the pear tree that stood before her house. His skin was the color of light cinnamon. His many falls and scrapes had left no more trace than two scars on his knees.

His hands were narrow, the fingers long and elegant. One would never have guessed his feet had never known shoes.

In spite of his size, he seemed to her as vulnerable as a baby chick flitting terrified across the barnyard. The sight of him moved her, but she did not want to pity him. She wanted to help him—and pity made poor counsel.

She found it hard to leave him behind, even if only for a few weeks, but U May had offered to look after him for a while. U May felt the company of the other boys would do him good. The communal meditation and the lessons, the peace and predictable routines of the monastery would strengthen his sense of security and confidence.

T he novices took him into their midst, pressed a black bowl into one hand and a bamboo staff into the other. The monk standing in front of him in the line clenched one end of this staff under his arm. This is how they intended to lead Tin Win around. In a matter of moments the line of monks was on its way, taking small, cautious steps so that the blind one, too, might easily follow along. The novices marched through the gate, then turned right, making slowly for the main thoroughfare. Though Tin Win would not have noticed it, they were accommodating themselves to his tempo, moving more quickly when he picked up the pace or easing up when uncertainty slowed his steps. In front of nearly every house stood a man or a woman with a pot of rice or vegetables they had cooked for the monks in the wee hours of that morning. The procession halted again and again. The benefactors would fill the novices' bowls and bow humbly.

Tin Win clung to his thabeik and his staff. He was used to wandering across the fields with a long stick when he was out on his own. He would swing it back and forth in front of him like an extended arm scanning the ground for ruts, branches, or stones. The bamboo staff in his hand now was no substitute for his own. This one made him dependent on the monk in front of him. It upset him to be out and about without Su Kyi. He missed her hand, her voice, her laughter. The monks were so quiet. Apart from a modest "thank you" for anything put in their bowls, they said nothing, and their silence only agitated him further. After only an hour or so Tin Win noticed that his bare feet were gradually gaining confidence on the sandy ground. He had not stumbled. He had not fallen. Neither the bumps nor the holes in the street had thrown him off balance. His hands relaxed. His stride grew longer and quicker.

Back at the monastery they helped him up the steps to the veranda. The staircase was steep and narrow, without a handrail, and Tin Win wished he could climb it himself. But two monks took him by the hands, a third held him firmly from behind, and Tin Win took one step after another, learning to walk.

Crouching on the floor in the kitchen, they ate the rice and vegetables. Flames blazed in the fire pit, over which a sooty and dented kettle of water boiled. Tin Win sat in their midst, not hungry but tired. He could not say which strain had been greater: the long march or having to rely on the monk in front of him. He was so exhausted that he could hardly follow U May's lesson, and fell asleep while meditating in the afternoon. He was roused by the monks' laughter.

Only lying awake later that evening did he recall the marvelous sounds of the morning. Had that been a dream? If his ears had not deceived him, where were those sounds now? Why could he hear nothing but the snoring of the other monks, no matter how hard he concentrated? He longed to recover the intensity he had experienced only hours earlier, but the harder he tried, the less he heard, until in the end even the snuffling and snoring all around reached him only from a great distance.

I n the weeks that followed, Tin Win did his best to participate in the monastic routine. With each passing day his confidence in the bamboo staff increased, and he enjoyed walking around town without fear of fall or mishap. He learned to sweep the courtyard and to wash clothes, and he spent many afternoons with a tub and washboard ringing out the robes until the cold water made his fingers ache. He helped clean up the kitchen and demonstrated an extraordinary knack for making firewood. One cursory feel sufficed for him to advise the others whether they had better break a given piece of wood on their knees or over a stone. Soon he recognized the monks not only by their voices but also by their lip-smacking, their coughing and belching, their tread across the floorboards, the sounds of their soles on the wood.

He was happiest during the hours spent with U May. The boys would crouch in a semicircle, Tin Win always in the first row and not two yards away from the old monk, whose voice still held the same power and magic that had moved him so profoundly at their first meeting. Even when U May said nothing, allowing the young monk who assisted him to lead the class, Tin Win sensed his proximity. It reassured him. Often he would remain seated when the other children rose and left, edging closer to U May and barraging him with questions.

"How come you can't see anything?" Tin Win asked him one day.

"Who says I can't see anything?"

"Su Kyi. She says you're blind."

"Me? Blind? It's true I lost my eyesight many years ago. But that doesn't mean I'm blind." He paused, then asked: "And you? Are you blind?"

Tin Win considered. "I can tell light from dark, nothing more."

"Have you a nose to smell with?"

"Of course I do."

"Hands to feel with?"

"Certainly, yes."

"Ears to hear with?"

"Of course." Tin Win hesitated. Should he tell U May? But that'd been weeks in the past, and sometimes he was no longer certain that he hadn't imagined the whole thing. "What more do you need?" asked U May. "The true essence of things is invisible to the eyes." A long silence, then: "Our sensory organs love to lead us astray, and eyes are the most deceptive of all. We rely too heavily upon them. We believe that we see the world around us, and yet it is only the surface that we perceive. We must learn to divine the true nature of things, their substance, and the eyes are rather a hindrance than a help in that regard. They distract us. We love to be dazzled. A person who relies too heavily on his eyes neglects his other senses—and I mean more than his hearing or sense of smell. I'm talking about the organ within us for which we have no name. Let us call it the compass of the heart."

The monk reached out his hands to him and Tin Win was surprised at how warm they were. "A person without eyes must be aware," U May told him. "It sounds easier than it is. You must attend to every movement and every breath. As soon as I become careless or let my mind wander, my senses lead me astray. They play tricks on me like ill-mannered children looking for attention. Whenever I am impatient, for example, I want everything to happen more quickly. My movements become hasty. I spill the tea or the bowl of soup. I don't hear properly what others say because I am already elsewhere in my thoughts. Or when rage clamors within me. I once got angry with a young monk, and shortly thereafter I stepped into the kitchen fire. I hadn't heard it crackling; I hadn't smelled it. Rage had muddled my senses. Eyes and ears are not the problem, Tin Win. It is rage that blinds and deafens us. Or fear. Envy, mistrust. The world contracts, gets all out of joint when you are angry or afraid. For us as well as for anyone who sees with their eyes. Only they don't notice it. Be patient."

Tin Win turned toward the old monk.

"Be patient," he said again.

U May attempted to rise. Tin Win sprang up to help him. The old man leaned on his shoulder, and the two walked slowly through the hall onto the veranda. It was raining. Not an ardent shower, but a soft, mild veil of summer rain; the water from the roof dripped at their feet. U May leaned forward so that it rained onto his bald head, running down his neck and back. He drew his pupil out with him. The water ran down Tin Win's forehead, cheeks, and nose. He opened his mouth and stuck out his tongue. The rain was warm and a little salty.

"So what are you afraid of?" U May asked him.

"Why do you think I'm afraid?"

"Your voice."

Of course U May was right, but Tin Win didn't know what he was afraid of; it was almost always there, pursuing him like a shadow on a sunny day. Sometimes it was small, barely perceptible, and he could keep it in check. On other days it would resurge, increasing beyond measure until his hands were clammy with cold sweat and his body trembled as if smitten with ague.

The two stood silently side by side. Doves cooed under the eaves. After a few silent minutes, the old monk asked again: "What are you afraid of?"

"I don't know," answered Tin Win softly. "Of the plump beetle crawling though my dreams and gnawing at me until I wake. Of tree stumps on which I sit and from which I fall without ever hitting the ground. Of fear."

U May stroked the boy's cheeks with both hands.

"Every one of us knows fear," he said. "So well! It encircles us like flies around ox dung. It puts animals to flight. They bolt and run or fly or swim until they believe themselves safe or until they keel over dead from exhaustion. Humans are no wiser. We see that there is no place on earth where we can hide from fear, yet still we attempt to find one. We strive for wealth and power. We abandon ourselves to the illusion that we are stronger than fear. We try to rule—over our children and our wives, over our neighbors and our friends. Ambition and fear have something in common: neither knows any limits. But with power and wealth it is just as with the opium I sampled more than once in my youth—neither keeps its promises. Opium never brought me eternal happiness. It only demanded more and more of me. Money and power do not vanquish fear. There is only one force more powerful than fear."

That evening Tin Win lay motionless on his straw mat. Except for U May, all the monks slept in one large room next to the kitchen. They spread out their mats on the wooden floorboards and buried themselves in their woolen blankets. Up through the cracks in the floor crept the cold of the night. Tin Win listened hard. He heard one dog barking and another answering. Then a second and a third. The fire in the kitchen still crackled softly. On the roof the little gold bells tinkled until the breeze finally settled and they, too, were quiet. Tin Win observed how one monk after the other fell asleep, heard their breathing become quiet and regular, until all at once all sound completely disappeared. A silence prevailed more complete than Tin Win had ever experienced. It was as if the world had melted away. Tin Win plummeted into an abyss, turning in the air, tumbling, stretching out his arms, looking for something to hold on to, a branch, a hand, a sapling, anything to break his fall. There was nothing. He fell deeper and deeper until suddenly he heard again the breathing beside him. And the dogs. And the rattle of a motorcycle. Had he drifted into a dream? Or had he been awake without hearing anything for a few seconds? Had his ears failed? Just like that? Was he going to lose his hearing as well as his eyesight?

Fear beset him, and he thought of U May. There was only one force more powerful than fear. The old man had comforted him. He would find it. Only he must not look for it.

# Chapter 4

SU KYI WALKED across the monastery courtyard. In the shadow of a fig tree six monks greeted her with a bow. She spotted Tin Win in the distance, sitting on the topmost step of the veranda stairs, a fat book on his knees. His fingers rushed over the pages, his head slightly tilted, his lips moving as if he was talking to himself. Every afternoon for nearly four years she had found him reading whenever she came to fetch him from the monastery. The things that had happened over those few years! Just last week U May confirmed again how much Tin Win had changed, how gifted he was. He was the best and most industrious student. He possessed an extraordinary capacity to concentrate and often astounded his instructor with a memory, an imagination, and a power of deduction unlike any U May had ever witnessed in a soon-to-be-fifteen-year-old. Tin Win could recite the contents of lessons days after the fact, effortlessly and completely. In a matter of minutes he would solve math problems in his head for which others required a slate and half an hour. The old monk regarded him so highly that after one season he had begun to give him additional, private instruction in the afternoon. Out of a crate he had pulled books in Braille given to him years ago by an Englishman. Within a few months Tin Win had mastered the alphabet. He read everything that U May had collected over the years, and it wasn't long before he knew every book in the monastery. Fortunately, thanks to U May's friendship with a retired British officer whose son had been born blind, it was possible to provide Tin Win with a steady supply of new books. He devoured fairy tales, biographies, travel accounts, adventure novels, plays, even philosophical treatises. He lugged a new book home nearly every day, and just the previous night Su Kyi had been wakened once again by his murmuring. She found him squatting in the dark beside her, a book on his lap, his hands sweeping across the pages as if caressing them, while he quietly whispered every sentence his fingers felt out.

"What are you doing?" she asked him.

"Traveling."

She smiled, tired though she was. Only a few days earlier he had explained to her that he did not merely read books but traveled with them, that they took him to other countries and unfamiliar continents, and that with their help he was always getting to know new people, many of whom even became his friends.

Su Kyi shook her head, because in his life outside of books he was apparently quite incapable of making friends. Whatever else the school might have done for him, he remained aloof and shy. And in spite of his engagement with the lessons, he had only superficial and sporadic contact with the other boys. He was courteous to the monks but maintained his distance, and Su Kyi worried increasingly that no one could really get through to him. No one, perhaps, but herself and U May, and even there she was not so sure. No, Tin Win lived in his own world, and sometimes she caught herself foolishly wondering whether he was sufficient unto himself, whether he had any need at all for companionship.

Su Kyi stood at the bottom of the stairs clicking her tongue, but Tin Win was so engrossed in his book that he failed to notice. She watched him and realized for the first time that there was nothing more of the child about him. He had shot up over the heads of the other monks. He had the powerful upper arms and broad shoulders of a farmer but the delicate hands of a goldsmith. In his features she could recognize the young man he was soon to be.

"Tin Win," she said.

He turned his head in her direction.

"I still have to get something at the market before we go home. Do you want to come with me or wait here?"

"I'll stay." He dreaded the crowds that jostled among the booths. Too many people. Too many unfamiliar sounds and strange scents that might bewilder him and make him stumble.

"I'll hurry," Su Kyi promised.

Tin Win stood up. He tugged at the new green longyi he had tied with a strong knot about his waist, then walked across the veranda into the monastery hall. He was on his way to the fire pit in the kitchen when he heard a sound he did not recognize. At first he imagined that someone was striking a piece of wood to the beat of a clock, but it was neither dull enough nor hard enough for that. An entirely distinctive monotone rhythm. Tin Win stood still. He knew every room, every corner, every beam of the monastery, and such a sound he had never yet heard. Neither here, nor anywhere else. Where did it come from? The middle of the hall?

He listened hard. He took one step and froze. Listening. There it was again, louder and clearer than before. It sounded like a knocking, like a quiet, gentle knocking. A few seconds later it was joined by the shuffling steps of the monks, their belching and farting from the kitchen, the creaking of the floorboards and the jarring of the shutters. The doves under the eaves. Above him there was rustling: a cockroach or a beetle crawling across the roof. What kind of chirping was that at the wall? Flies rubbing their hind legs together? Something drifted down from above. A feather. Wood worms gnawed the beams beneath him. A breath of wind in the courtyard lifted grains of sand into the air and set them down again. From afar came the snorting of oxen in the fields and the din of voices at the market. It seemed to him as if a curtain drew slowly back to reveal again the world he had briefly encountered once before, then lost. The hidden realm of the senses for which he had so longed. Here it was again.

And through all that crackling, through the creaking, whispering, and cooing, the dripping, trickling, and cheeping, came that unmistakable soft knocking. Slow, calm, and even. Somehow the source of all sounds, tones, and voices in the world. It was at once strong and delicate. Tin Win turned toward it and hesitated. Did he dare approach it? What if he frightened it off? Carefully he lifted one foot. Held his breath. Listened hard. It was still there. He ventured a single step, then a second. He set one foot in front of the other, cautiously, as if he might otherwise tread on the thing. After each movement, he paused momentarily, making sure he had not lost it. It grew clearer with every step. Then he stood still. It had to be right in front of him.

"Is someone there?" he whispered.

"Yes. Right at your feet. You're about to trip over me."

It was a girl's voice. One he did not recognize. He tried in vain to call up her image.

"Who are you? What's your name?"

"Mi Mi."

"Do you hear that thumping noise?"

"No."

"It must be here somewhere." Tin Win knelt down. Now it was nearly next to his ear. "I hear it more and more distinctly. A soft pulsing. You really don't hear it?"

"No."

"Close your eyes."

Mi Mi closed her eyes. "Nothing," she said, and laughed. Tin Win leaned over and felt her breath on his face. "I think it's coming from you." He crept closer to her and held his head just in front of her chest.

There it was. Her heartbeat.

His own heart began to race. He felt almost as if he was eavesdropping, as if he had no right to the information to which he was now privy. He felt fear rising in him, until she laid her hand on his cheek. Its warmth flowed through his body, and he wished she would never take it away. He sat up straight. "Your heart. It's your heartbeat I'm hearing."

"From such a great distance?" She laughed again, but she was not mocking him. He heard it in her voice. It was a laugh he could trust.

"You don't believe me?" he asked.

"I don't know. Maybe. How does it sound, then?"

"Wonderful. No, more beautiful than that. It sounds like . . ." Tin Win stammered, searching for words. "I can't describe it."

"You must have good ears."

He might have thought she was having a laugh at his expense. Her tone revealed to him that she was not.

"Yes. No. I'm not sure if it's our ears that we hear with."

For a few moments, neither said a word. He did not know what to say. He was afraid she might stand up and run off. Perhaps he ought to talk and talk and hope that his voice would captivate her. Mi Mi might stay and listen as long as he kept talking.

"I've never . . ." He wondered how to put it. "Noticed you in the monastery," he said finally.

"I've seen you many times already."

A woman's loud voice interrupted her. "Mi Mi, where are you hiding?"

"In the hall, Mama."

"We have to go home."

"I'm coming."

Tin Win heard that she lifted herself but did not stand up. She extended her hand and quickly stroked his cheek once.

"I have to go. See you soon," she said, and he heard her moving away, but she was not walking. She was crawling on all fours.

# Chapter 5

TIN WIN SAT on the floor, his legs pulled up to his chest, his head on his knees. He would have liked nothing better than to sit there the rest of the day and the night and the next day, too. As if any movement might destroy what he had experienced. Mi Mi was gone, but the beating of her heart had stayed with him. He remembered it, heard it, as if she were sitting next to him. And what of the other tones and sounds? He lifted his head, turned it from one side to the other, and listened around. The rustling continued quietly on the roof. The cheeping at the wall and the gnawing in the wood were still there. The snorting of the water buffalo in the fields, the laughter of the patrons in the teahouses—Tin Win was certain he heard them clearly. He stood up carefully and could hardly believe it. This intense hearing had stayed with him. The noises, whether familiar or strange, were still there. Some were louder, others quieter, but their power and intensity were undiminished. Would they help him find his way in the world?

Tin Win went to the door, passed down the veranda steps, and crossed the courtyard. He wanted to walk around, up and down the main street. He wanted to explore the town, to have a good listen. New, unfamiliar noises were rushing at him from all sides. The world was thumping, thudding, crackling, and rustling. He heard it hissing and gurgling, squeaking and croaking, and none of this deluge of impressions frightened him. He observed that ears functioned in much the same way as eyes. He remembered looking at the forest, seeing dozens of trees with their hundreds of branches and their thousands of needles and leaves simultaneously, not to mention the meadow in the foreground with its flowers and bushes, and he recalled that somehow none of it had confused him in the least. His eyes had focused on a few details of the scene. The rest was peripheral. And with each minute shift of his pupils he could change his focus and consider new details without losing sight of the others. That is what he was experiencing now. He was perceiving such a multitude of noises that he would not have been able to count them, yet they did not blend into one another. Just as previously he had directed his gaze to a blade of grass, a blossom, or a bird, so now he could train his ears on a particular sound, listen to it at leisure, and always detect new tones within it.

He walked along the monastery wall, stopping time and again to listen. He could not get enough of all the noises that filled the air. From a house on the far side of the street he heard a fire blazing. Someone was peeling and chopping garlic and ginger into little pieces, cutting scallions and tomatoes, pouring rice into boiling water. He recognized these sounds from home, from Su Kyi's cooking, and he heard them distinctly, though the house must have been at least fifty yards away. In his mind an image arose—he could not have seen it more clearly with his eyes—of a young woman sweating in her kitchen. Beside him he heard a horse snuffling and a man spitting the juice of chewed betel nuts onto the street. And what of the many other noises he could detect? The melodic chirping, the gnashing, the croaking? Even when he recognized the sound, he did not know to whom or what it belonged. He heard the snapping of a twig, but was it the branch of a pine, an avocado, a fig, or a bougainvillea that was breaking? And the rustling at his feet? Beetle? Snake? Mouse? Something he could never even have imagined making a noise? By itself his extraordinary ability was of little use. He needed help. These sounds were the vocabulary of a new language, and he needed a translator. Someone upon whom he could rely, someone to whom he could entrust himself, someone who would tell him the truth and who would take no pleasure in leading him astray.

He had reached the main thoroughfare now, and the first thing he noticed was a perpetual thrumming on all sides. All the hearts of passersby. To his astonishment he observed that no two sounded alike, just as no two voices did. Some were clear and light, like children's voices, while others beat wildly, hammering like a woodpecker. There were those that resembled the excited peeping of a young chick, and still others whose calm, even beats reminded him of the wall clock Su Kyi wound every evening in his uncle's house.

"Tin Win, what are you doing on the main street by yourself?" It was Su Kyi, coming to collect him. She was shocked. He heard it in her voice.

"I thought I would go to the corner and wait for you there," he replied.

She took his hand, and they walked down the street, past the teahouses and the mosque, turning off behind a small pagoda and slowly ascending the hill on which they lived. Su Kyi was telling him something, but Tin Win was not paying attention to her words. He was listening to her heart. At first it sounded strange. It beat so irregularly, a light tone following a dark one, and the contrast with the familiar voice confused him. After a few minutes, though, he grew accustomed to its rhythm and found that it suited Su Kyi, whose mood and temper, like her voice, sometimes changed abruptly.

At home he could hardly wait to ask Su Kyi for help. He sat down on a stool in the kitchen and listened. Su Kyi was chopping wood outside the door. Cackling hens were running all about her. Pines rocking in the wind. A few birds were singing. Noises that he could recognize and classify. Then he noticed a soft rustling, or was it more a buzzing, a curious tweeting? Was it a beetle or a bee? If Su Kyi could discover the source of this sound for him, he would have learned his first vocabulary word.

"Su Kyi, please come here," he cried excitedly.

She set the ax aside and came into the kitchen. "What is it?"

"Do you hear that buzzing?"

Both paused and listened. He could hear from her heartbeat, quick and loud, how she strained and concentrated. It beat now much as it had a few minutes ago when they were walking uphill.

"I don't hear any buzzing."

"It's coming from up there, above the door. Do you see anything there?"

Su Kyi went to the door and stared at the ceiling. "No."

"Look closely. What's there?"

"Nothing. Wooden slats and dust and dirt. What were you expecting?"

"I don't know, but the noise is coming from there, from the corner I think, where the wall runs into the roof."

Su Kyi looked more closely at the wall. She couldn't see anything out of the ordinary.

"Try standing on a stool. Maybe you'll see better then?"

She climbed onto a stool and examined the wood. Admittedly, her eyes were not the best, and even objects right in front of her nose had begun to lose their clarity, but this much she could clearly see: In this dirty corner of her kitchen was nothing that by any stretch of the imagination buzzed—or made any other kind of noise, for that matter. A fat spider sat spinning her web. Nothing more.

"There's nothing here. Trust me."

Tin Win rose. He was discouraged.

"Will you come with me into the yard?" he asked her.

They stood in front of the hut. He took her hand and tried to concentrate on a single sound that was unfamiliar to him: a sucking, slurping noise.

"Do you hear the slurping, Su Kyi?"

She knew how important it was to him that she hear it, too. But she didn't hear anyone drinking or slurping anything.

"We're alone, Tin Win. No one's drinking anything in our yard."

"I'm not saying anyone is. I hear a noise that sounds like sucking or slurping. It's not far from us."

Su Kyi took a few steps.

"Farther, a little farther yet," he directed her.

She went farther, nearly to the garden fence, knelt on the ground and said nothing.

"Can you hear it now?" It was not a question, but a request, and she would have given her life to oblige. But she couldn't hear a thing.

"No."

"What do you see?"

"Our fence. Grass. Dirt. Flowers. Nothing that could make a slurping noise." She looked at the yellow orchids and at the bee crawling out of one of its blossoms and stood up again.

# Chapter 6

SAND COVERED HIS face. He felt it on his lips and between his teeth. Tin Win lay in the dust of the road, feeling as helpless as a beetle on its back. He was on the brink of tears. Not because he had really hurt himself, but out of shame and rage. He had asked Su Kyi not to pick him up that day, telling her that for once he intended to walk home alone from the monastery. He had been certain he could find his own way, after all those years.

He didn't know whether he had stumbled over a stone, a root, or a rut cut into the earth by the rain. He knew only that he had committed the most foolhardy of blunders: overconfidence. He had ceased to be attentive. He had set one foot in front of the other without concentrating, absentmindedly. He did not know whether the sighted could really pay due attention to several things at once or they merely claimed they could. He knew only that he could not.

On top of that, he had been angry, and that particular emotion had always wrought havoc in his world. U May was right. Rage and anger confounded his senses every time, making him stumble or walk into trees or walls. Tin Win pulled himself up, wiped the dirt off his face with his longyi, and went on. His steps were uncertain. He paused after each one, probing the path with his staff as if he were crossing enemy territory.

He wanted to get home as quickly as possible. Initially he had intended to follow his ears, to explore the area further, to discover new noises and to investigate them; indeed, perhaps even to venture into the market Su Kyi had spoken of so often. Now, though, he felt only fearful of the veil of noise surrounding him. Chirping, hissing, gnawing, and chattering . . . every individual sound frightened him. He was in retreat and would most have liked to flee as quickly as possible. Instead he had to grope his way forward, creeping step by step along the wall, stealing down the main street, clinging all the while to his staff like a castaway to a plank. He turned to the right and noticed that the incline began. A stranger called his name.

"Tin Win. Tin Win."

He took a deep breath.

"Tin Win."

Now he recognized the voice.

"Mi Mi?" he asked.

"Yes."

"What are you doing here?"

"I'm sitting by the little white pagoda waiting for my brother."

"Where is he?"

"We sell potatoes at the market every week. Now he's taking rice and a chicken to a sick aunt who lives on the hill. He'll come back for me after that."

Tin Win felt his way cautiously to the pagoda. He had stumbled so often that someone might as well have been setting stones and sticks directly in his path. He could only hope he would be spared the humiliation of falling in the dirt right before Mi Mi's eyes. He heard by the sound of his staff that he had reached the pagoda, and he sat down beside her. Then he heard her heart beating, and with each pulse he grew calmer. He could not imagine a more beautiful sound. Her heart was different from the others—softer, more melodic. It didn't beat; it sang.

"Your shirt and longyi are filthy. Did you fall?" she asked.

"Yes. It's not bad."

"Did you hurt yourself?"

"No."

Tin Win was regaining his confidence. Each noise was returning to its accustomed volume. Mi Mi nudged closer to him. Her scent reminded him of pines after the first shower of the rainy season. Sweet, but not heavy, very fine, multiple whisper-thin layers. For a while they said nothing, and Tin Win ventured again to listen hard. He heard a kind of soft drumming or dripping. It came from the other side of the pagoda. Ought he to ask Mi Mi whether she could hear it, too? And if she could, whether she would look to see what it was so that he would know how to classify it in the future? He hesitated. What if she heard and saw nothing? Then he would feel still lonelier than he had yesterday with Su Kyi. Besides, he did not want to make a fool of himself in front of Mi Mi. Better not to ask. But the temptation was too great. In the end, he decided to lead up to it question by question, depending on how she reacted.

"Do you hear that dripping sound?" he asked tentatively.

"No."

"It might not be dripping, exactly. It sounds more like a delicate hammering." He tapped very quickly with his fingernail on his staff. "Something like that."

"I don't hear anything."

"Could you take a quick look behind the pagoda?"

"There's nothing there but shrubs."

"And in the shrubs?" Tin Win was finding it difficult to mask his excitement. If only she could help him, at least to solve this one riddle.

Mi Mi turned around and crept behind the little temple. The undergrowth was thick and the sharp twigs scratched her face. She couldn't find anything that made the kind of noise Tin Win had described. A bird's nest was all she saw. "There's nothing here."

"Tell me exactly what you see," asked Tin Win.

"Branches. Leaves. An old bird's nest."

Tin Win considered. "What's in the nest?"

"I don't know, but it looks abandoned."

"The noise is definitely coming from the nest. Can you look more closely?"

"It won't work. It's too high. I can't stand up here."

Why couldn't she just get up and look in the nest? It was right in front of her. A glimpse would suffice—just a quick glance and he would know for sure whether he could trust his ears.

She crept back around the corner. "What do you expect is in there?"

He paused. Would she believe him? Would she scoff at him? Did he have any choice?

"An egg. I think the drumming is the heartbeat of an unhatched chick."

Mi Mi laughed. "You're joking. No one can hear that clearly."

Tin Win said nothing. What could he say to that?

"If you help me, I can check whether you are right," said Mi Mi after a pause. "Can you carry me on your back?"

Tin Win squatted down, and Mi Mi put her arms around his neck. Tin Win straightened up slowly. He stood uneasily, swaying from side to side.

"Am I too heavy?" she asked.

"No, not at all." It wasn't the weight that unsettled him. It was the unaccustomed sensation of having a person on his back. She swung her legs around his hips, and he folded both arms behind his back to brace her. Now he had no free hand for his staff, and he did not know the ground in front of him. He went weak in the knees.

"Don't be afraid. I'll guide you." Tin Win took one small step. "Good. And another. Careful, there's a stone just ahead. Don't be startled."

Tin Win felt for the stone with his left foot, examined it, and set his foot on the earth beyond it. Mi Mi directed him behind the little temple. With one hand she tried to keep the branches out of his face.

"There it is. One more step. One more." He felt her supporting herself with her hands on his shoulders, stretching up and leaning forward. His heart raced, and only with great effort could he maintain his balance.

"One. Not big."

"Are you sure?"

Tin Win took no pains to hide his jubilation. They were squatting again by the side of the street, and he could hardly keep still. Mi Mi had opened the door a crack. She had let a shaft of light into his darkness. He would have liked nothing better than to run off with her then and there. To investigate every tone, every sound, every noise he could find. He had learned his first word. Now he knew the heartbeat of a chick in the egg, and eventually he would discover how to recognize the wing beats of a butterfly, why there was gurgling all around him—even when there was no water in the vicinity—and why even in a dead calm he still could hear a rustling. With Mi Mi's help he would solve one riddle after another, and in the end, perhaps, a world would emerge.

"Mi Mi," asked Tin Win, "why didn't you want to look into that nest by yourself?"

She took his hands and laid them on her calves. Tin Win had never felt skin so soft. Softer even than the moss in the woods that he had previously so loved to stroke his cheeks against. His fingers moved slowly down her legs to her ankles, which were slender, but then oddly misshapen. Her feet were immovable. They were stiff and turned inward.

# Chapter 7

YADANA OFTEN REFERRED to the birth of her daughter as the most beautiful moment of her life, intending no offense to her five older sons. Perhaps it was because she had already thought herself too old for a further pregnancy but had always wished for a little girl. Or because now, at thirty-eight, she appreciated the birth and her child for what they were: a singular and incomparable gift. Perhaps it was because during the nine months the child was growing within her, she experienced no physical discomfort. Not a day passed when she had not stood straight up in the field to pause, close her eyes, stroke her belly, and rejoice. At night she often lay awake feeling the child flourish inside her, twisting or turning or kicking and knocking on the wall of her womb. No moment was more beautiful. Had she been prone to sentimentality, she would have wept. Or was it that she could not forget the first look from her daughter, out of those big deep-brown, nearly black eyes? How beautiful she was! Her brown skin was much softer than that of Yadana's other children. Her little head was round, not at all distorted by the exertions of birth, and her face was well proportioned. Even the midwife said she had never held such a beautiful newborn in her hands. So Mi Mi lay in Yadana's arms, the daughter gazing at the mother, who at that moment felt even more at one with her child than at any time during the previous nine months. And then the child smiled. A smile like none Yadana had seen before or since. And thus it was Moe, her husband, who first noticed the defective appendages. He let out a brief cry of shock and showed his wife the tiny, crippled feet.

"Every child is different," she answered him. And for Yadana that was the end of the story. Nor did the rumors that circulated through the village in the following weeks do anything to alter her position. People suggested her daughter was the reincarnation of a Scotsman's donkey, one that had broken both forelegs a few months earlier and had been shot. People supposed the child was not long for this world. The neighbors reckoned the poor girl was a come-uppance for the good harvests the family had enjoyed in recent years, the profits of which had enabled them to build a wooden house on stilts with a tin roof. So much good fortune did not come without a price. Others were sure the girl would bring calamity on the community, and there were even those who privately advocated that she be abandoned in the woods. Her husband's family pressed Yadana to seek the counsel of the astrologer. An astrologer could tell for certain what suffering lay in store for the child and whether it might not be more merciful to consign her to her fate. Yadana would not hear of it. She had always relied more on her instincts than on the stars, and her instincts left no room for doubt: She had borne a very special child with extraordinary capacities.

Nearly a year passed before her husband came around to a similar point of view. At first he hardly dared touch his daughter, preferring instead to hold her at arm's length and forbidding his sons to approach her. Until one evening his wife snapped at him: "Crippled feet are not contagious."

He attempted to appease her. "I know, I know."

"Why then have you not even looked at your daughter in nearly a year?" She tore the blankets from Mi Mi's body with a few swift hand movements.

Moe looked from his daughter to his wife and back. Mi Mi lay naked in front of him. It was cold, and a shiver ran over her, but she did not cry. She just looked at him expectantly.

"Why?" repeated Yadana.

He reached out his arms and touched the little belly. He brushed his fingers along the slender thighs, the knees, gliding downward until he held the little feet in his hands. Mi Mi smiled at him.

Her eyes reminded him of his wife's gaze when they first met. Her smile, too, had that magic that even today he could not resist. Moe was ashamed.

Yadana wrapped the child back in its blankets, bared her breast, and nursed Mi Mi.

Soon it was clear to Moe that his daughter had inherited not only her mother's beautiful eyes but also her satisfied, even-tempered, and cheerful disposition. She never cried, rarely screamed, slept through the night, and gave the impression of an individual in tune with herself and her surroundings.

Nor did any of this change when, after more than a year, she tried for the first time to pull herself up. She had scrambled to the railing of the little porch at the front of the house. Moe and Yadana, who were standing in the yard feeding the chickens and the sow, watched their daughter hoist herself onto the uprights of the railing. She tested her weight on her twisted feet, and for one short moment she stood, staring terrified at her parents, and then she fell. She tried it again and yet again, and Moe wanted to rush to her, to help her, though he didn't know how. Yadana held him firmly back. "Her feet will not support her. She needs to learn that," she said, knowing that no one could alter that fact.

Mi Mi did not cry. She rubbed her eyes and examined the railing, as if there were something wrong with the wood. She tried it again, struggling to keep her balance. On her sixth try, though, after landing on the planks again, she gave up, crawled to the staircase, sat herself up, looked at her parents, and smiled. It was the first and only time she tried to stand and walk. From that point on she laid her claim to the house and the yard on all fours. She would scramble along the porch steps so quickly that her parents could hardly keep up. She ran after the chickens, and on hot summer days, when rain had softened the ground in the yard, she loved to wallow in the mud. She would play hide-and-seek with her brothers, crawling into the remotest corners of the yard, where it was rare that anyone found her.

By all appearances, Mi Mi retained her equanimity even later, when she came to understand more clearly how useful feet could be. When she would sit on the porch watching the neighbor children frolicking across the yard or climbing in the massive eucalyptus trees that separated the properties. Yadana sensed that her daughter accepted the constraints nature had imposed on her, which did not, however, mean that she turned away or withdrew from life. On the contrary, her freedom of movement might have been limited, but her curiosity and her talents in other aspects of life seldom knew any bounds.

Most remarkable of all was her voice. As an infant Mi Mi spent most of her time firmly tied to her mother's back, and Yadana had made a habit of singing to her daughter while working in the fields. Soon Mi Mi knew most of the songs by heart, and mother and daughter would sing in chorus. Mi Mi's voice grew ever lovelier, and when the seven-year-old sang in the evening while helping her mother cook, the neighbors would gather to sit in rapt silence on the ground in front of the house. From week to week their numbers increased. Soon they filled the whole yard, standing even on the path that passed by the house or sitting in the tops of trees bordering the property. The more superstitious among them even asserted that Mi Mi's voice possessed magical powers. They loved to tell of the sick old widow living within earshot who had not left her hut for two years, until one day in the twilight she had mingled with the crowd and begun to dance. Then there was the boy living in a shack across the way, whom everyone called the Fish. His skin was dry and covered everywhere with white eczema and scales. Not six months after Mi Mi's song rang for the first time through the dusk, every last pustule had vanished.

At the market where she bought potatoes and rice with her mother, her songs drew such a concourse of people that two police officers came and asked her to desist, in the interest of public security and order. An Irish drunkard—who had nevertheless achieved the rank of major in Her Majesty's Army and who was now spending the twilight of his life in Kalaw—requested that she sing at his deathbed. Mi Mi was invited to weddings and births, and in return her family was richly rewarded with tea, chickens, and rice. Just when Moe was seriously considering leasing his fields, though, Mi Mi announced to her parents that she would not be singing any longer.

They were sitting on a plank in the yard. It was not yet dusk, but the cool of the evening had already asserted itself. Yadana draped a heavy jacket around her daughter's shoulders. Mi Mi was grinding the bark of a thanakha tree in a mortar, and her mother was washing tomatoes and scallions. The pig was grunting under the house, and the water buffalo was defecating in front of the garden gate. They could smell the stench from where they sat. Moe assumed she was joking.

"Why would you want to stop singing?"

"It's no fun anymore."

"What do you mean? What happened?"

"Nothing happened."

"But your voice sounds more beautiful every day."

"I can't stand to hear it anymore."

"You mean you never want to sing again?"

"I want to save my voice."

"Save it? What for?" Moe was doubtful.

"I'm not sure."

Moe knew there was no point arguing with his daughter. She had her mother's obstinacy. She rarely insisted on anything, but once she had made up her mind, it was impossible to talk her out of it. Privately, he admired that in her.

Yadana in particular was aware how much Mi Mi had changed recently. She had just turned fourteen, and her body was gradually assuming womanly contours. It was not only her voice that grew lovelier from day to day. True, her eyes no longer dominated her face, but they were still as radiant as ever. Her skin was the color of ground tamarind, and her hands, though she used them to prop herself up and to move about, were not stout, hard, or callused but long and slender. Her fingers were so nimble that Yadana could hardly follow them when Mi Mi helped her cook, peeling a ginger root and finely slicing or chopping it. Two years ago she had taught her to weave, and it hadn't been long before Mi Mi had surpassed her mother in that art. Most of all, though, Yadana admired the confidence with which her daughter moved. In the past Yadana had had nightmares. She would see Mi Mi crawling like an animal through the filth or across the marketplace while onlookers ridiculed her. Sometimes she would still dream that Mi Mi wanted to take the train to Thazi and was crawling along the platform to her car when the steam engine would start rolling. Mi Mi would try to crawl faster and faster. She never caught the train.

Even during the day Yadana would catch herself worrying how Mi Mi, the grown woman, would welcome guests into her home. Crawling to them on all fours? How mortifying!

And now she could hardly believe how much poise her daughter commanded and with what self-assurance she moved about. There was nothing bestial or humiliating in the way she crawled. She wore only the most beautiful self-woven longyis, and although she slid across the filthy floor in them, they were never unpresentable. When she moved, gingerly placing one hand, one knee in front of the other, she radiated such dignity that people at the market would step aside and treat her with great respect.

# Chapter 8

THE JULIA THAT I had known until now—and with whom I considered myself on intimate terms— would have leapt up at this point. She would have been outraged. She would have cast U Ba a disdainful, piercing glance and grabbed her little backpack without a word. Or she would have laughed in his face and declared the whole thing a lot of sappy nonsense. She would have left.

But I did not move a muscle. Though I felt an impulse to stand up, it was a powerless one, like a reflex from another time. I didn't know what to think of U Ba's tale. It was too much for me. Was I supposed to believe that my father had not only been blind as a young man, but had lost his heart to a cripple? Was this woman supposed to be the reason he left us, his family, high and dry after nearly thirty-five years? After fifty years of separation? It seemed absurd to me. At the same time, I couldn't help thinking of something my father had said: There is nothing, for good or for evil, of which a person is incapable. That was his response when we learned that one of my mother's cousins, a pious Catholic, had had an affair with the sixteen-year-old babysitter. My mother couldn't get over it: That's just not like Walter, she said again and again. My father thought that was a mistake. He seemed to think anyone was capable of anything, or at least he wouldn't exclude the possibility just because he thought he knew the person. And he insisted that this did not represent the worldview of an embittered pessimist. On the contrary, he had said. It would be much worse to expect good from other people, only to be disappointed when they didn't measure up to our high expectations. That would lead to resentment and contempt for humanity.

In many of the traits and mannerisms U Ba described, I was beginning to discern the outlines of my father. I felt as if I was eavesdropping on a quarrel between opposing, internal voices. One voice was the attorney. She remained skeptical. She wanted facts. She was looking for guilty parties, a judge who could pass sentence or who would, by dint of his authority, put an end to the charade. The other was a voice I'd never heard before. Wait, it cried, don't run away. Don't be afraid.

"You must be hungry." U Ba interrupted my thoughts. "I took the liberty of having a little something prepared for us." He called a name I didn't understand, and almost immediately a young woman came out of the kitchen with a tray. She bowed with just the hint of a curtsy. U Ba rose and handed me two chipped plates. On one lay three thin, round flatbreads. The other held rice, brown sauce, and pieces of meat. With it he gave me a frayed white napkin and a thin bent spoon.

"Burmese chicken curry. Very mild. We eat it with Indian flatbread. I hope it's to your liking."

I must have looked doubtful. U Ba laughed and tried to reassure me. "I have asked my neighbor to pay special attention to cleanliness in the preparation of this meal. I know that our food does not always agree with our guests. But even we are not immune. Believe me, I, too, have spent countless hours of my life chained to a toilet."

"That's not exactly a comfort," I ventured, biting into one of the breads. I had read in my travel guide that one ought to be wary especially of salads, raw fruit, untreated water, and ice. Bread and rice, by contrast, were thought to be comparatively unproblematic. I tried some rice with sauce. It was a little bitter, almost earthy, but not bad. The chicken was so tough I could hardly chew it.

"Where's my father?" I asked after we had eaten for a while in silence. It sounded more severe and demanding than I'd meant it to. The voice of the attorney.

U Ba regarded me for a long time. With the last piece of flatbread, he wiped his plate clean. "You are getting closer to him all the time. Can't you feel it?" he said, and wiped his mouth with the old napkin. He took a sip of tea and leaned back in his armchair. "I could tell you in one sentence where he is. But now that you have waited so long, more than four years, what difference will a few hours more or less make? You will never again have the chance to learn so much about your father. Wouldn't you like to know how he and Mi Mi fared? How she changed his life? Why she meant so much to him? Why she will change your life, too?"

U Ba did not wait for my response.

# Chapter 9

SU KYI NOTICED at once that something extraordinary had happened to Tin Win. She was sitting in front of the garden gate waiting for him and had just begun to worry. The road was in a wretched state. Continued heavy rains two days earlier had softened the ground, and the oxcarts had subsequently cut deep tracks in the muck. The sun had dried the mud, and now the surface was hard and crusted over and riddled with depressions and ruts—tricky enough even for a sighted person. Had it been a good idea to let him walk alone, today of all days? Then she recognized his red and green longyi and his white shirt coming up the hill. But his gait was different. Was that really Tin Win?

That evening he was talkative as never before. He regaled her with full details of U May and how excited he, Tin Win, was as he stepped all alone from the monastery gate into the street, how in his distraction he fell and grew angry, but how from now on he intended to manage the trip entirely without her help. He told of noises, of bird feathers and bamboo leaves he had heard floating to the ground, of beating hearts that sounded like voices in song. Su Kyi delighted in his imagination.

Concerning Mi Mi he said nothing, and so poor Su Kyi was also at a loss to explain what was happening to Tin Win. He, who regularly hunched silently in a corner for hours at a time, was hardly able to sit still. He marched restlessly through the house and yard. He took a sudden interest in the market, wanting to know why it convened only every fifth day and inquiring repeatedly when it would be time again. His appetite waned from meal to meal until on the third day he would drink only tea. Su Kyi didn't know what to do. Tin Win was ill, that much was certain, but he complained of no ailment. Gradually, the tales of the noises he was hearing began to trouble her. Clearly he was losing his mind.

Tin Win counted the days—and the hours and the minutes—until the next market. How long a day could be. Why did it take an eternity for the earth to turn once about its axis? Time crept by as slowly as a snail across the forest floor. Could he do nothing to hasten its passage? He asked U May, who merely laughed.

"Be patient," he said. "Sit down and meditate. Then time will lose its meaning."

Meditation had served Tin Win well in the preceding few years, but little good it did him now. He tried sitting amid the monks in the monastery, in a meadow, and on the stump in front of his house. Whatever he tried, wherever he was, he heard her heart knocking. He heard her voice. He felt her skin. He felt her weight against his back.

The scent of her filled his nose. That soft, sweet, unmistakable fragrance. On the eve of the next market day he could get no rest. He heard Su Kyi lowering herself onto the mat next to him, turning onto her side, and pulling the covers up to her ears. Shortly thereafter her heart, too, settled down for its nightly repose. It beat slowly and evenly, as if it would never cease. His own heart raced. A wild and fierce beating. He did not even know what was exciting him so; it was a world in which eyes played no part in seeing, where motion did not depend on feet.

How best to locate Mi Mi that morning among all the booths and people? From Su Kyi's descriptions Tin Win imagined the market like a flock of birds descending on a field. A tumult of voices, sounds, and smells. It'll be crowded, he thought, and they'll push and shove, and no one will be watching out for me. Curiously, the thought did not frighten him, he who was otherwise so wary of people. He felt certain he would find Mi Mi quickly. He would recognize the sound of her heartbeat. He would follow her scent. He would hear her voice, even if she merely whispered something into her brother's ear.

For a few minutes Tin Win stood motionless by the side of the road. He retied his longyi. Sweat stood in little beads on his brow and nose. Voices of the market were both louder and more intimidating than he had anticipated, like a rushing brook swollen into a threatening and impassable torrent. How to get his bearings? He did not know the paths between the booths. He did not know the quirks of the ground. Not one voice was familiar to him.

He set one foot in front of the other, slowly but without hesitating. He would let himself be swept along by the stream of people. Someone shoved him from behind. He felt an elbow in his ribs. "Watch where you're stepping," a man barked at him. The betel nut chewers smacked their lips and spit juice onto the street. An infant whimpered. So many voices and hearts snorted, groaned, coughed, and rattled around him. Their guts rumbled. It was so loud, that he was unable to distinguish one from the other. But he would find her. He knew this. Nothing was troubling him but the heat. He'd had too little water at the monastery and was sweating more than usual. His shirt was wet, his mouth dry. Suddenly he noticed that the throng was splitting off into two directions, and he tried to stand his ground, but the pressure from behind was too great. He followed those turning to the right.

"Watch out," yelled a woman. He heard a cracking sound and felt something soft and moist on his feet and between his toes. Eggs.

"Are you blind?"

He turned toward her. She saw the milky white in his eyes and mumbled a shocked apology. Tin Win was swept along. These must be the fish stands. He caught the salty tang of dried fish. Next he had the bitter scent of coriander in his nose, then the spicy-sour goldenseal, an aroma that went right to his head and burned on his mucous membranes when he inhaled. He caught the fragrances of cinnamon, of curry, and of chili pepper. Of lemongrass and ginger. Interspersed again and again with the luscious, heavy, cloying fragrance of overripe fruit.

As soon as he honed in on it, people stopped jostling him. Those coming from behind parted around him as if sensing that pushing and shoving were of no further use. Tin Win listened hard. There it was. So tender and fragile, so steady. It would catch his ear amid all the noise in the world. From a distance he felt her skin in his hands. Her arms about his neck. He followed the beating that came to him from a remote corner of the market.

# Chapter 10

MI MI SAT out of the way, beside a heap of potatoes. In her left hand she held a small round parasol to protect her from the sun. It was the dark red, nearly brown shade of monks' robes. She was wearing her most beautiful longyi, red with a green pattern. She had finished weaving it only the previous evening. She wore her black hair in a braid. That morning she had asked her mother to paint two round yellow circles on her cheeks. All the older girls and women made themselves up this way, but Mi Mi had always put it off until now. Her mother smiled and asked no questions. Once Mi Mi was settled on her brother's back, Yadana sent her daughter off with a kiss on the forehead. True, she did the same thing every time they parted, but this kiss had been different. Mi Mi sensed it, though she would have been hard pressed to articulate the distinction.

Now she was sitting on her handmade blanket and waiting. Indeed, she had done nothing else for the past four days. Whether crawling across the yard to gather chicken eggs or picking strawberries behind the house, whether helping her mother with the cooking, sorting potatoes, or weaving, she was waiting. For market day. For Tin Win.

She never minded the waiting. She had learned early on that it was a natural part of life for anyone who couldn't walk, who depended on the help of others. Waiting was so interwoven with the rhythm of her life that it almost disturbed her when anything happened right away. She was mystified by people who were always hurrying things along. A time of waiting offered moments, minutes, sometimes even hours of peace, of rest, during which, as a rule, she was alone with herself. And she needed these breaks to prepare herself for anything new, for any kind of change. Be it a visit to her aunt on the other side of the village or a day in the fields. Or the market. She could not understand why it did not overtax her brothers to hurry with quick steps from place to place, from person to person. If ever she chanced to be carried unexpectedly and without waiting to see friends on the next hilltop, it always took some time before she really arrived. She would sit silently during the first few minutes in the new place. As if her soul were following more slowly across the valley. She felt that each and every thing required a certain amount of time. Just as the earth needed its twenty-four hours to turn once about its axis, or three hundred sixty-five days to orbit the sun, she felt that each and every thing required a certain amount of time. Her brothers nicknamed her Little Snail.

Worst of all were the trains and cars in which some of the British would travel through Kalaw, reportedly even as far as the capital. She was not frightened by the dreadful, loud clatter with which they rumbled through the village so that chickens took flight and horses and oxen recoiled. Nor was she much put out by the stench they drew in their wake. It was the speed that frightened her. Was it really possible for a person to shorten the time it took to get from one place or person to another? How could anyone think so?

Mi Mi was happy that four days would pass before the market, even if she would have liked most to see Tin Win again the very next day. Waiting meant she would be free to think about him at leisure, taking time to recall every detail of their last meeting. That, too, was an advantage of waiting—it gave her the chance to clear her mind. As always, whenever she let her thoughts roam, pictures arose in her mind, pictures she examined with care, as if they were gems or precious metals whose authenticity must be ascertained: She saw Tin Win approaching her; saw herself clamber onto his back; saw him later sitting beside her, quivering with excitement and joy. It had felt to her as if he was ready to take her on his back and run off with her, hot on the trail of ten thousand things unknown.

At home, then, she had sat for a long time on the porch with her eyes closed, trying to do as Tin Win had done. She listened hard. The pig was grunting beneath the house.

The dog was snoring. There were the birds and the voices of the neighbors . . . but not the beating of their hearts. She wanted to ask Tin Win if there was a trick to it and if he might be able to teach her this art of hearing. At least the rudiments.

She told her youngest brother the story of the bird's nest, but he made fun of her. How on earth could she believe that anyone's hearing could be so acute? Someone probably told him ahead of time that there was an egg in the nest. Tin Win just wanted to impress her.

This left Mi Mi angry—more at herself than at her brother. She ought to have known. There were things a person who walked through the world on two sound feet simply couldn't understand. They believed that people saw with their eyes. That footsteps overcame distances.

# Chapter 11

THE MIDDAY SUN burned almost directly over the marketplace. Tin Win and Mi Mi sought shelter under the little parasol and edged closer together. Mi Mi's brother stuffed the remaining potatoes into a sack. He would go ahead and come back for his sister.

"I can carry Mi Mi home. It'll save you from making two trips," said Tin Win.

The brother looked at his sister as if to say: How is this blind fellow supposed to carry you up the mountain? Mi Mi nodded to him: "Don't worry."

Her brother shouldered his sack of potatoes, mumbled something incomprehensible and set off.

"Would you mind if we took a detour through the town?" asked Tin Win.

"Wherever you like," said Mi Mi. "You're the one who has to carry me, not the other way around." She laughed and draped an arm around his neck. He stood slowly. They went down a side street where several oxcarts and wagons were parked. Men and women crisscrossed the road, loading their vehicles with sacks of rice and potatoes and baskets full of fruit. The animals were restless. The horses whinnied and pawed the earth or stamped their hooves. The oxen snorted and shook themselves so that their yokes creaked. They are tired from the sun and from waiting, and they're hungry, too, thought Tin Win. He heard their stomachs growling. The wagons stood this way and that in the street, and together with the many unfamiliar noises they seemed to him to form a wall he would surely bump into any moment now. Where was the guide who helped him to avoid the most grievous mishaps? Who warned him of pits and ditches, of stones and branches, houses and trees, at least when he paid attention? Now he felt as if he were creeping through a labyrinth in which high walls blocked his way. In which corners and edges waited to undo him. A maze in which he could not help but get lost. How would he ever bring Mi Mi safely home?

Never before had his blindness so burdened him. His knees went weak and he swayed. He lost his sense of direction. Where was he? Was he going in a circle? Was he walking toward an abyss? How was he to know that his next step would not be his last? Soon he would feel no ground beneath his feet. He would lose his balance and pitch forward into the great void he had always dreaded.

"Careful. Two more steps and you'll bump into a basket of tomatoes." Mi Mi's voice was next to his ear. She was whispering.

"Another little bit to the left. Good. Straight ahead. Stop." She pressed his shoulders gently to the right. He hesitated a moment before turning himself ninety degrees. There must be an ox right in front of them. Its mighty heart beat like the muted drum the monks sometimes struck at the monastery. The animal's breath was moist on his skin.

"Straight ahead?"

"Straight ahead." He shuffled his feet, not daring to lift them. A few steps later she pulled gently on his left shoulder, and he turned that way. He bumped into something wooden and winced.

"Sorry, the cart. I thought we were past it. Does it hurt?"

He shook his head and walked slowly on until she tugged again on one shoulder and cautiously changed their course.

"Step up, there's a sack of rice."

He lifted his leg, felt for the sack with his toes, and took a big step.

"Good," she said, and squeezed him briefly.

They went on, Mi Mi conducting him through the streets with her gentle movements as if guiding a boat through rapids. With each arc, each turn, each obstacle overcome, Tin Win's steps became firmer and more confident. Her voice, so close to his ear, comforted him. He trusted her instructions. He, who so often could not trust even his own senses, found himself relying on her eyes.

She dried his neck with her longyi.

"Am I too heavy?" she asked.

"Not at all." How could he explain that he felt lighter with her on his back?

"Thirsty?"

He nodded.

"We can get fresh sugarcane juice over there." It was expensive, but her mother had allowed her to drink one juice a month after the market, and she would certainly have no objection to her treating Tin Win. He noticed that they had stepped into the shade of a large tree. "Stop here," she said. "Set me down."

He lowered himself onto one knee. She slid slowly from his back to the ground and settled onto a wooden stool that belonged to the juice stand. She placed a second stool behind Tin Win and tugged at his hand. He sat down without hesitating.

They sat under the broad crown of a banyan tree, and Mi Mi ordered two juices. He heard the sugarcane crushed in the press, something like the cracking sound a cockroach made when you stepped on it in the kitchen. Had Mi Mi noticed his fear? Did it matter? She had led him through the labyrinth. They had neither run into a wall nor fallen into an abyss. She had built bridges and torn down walls. She was a magician.

Mi Mi took a sip of her juice. She couldn't imagine anything tasting better. She looked at Tin Win. She wouldn't have guessed that a face with unseeing eyes would be capable of expressing so much joy. She smiled, and he smiled back. She didn't even notice how odd that was.

"Tin Win, what do you hear now? My heart?" asked Mi Mi.

"That, too."

"Can you teach me?"

"What?"

"To hear hearts."

"I don't think so."

"Please try."

"I wouldn't know where to start."

"But you know how to do it."

Tin Win considered. "Close your eyes." Mi Mi closed her eyes. "What do you hear?"

"Voices. Footsteps. The tinkling of harness bells."

"Nothing else?"

"Well, sure. I hear birds and someone coughing and a child crying, but I don't hear any hearts beating."

Tin Win was quiet. Mi Mi listened more. After a few minutes the noises ran together, as obscured as pictures to a weeping eye. She heard the blood coursing in her ears, but not her heart, much less Tin Win's or anyone else's.

"Maybe it's too loud here," said Tin Win after a long pause. "We might need more quiet. Let's go, and we can try it again when we find some place where we hear nothing but the birds, the wind, and our breath." He knelt before Mi Mi. She took hold of his shoulders. He stood up, and she crossed her legs in front of his belly.

They were walking down a quieter street. Her breath on his neck. How light she was. He nearly stepped on a sleeping dog taking shelter from the sun in the shade of a house.

"Sorry. I didn't see him," she said.

"Neither did I," he said. They laughed.

Just beyond the train station, Mi Mi directed him away from the street. "I know a shortcut," she said. A few yards later they were standing on a small hillside surrounded by hibiscus bushes. Tin Win recognized their sickly sweet scent. He extended his foot and realized they would be going downhill. Not steeply, but enough to throw him off balance.

"Maybe backwards is easier," suggested Mi Mi. She was accustomed to dashing down hills like this in a few quick leaps on her brothers' backs. He turned around and began his cautious descent. Mi Mi, reaching with one hand into the bushes, had taken firm hold of the branches. Together they slid slowly down the slope, and soon Tin Win had stones beneath his feet.

"Where are we?" he asked.

"On the railroad embankment," she explained to him. "We can walk on the wooden ties between the rails. My brothers do it all the time."

He stood still. She might as well have said Mandalay. Or Rangoon. Or London. Until now, the embankment had been for him a place beyond all reach. He knew it only from the stories of other boys at school. They often boasted of their escapades on the tracks while waiting for the black steam engine. How they would set pinecones or the odd bottle cap on the rails, or how they would test their courage by creeping as close as they could to the passing train. At one time Tin Win had dreamed of joining in. Later he'd given up hope. The embankment was not part of his world. It belonged to the sighted.

Now he was the one walking between the rails, and soon he found a rhythm that allowed him to set his feet confidently on a tie at every step. He need not worry here about walking into a tree or a bush or about tripping over anything. He was climbing a ladder out of a cold, damp cave and the world grew brighter and warmer with every step. He walked more quickly, and soon he skipped one tie and then started to run. Mi Mi said nothing. Eyes closed, she was holding on tightly and rocking in time with his strides as if on horseback. Tin Win took great long steps, running as fast as he could. He had already stopped worrying about the distance between the ties, and he heard nothing but the beating of his heart, a drumbeat that spurred him on. Ever louder and harder, mighty and wild. A clamor that rang up the valley and beyond the mountains. Not even a steam train was louder, he thought.

When he finally came to a standstill, it was like waking from a dream. "I'm sorry," he said, completely out of breath.

"What for?" asked Mi Mi.

"Weren't you afraid?"

"Of what?"

~~~~~~~

They lay in the grass, and Mi Mi looked up at the sky. It was late, and the sun would soon be setting. Second only to the early-morning hours, Mi Mi found this the most beautiful time of day. The light was different, clearer, and the contours of the trees and mountains and houses were more defined than at midday. She liked the voices of the evening and the scent of the fires that burned in front of the houses before nightfall.

"Do you have any idea what a heart sounds like?" asked Tin Win.

Mi Mi considered whether she had ever heard a heart beating. "I once pressed my head to my mother's breast because I wanted to know what was making that knocking. But that was a long time ago." At the time she had thought there was an animal in her mother's chest, knocking on her ribs to be let out.

# Chapter 12

HE COULDN'T FALL asleep that night. Nor the next, nor the one after that. He lay beside Su Kyi and thought about Mi Mi. He spent three wakeful nights, yet was not tired. He felt more alert. His senses, thoughts, and recollections were clearer than ever before. They had spent one afternoon together. One afternoon that he cherished like a talisman. He remembered every word that had passed between them, every shade of her voice, every beat of her heart.

On that afternoon, with Mi Mi on his back, her voice in his ear, her thighs around his hips, he had, for the first time, felt something akin to ease, a touch of joy. An emotion so foreign to him that he did not even know what to call it. Happiness, lightheartedness, fun—these were for him words without content, speech without meaning. He realized how much energy each day cost him. Waking in that milky white fog. Groping his way through a world that had turned its back on him. He suddenly found the loneliness in which he lived unbearable, though he did have Su Kyi and U May. He revered both, trusted both, was infinitely grateful to both for the attention, the affection, they showed him. And yet, as with everyone he met, he felt an odd distance between them and himself. How often had he sat around the fire in the monastery with the other pupils or monks, wishing that he belonged, that he were part of some group, some system. Wishing that he felt something for the others—fondness, anger, or even just curiosity. Anything. But he felt little more than an emptiness, and did not know why that was. Even when someone touched him, put an arm around his shoulder, or took him by the hand, Tin Win was unmoved. The same fog that clouded his eyes seemed to have insinuated itself between him and the world.

But with Mi Mi—her eyes saw for him. With her help he did not feel like a stranger in his own life. She made him feel a part of things. Of the happenings at the market. Of the village. Of himself.

With her, he turned toward life.

In the coming months, the two spent every market day together, exploring Kalaw and its vicinity as if they had discovered an uncharted island. They investigated the place with the meticulous care of two scientists, street by street, house by house. Often they would crouch for hours by the side of the road. On most of their expeditions they covered little more than a single street, a bit of meadow.

Over time they established a fixed ritual for unlocking the secrets of this new world. Having taken a few steps, they would pause, silent and motionless. Their silence might last a few minutes, half an hour, or even longer. Tin Win was soaking up the sounds, tones, and noise. Then he would describe in detail what he heard, and Mi Mi would tell him what she saw. Like a painter she sketched the scene for him, at first roughly, then with increasing precision and detail. When images and tones did not coincide they launched a search for the sources of the unfamiliar sounds. She crawled through hedgerows and bushes, dragged herself across flowerbeds and under houses, took apart stone walls and put them back together. She rummaged through woodpiles and dug with her hands in meadows and fields until she found what Tin Win heard: sleeping snakes and snails, earthworms, moths. With each passing day Tin Win came to know the world better. Thanks to Mi Mi's descriptions, he could connect sounds with objects, plants, and animals. He learned that the wing beats of a swallowtail butterfly sounded brighter than those of a monarch; that the leaves of a mulberry tree rustled differently in the wind from those of the guava; that the chomping of a wood worm was not to be confused with that of a caterpillar; that the rubbing of hind legs was distinct from fly to fly. It was a whole new alphabet.

He had more trouble when it came to the tones produced by people. Soon after losing his eyesight Tin Win had begun to pay attention to voices, learning to differentiate and interpret them. They became for him a kind of compass to guide him through the world of human emotions. If Su Kyi was angry or tired, he heard it in her voice. Whether his fellow students envied him his accomplishments, whether he was annoying the monks, whether a person liked him or not: all was revealed to him by the tone in which a person spoke to him.

Every voice had its distinctive repertoire of expressive forms, and so, too, did every heart. Recognizing strangers by their heartbeat on a second or third meeting posed no difficulty for Tin Win, even though the beating was never absolutely identical. It betrayed much about body and soul and altered with time or according to the situation. Hearts could sound young or decrepit, boring or bored, mysterious or predictable. Yet what was he to think when an individual's voice and heart were at odds, each telling a different, mutually incompatible story? Take U May, for instance. His voice had always sounded strong and robust, as if untouched by the years. Tin Win had always pictured him as a great old pine with a mighty trunk, impervious even to the storms that occasionally swept the Shan Plateau. One of those trees under which he had previously felt secure and loved to play. U May's heart, however, sounded neither strong nor robust. It sounded fragile and weak, spent and weary. It reminded him of the emaciated oxen he had seen as a child, passing by their house, behind them a heavy cart loaded with sacks of rice or wooden beams. He had gazed after them, convinced they would fall dead before they reached the summit of the mountain. Why did U May's voice not match his heart? Which should he trust? The voice or the heart? These were questions to which he knew no answer. Though he believed, somehow, that with Mi Mi's help he would resolve them. Some of them, at least.

# Chapter 13

MI MI REMEMBERED precisely when she first heard of Tin Win. Two years earlier one of her brothers had gone into the monastery as a novice. While she was visiting him with her mother, he spoke of a blind boy who had fallen that morning with a thabeik in his hands. For fear of spilling the food, he had not let go of the bowl and so landed hard on his face, bled from his nose and mouth, and—to make matters worse—lost a whole day's rice in the dirt. He was supposedly extremely clumsy, being blind, after all, but in class he was the best. The story had saddened her, though she couldn't say why. Did that mishap remind her of her own attempts to take a few steps on her crooked feet, behind the house, where none might see her? Of the pain and the two steps she managed before falling to the dusty ground? She wondered why Tin Win had tumbled, whether it happened often, and how he managed to get around at all. How must he have felt? Lying in the dirt, everyone's food gone to waste. She couldn't help but think of a day she played marbles with her friends in front of the house. The other children marveled at the glass balls an Englishman had given her. They rolled them into little depressions, and Mi Mi was proud to show them how the game worked. One girl suddenly leapt up, declaring she was bored. Why didn't they have a running race instead? First one to the eucalyptus tree was the winner. And off they ran. Mi Mi slowly collected her marbles. Only once had she asked the question: Why? And she had known that there would never be an answer. Her feet were a whim of nature. It would have been silly to look for causes or to rebel. She would not bicker with fate. Still, it hurt.

Worse than the pain was the distance she felt from her family at such moments. She loved her parents and brothers above all else, but the fact that they did not really understand what went on inside her isolated Mi Mi nearly as much as her feet did. Her brothers' care was touching. They took turns carrying their sister to the field or to the lakes, hauling her through the village, to the market, or to relatives on a distant farm in the mountains. They never thought of it as a sacrifice, but as something quite routine, like chopping wood in the morning, carting water, or harvesting potatoes in the fall. They expected no gratitude in return, of course not. Yet if Mi Mi was ever sad, if she wept for no obvious reason—a thing that was rare but not unheard of—they stood around not knowing what to say or do. With puzzled expressions. As if to say: We're doing everything to make your life good. Why is that not enough? Not wanting to seem ungrateful, she would swallow her tears as best she could. It was the same way with her mother. Yadana marveled at her daughter. Mi Mi knew that. She was proud of the strength and grace with which her Little Snail bore her handicap. And Mi Mi wanted to be strong, if sometimes only not to disappoint her mother. Yet she also longed for moments when she might be weak, when she need not prove anything to anyone. Not to her parents. Not to her brothers. Not to herself.

A few days later she was sitting on the monastery porch, and her brother pointed out Tin Win as he was sweeping the courtyard.

Mi Mi couldn't take her eyes off him. She was amazed at the thoroughness with which he cleaned a place that he could not see. At times he stopped and lifted his head, as if he smelled or heard something in particular.

In the days that followed she thought of him often, and on her next visit she lingered on the steps until she saw him again. He came with an armful of firewood, mounted the steps right next to her, and went into the kitchen without ever noticing her. She followed him and watched him from a distance. He broke a few sticks and set them in the flames. He put water in a kettle and hung it over the fire. It seemed effortless. She was impressed by the calm, thoughtful manner in which he moved, the quiet dignity he radiated. As if he was grateful for every step he took without falling, for every move he made without injuring himself. Was life without sight as easy for him as it appeared? Or did it cost him as much effort as her daily life without feet? Might he understand what went on inside her when the other children ran to the eucalyptus tree? When her mother looked at her full of pride while she felt anything but strong? When her brothers carried her past the neighbor girls sitting with young men by the side of the road, singing songs, shyly holding hands? Several times she wanted to speak to him or crawl into his path so that he would stumble over and thus become aware of her. She resisted the urge. Not out of shyness, but because she was convinced it was unnecessary. They would meet. Every life had its own course, its own rhythm, on which Mi Mi thought it was impossible to exercise any decisive influence.

She was not surprised that afternoon in the monastery when Tin Win came to an abrupt halt on his way to the kitchen, made half a turn as if picking up a trail, walked over to her, and crouched down. She looked right at him and read more in his milk-veiled eyes than she ever could with her parents or brothers. She saw that he knew what loneliness was, that he understood why it might be raining inside a person even when the sun shone, that sadness needed no immediate cause. She was not even surprised when he told her about the beating of her heart. She believed every word.

She lived from one market day to the next, was impatient for the first time in her life, counted the hours and minutes, could not wait until they saw each other again. Her longing was so great that after a few months she wanted to pick Tin Win up after his lessons at the monastery. Would he be happy, or would she be intruding? She could act as if she were coincidentally passing by with her brother. When he heard her waiting on the veranda he came straight over to her. His smile dispelled her doubts. He was at least as happy as she was. He sat down beside her, taking her hand without saying a word. From then on they saw each other every day.

Tirelessly he carried her through the village and across the fields, up the mountains and back down again. He carried her in the scorching midday heat and in the most torrential downpours. On his back, in his company, the limits of her small world evaporated. They roamed and roamed, making up for all those years when her horizon had been the garden fence.

During the monsoon months, on days that threatened to sink them into the mud, they'd stay in the monastery and take refuge in Tin Win's books. His fingers flew over the pages, and now it was his turn to conjure images before her eyes. He read aloud, she lay beside him and surrendered to his voice, irresistible as it was. She toured with Tin Win from one continent to the next. She, who on her own feet would not have made it to the next village, circled the globe. He carried her up the gangways of ocean liners, from one deck to the next, all the way to the captain's bridge. On arrival in the ports of Colombo, Calcutta, Port Said, or Marseilles it rained confetti and the ship's band played. He carried her through Hyde Park, and they turned heads in Piccadilly Circus. In New York they were nearly struck by a car, Tin Win insisted, because Mi Mi was always looking up instead of concentrating on the traffic and on guiding him through the canyon-like streets. She was no burden. She was needed.

With great patience, Tin Win was teaching her to hear. Of course, her ears were not as sensitive as his. She was not going to hear his heart beating without laying her head on his chest. Nor could she distinguish dragonflies by their humming, or frogs by their croaking, but he did teach her to attend to sounds and voices, not only to hear them but also to pay them reverence.

Now when anyone spoke to her she focused first on the timbre, what she called the color, of the voice. The tone often said more than the words spoken. At the market she knew right away whether customers were intent on bargaining or would accept her price for the potatoes. She bewildered her brothers by knowing in the evening after only a few sentences how their day had been, whether they were happy, bored, or irritated. Little Snail became Little Psychic Snail.

When Mi Mi was not waiting for him on the monastery steps one day at noon, Tin Win was immediately alarmed. They had seen each other every day for more than a year, and she had said nothing the evening before about not being there today. Was she sick? Why had none of her brothers come to let him know? He set off at once for their farm. It had rained heavily in the night, and the ground was wet and slippery. Tin Win made no attempt to hear the puddles in advance. He sloshed through them, crossed the empty marketplace, and hastened up the mountain. He slipped several times, fell, and got up, sparing no thought for his drenched and muddied sarong. He plowed into an old peasant woman. In his agitation he had heard neither her voice nor her heartbeat.

The house was empty. Even the dog was gone. The neighbors hadn't a clue.

Tin Win tried to calm himself. What could possibly have happened? Probably they were out in the field and would arrive soon. But they didn't. At dusk his anxiety returned. Tin Win heard himself calling out her name. He shook the stairway railing until it broke off. He imagined he could see again. A giant butterfly dropped down from heaven like a bird of prey, landed in the meadow, and crept toward him. Tin Win climbed a tree trunk. Red points came hurtling toward him. A searing pain shot through him each time one hit. He tried to dodge them, running across the yard, bloodying brow and chin. Three neighbor boys brought him home.

# Chapter 14

IT WAS A wail like none Su Kyi had ever heard. It was loud, but that was not the strange or alarming thing about it. This was no wretched lament. It was a violent revolt, a scream of rage and doubt. It hurt the soul, not the ears.

She woke at once and turned to the source of the noise. Beside her sat Tin Win, mouth open wide, howling loudly. She called his name, but he didn't respond. She wasn't even sure he was awake. She grabbed his shoulders and shook him. His body was tense, almost rigid. "Tin Win. Tin Win," she cried, stroking his face and taking his head in her hands. That soothed him. After a few seconds he dropped slowly back onto his sleeping mat, where he curled up, his knees to his chest, and slept on, his head resting on her hands.

When Su Kyi woke in the predawn light, Tin Win lay whimpering beside her. She whispered his name, but he did not answer. She slipped into her longyi, pulled a blouse and sweater over her head, and spread a blanket over him. Maybe he'd caught a cold, she thought. He had not come home until after dark last night. Three young men had brought him. Tin Win had looked dreadful—muddied, bloody, cuts all over his head. He had lain down on his mat without a word.

She went into the kitchen and made a fire. Yesterday's hot chicken soup and rice with a bit of curry would do him good.

At first she did not notice the gagging and gasping. When she came into the bedroom he was kneeling in front of the open window, vomiting, and it sounded as if his body were forcefully ridding itself of everything he had ever eaten. The heaving came in waves, and the less he brought up, the more violently it shook him. Su Kyi could see how eventually it took hold of his entire body, until in the end nothing but a greenish, foul-smelling substance was coming out of his mouth. She dragged him back to his bed and tucked him in. He groped about for her hand. She sat down next to him and took his head in her lap. His lips were twitching. His breathing was labored.

Tin Win didn't know whether he was dreaming or awake. He lost all awareness of time and space. His senses turned inward. The fog before his eyes gave way to a sinister darkness. In his nose was an acrid stench, the smell of his own viscera. His ears registered nothing but the sounds of his body. The rush of his blood. A bubbling and burbling in his stomach, gurgling in his bowels. His heart. Above it all hovered fear. It had no name and no voice. It was simply there. Everywhere. Like the air he breathed. It ruled his body, lorded over his thoughts and his dreams. In his sleep he heard the beating of Mi Mi's heart and called her name, but she didn't answer. He searched, running in the direction of the beating, but never reached it. He ran faster and faster without ever getting closer to her. He ran until he collapsed from exhaustion. Or he saw Mi Mi sitting on a stool, walked over to her, and suddenly the earth opened and swallowed him. It went dark, and he fell, and there was nothing he could hold on to. He got hotter and hotter until he noticed that he landed and was sinking in a simmering bog. Then the dream would start all over again from the beginning. Why was he unable to dream his own death?

But it was not dying that frightened him. It was everything else. Every touch. Every word. Every thought. Every heartbeat. His next breath.

He couldn't move. He couldn't eat. He spat out the tea that Su Kyi poured into him. He heard her voice, but she was far away. He felt her hand and yet was not certain she was really touching him.

Again and again, the words of U May went through his head. "There is only one power that mitigates fear, Tin Win." But what power can mitigate the fear of love, U May?

Three days later he still showed no sign of improvement. Su Kyi massaged him for hours. She rubbed him down with herbs. She hadn't left his side in seventy-two hours. He complained of no pain, was not coughing, and his body seemed to her rather too cold than too hot. She had no idea what was ailing him, but she was sure of this: It was grave, and it seemed to want his life. She wondered whom to turn to for advice. She was as wary of the nurses and doctors at the little hospital as of the astrologers and medicine men of the Danus, Paos, and Palongs. If anyone could help, it was U May. Perhaps, she thought, Tin Win was not suffering from any illness at all. Perhaps ghosts and demons had been wakened, who—as far as Su Kyi knew—dwelt in all of us, waiting only to emerge from hiding or to unmask themselves. So she set some tea beside the sleeping Tin Win and hurried to the monastery.

She painted the past three days and nights for U May in all their detail, but the story did not seem to trouble him particularly. He mumbled something about a virus, the virus of love, the infection which, if she had understood him correctly, everyone carried, but which only ever afflicted a few. When it was triggered, however, it was accompanied in the beginning by considerable fear, by tumultuous states that would confound both body and soul. In most cases, these symptoms would subside in due course.

In most cases, he had said. And Su Kyi could not help but think of an old story—this of her great uncle who had not left his bed for thirty-seven years, who for years at a time lay motionless on his mat, staring at the ceiling, making not a sound, refusing to eat on his own and surviving only because his relatives, with the patience of angels, fed him daily. And all of this because the neighbors' daughter, whom he had desired in his youth, had been married off by her parents to another man.

And there was another such story—this of Su Kyi's nephew who lost his heart to a girl in the village and who sat singing love songs in front of her family's house every evening at dusk. That in itself was nothing unusual, a custom practiced by most young couples in Kalaw. But her nephew never stopped singing, even when it became unmistakably apparent that the girl's family did not welcome his overtures. After a while he would sing not only in the evening hours but throughout the day, and when he started singing at night as well his brothers had to come and—since he refused to go—carry him off. At home he climbed into an avocado tree and did not stop singing until his voice failed him for a good three weeks and six days later. From then on he moved his mouth in time with the melody, his lips forming the words of the song that told of his eternal love. The longer she thought about it, the more stories she remembered of peasants and monks, of merchants and traders, goldsmiths and wagon drivers—indeed, even of certain Englishmen—who had similarly lost their minds.

Perhaps it had something to do with Kalaw. Perhaps it was home to an extraordinarily virulent strain. Perhaps it was the mountain air or the climate. Something in this unassuming corner of Southeast Asia that made it particularly severe.

U May himself saw no reason for concern.

Upon her return, Tin Win lay still unmoved in his bed. Su Kyi ground eucalyptus leaves in her mortar and held them under Tin Win's nose, hoping they would stimulate his sense of smell. She tried the same with a bunch of hibiscus blossoms and jasmine. She massaged his feet and head, but Tin Win did not respond. His heart was beating, and he was breathing, but he exhibited no other signs of life. He had withdrawn into a world where she could not reach him.

On the morning of the seventh day a young man appeared at her door. On his back was Mi Mi. Su Kyi recognized her from the market and knew that Tin Win spent afternoons and weekends with her.

"Is Tin Win at home?" asked Mi Mi.

"He's sick," answered Su Kyi.

"What's wrong with him?"

"I don't know. He's not speaking. He's not eating. He's unconscious."

"May I see him?"

Su Kyi showed her the way through the kitchen into the bedroom. Tin Win lay there motionless, his face haggard, his nose angular, and his skin ashen and lifeless despite its brown color. The tea and rice had not been touched. Mi Mi slid from her brother's back and crawled to Tin Win. Su Kyi could not take her eyes off her. This girl moved with a grace Su Kyi had never before seen. As if her oddly formed feet had given her a different, heightened sense of her limbs and movements.

Mi Mi took Tin Win's head in her hands and laid it in her lap. She bent over him, and his face disappeared under her long black hair. She whispered in his ear. Her brother turned and went out. Su Kyi followed him. She made tea for the guests and scrounged up roasted melon and sunflower seeds from an old tin, then stepped into the garden and sat down in the shadow of the avocado tree. She gazed across the yard at the firewood chopped and piled neatly against the wall of the house, the tree stump on which from time to time she slaughtered a chicken, their vegetable garden, the slowly crumbling bench that Tin Win's father must have built. Their six chickens ran about picking at the ground. She recognized the onset of sorrow growing within her. Su Kyi knew this mood. She abhorred it and always fought hard to stave it off—in most cases successfully. But now she felt the emotion gaining weight and strength. She could see no cause, and groundless sadness was for her nothing but self-pity, a thing she had resisted her whole life long. Was it Tin Win's mysterious illness that troubled her so? The fear of losing him? Or the recognition, returning at long intervals, of how solitary, lost, and lonesome she was? Tin Win, too. Her sister. Everyone, really. Some felt it; some did not.

At that moment she heard the song. It came from the house, faint as if from across the valley. An elegant and gentle girl's voice singing a melody that Su Kyi did not know. Nor could she make out the lyrics—at least no more than isolated words. It was the melody and the passion that moved her so.

This is a song that can tame ghosts and demons, thought Su Kyi. She sat transfixed under the tree. As if the slightest movement might spoil the moment. Mi Mi's voice permeated the house and yard like a fragrance penetrating into every nook and cranny. To Su Kyi it seemed as if all other sounds—the singing of the birds, the chirping of the cicadas, the croaking of the frogs—were slowly ebbing away until only the song remained. It had the power of a drug. It opened every cell, every sense in her body. She thought of Tin Win. She need have no more fear on his account. This kind of song would always find him, even in the remotest hiding place.

Su Kyi sat motionless under the avocado tree until her eyelids fell shut.

The cool of the evening woke her. It was dark, and she had caught a chill. The voice sang on, just as gently, just as beautifully. Su Kyi rose and went into the house. A candle was burning in the kitchen, another in the bedroom. Mi Mi still sat beside Tin Win, his head in her lap. His face seemed fuller, his skin less pale. Her brother had left. Su Kyi asked whether she was hungry or wished to lie down. Mi Mi shook her head briefly.

Su Kyi ate a bit of cold rice and an avocado. She was tired and didn't feel there was much she could do. She returned to the bedroom, arranged a sleeping mat for Mi Mi, gave her a jacket and a blanket, then lay down herself.

When Su Kyi woke the next morning it was quiet. She looked around to make sure she was no longer dreaming. Tin Win and Mi Mi lay sleeping beside her. She rose and noticed—without understanding why—how hale and light she felt. Almost too light, she thought, walking into the kitchen. She made a fire and some tea, washed scallions and tomatoes, and cooked the rice for breakfast.

Tin Win and Mi Mi woke late that morning. It was warm but not too hot, and Su Kyi was working in the vegetable garden when she caught sight of Tin Win in the doorway, Mi Mi on his back. He looked older. Or maybe the exhaustion and the strain had left a mark on him. Mi Mi appeared to be giving him directions, for he walked around the firewood, a stool, and the ax as if he could see everything. They sat down on the bench along the kitchen wall. Su Kyi dropped her rake and rushed to them.

"Are you hungry?" she asked.

"Yes, rather," said Tin Win. His voice sounded somewhat deeper than usual, almost a bit unfamiliar. "And thirsty."

Su Kyi brought rice and curry and tea. They ate slowly, and he seemed to grow livelier and stronger with every bite.

After the meal, Tin Win announced that he would go for a walk with Mi Mi before bringing her home. He felt good, no longer tired at all. Su Kyi need not worry. His legs would support him, and he would be back before nightfall. He promised.

~~~~~

Tin Win and Mi Mi took the rough path up to the crest and then along the mountain ridge. He focused entirely on walking, wondering whether he would ever again be able to put himself entirely in her hands, whether she would still pilot him so artfully past all obstacles.

"Do you remember the past few days?" asked Mi Mi after they had been quiet for some time.

"Barely," he said. "I must have slept a lot. I never knew whether I was sleeping or awake. I heard nothing but whooshing and a dull cooing and gurgling."

"What was wrong with you?"

"I don't know. I was possessed."

"By what?"

"Fear."

"What were you afraid of?"

"When I got to your farm and no one was there and the neighbors didn't know where you were, I thought I would never see you again. Where were you?"

"We were visiting relatives up in the mountains. An aunt died, and we had to set out before daybreak." She put her mouth very close to his ear. "You don't need to be afraid. You can't lose me. I am a part of you, just as you're a part of me."

Tin Win was about to respond when his left foot stepped into nothingness. The hole in the ground was grown over with grass, and Mi Mi would presumably not have seen it even if she had been paying attention. Tin Win felt frozen in mid-stride, watching himself in slow motion. His foot groped for the ground, and it seemed an eternity before he found it. He tumbled, lost his balance, and noticed while falling how he suppressed the instinct to cover his own face with his hands, how instead he held Mi Mi closer. He did not know how far he would fall, when or where he would hit, whether he would land in the grass or on a stone or a bush that would scrape his face. His fall seemed endless, and the worst part was the uncertainty about what awaited him. He turned his head to the side and tucked his chin into his chest. Mi Mi clung tightly to him. They tumbled nearly headfirst. Tin Win sensed how he buried Mi Mi beneath him and how they then rolled sideways like a log down the grassy slope.

He had fallen, but he had landed. They came to a stop in a hollow.

Mi Mi was lying on top of him. Only now did Tin Win notice how tightly they clung to each other. He did not want to let go. Her heart was beating rapidly. He not only heard it; he felt it against his chest. Mi Mi felt very different lying on top of him. She was lighter than she was on his back, and he felt more than her arms around his neck. Her breast lay on his, her belly against his. Their longyis were disordered, their bare legs intertwined. An unfamiliar emotion took hold of him, a desire for more. He wanted to possess Mi Mi and to give himself to her. He wanted to be one with her, to belong to her. Tin Win turned aside, startled by his own desire.

"Are you hurt?" she asked.

"Not particularly. You?"

"No."

Mi Mi brushed the dirt from his face. She wiped his forehead and cleared the dust from the corners of his mouth. Their lips touched for a fraction of a second. Tin Win shuddered.

"Can you walk?" she asked. "I think we're in for some rain."

Tin Win stood up and lifted Mi Mi onto his back again. They crossed the field. A short time later they heard the rushing of the river, wild and full from all the rain in recent weeks. It had cut a little ravine into the land. Farther downstream was a bridge, but it wouldn't be easy to reach from here. Tin Win attempted to gauge the depth from the noise of the waters raging beneath them. It had to be about ten feet. "How wide is it here?" he asked.

"Six, seven feet, maybe more."

"How will we get across?"

Mi Mi looked around. "There's a tree trunk lying across the river over there." She guided Tin Win past a small boulder. It was a pine, thinner than Mi Mi had thought, no thicker than her thigh. The bark had been stripped, and someone had trimmed the branches close to the trunk. Mi Mi hesitated.

"What is it?" he asked.

"It's a long way down," she said.

"Only if you look. For me it's nothing."

He felt his way to the trunk and set one foot on it. His sole arched over the wood. Mi Mi tried to direct him with his shoulders, but he shook his head. "Trust my feet."

He had turned a bit to the side, one foot in front of the other. He was not taking proper steps but sliding the front foot forward a few inches at a time, feeling the wood until he had got the shape of it, then shifting his weight and dragging the other foot along. He could hear Mi Mi's heart, pounding. At the same time, the rushing of the water was loud and clear now. They must be right above the river. Creaking ominously, the slender trunk bent under their weight.

Tin Win moved slowly, but he never faltered. Not once. She felt dizzy and closed her eyes. He was right. It was easier that way. She just had to forget where she was.

Tin Win inched along until the river once again sounded a notch quieter. They had reached the other side. Mi Mi rocked with relief on his back and kissed his cheeks and neck. His knees buckled with the excitement. He stumbled and only with difficulty regained his balance. A few steps farther on they heard a mighty thunderclap close at hand. He was frightened. Thunderstorms still made him uneasy.

"There's a shack a bit farther down the valley," Mi Mi called out. "Maybe we can get there before it really opens up. Let's run alongside the river."

Tin Win moved as quickly as he could. Whenever he strayed too near the river or too far from the bank she would tug on the appropriate shoulder. The rain came. The water was pleasantly warm. It ran over their faces, dripped from their noses, and ran down their necks and bellies. Mi Mi snuggled into him, and he became aware of her breasts moving against his wet back.

The shack, a windowless shelter of wooden beams and boards, was no bigger than two or three sleeping mats and the floor was strewn with several layers of dried grass. Rain hammered on the tin roof like a thousand drumming fists. It fell so heavily that Mi Mi could barely see the river only a few yards away. The tempest was raging right above them now, and Tin Win shuddered with each thunderclap, but for the first time during a storm he did not feel ill at ease. It thundered so loudly that Mi Mi covered her ears. Tin Win flinched but wasn't afraid.

Inside the hut it was hotter and even more humid than outside. Mi Mi stretched out on the strewn grass. Tin Win sat cross-legged with her head between his thighs. He ran his hands through her hair, across her forehead, feeling her eyebrows, nose, and mouth, caressing her cheeks and throat.

His fingertips electrified her. With every movement her heart fluttered more rapidly. He bent down, kissed her forehead, her nose. His tongue ran across her throat and her ears. Mi Mi could hardly believe how she was enjoying her body, every place that Tin Win touched. His hands brushed her face, her temples, the ridge of her nose. They traced her lips, stroked her eyes and mouth. She opened it a little, and it was as if he had never touched her before.

He nestled her head on a bed of grass and took off his shirt. Mi Mi closed her eyes and breathed deeply in and out. He caressed her feet. His fingers explored her toes, brushed across her nails and the little bones beneath the taut skin, across the ankles. Up her calves to her longyi, then back again. Once. Twice. Mi Mi lifted her hips and pulled her shirt up a little, took his hand and laid it on her bare belly. His heart pounded, not quickly, but loudly and vigorously.

He sensed her breath quickening. His fingers flitted over her body, barely touching her. Between fingertips and skin there arose a tension that was more exhilarating than any contact. He gradually worked his way along, lower and lower beneath her longyi until he felt the edge of her pubic hair. He knelt beside her. She saw his longyi stretched to a small tent around his hips and was shocked—not by the sight, not by his fingers, but by her desire, by her breath and her heartbeat, ever quicker and fiercer. Cautiously he withdrew his hand. She wanted more and caught hold of him, but he lay his head on her breast and did not move. He waited. Her heartbeat did not settle for a long time.

It was a sound he would never take for granted. The reverence and respect he felt for every beat made him shudder. There it was, just inches from his ear. He felt as if he were peering through a chink into the lap of the world.

# Chapter 15

NEARLY FOUR YEARS passed this way between Mi Mi and Tin Win. After those first few weeks they had not let a day go by without seeing each other. She waited for him after school, or he went to the market after his lessons. On weekends he would collect her at home first thing in the morning. You're quite inseparable, her mother had said once, half in jest. *Inseparable.* In her usual fashion, Mi Mi had reflected on that word for a long time. She had turned it this way and that in her mind to see whether the sound of it appealed to her, whether it fit, and after a few days had come to the conclusion that there was no better description. They were inseparable. Her heart would flutter at the mere sight of him, and some part of her was missing when he was not around. As if the world stopped turning in his absence. She felt the lack of him in her entire body. Her head would ache. Her legs and arms would grow heavy and lame. Pangs shot through her belly and breast. Even breathing was laborious without him.

During their third summer together, Mi Mi guided Tin Win to the lakes, to swim, and it became their favorite retreat. They always went to the smallest of the four ponds. It lay off the beaten track behind a small stand of pines. Other young people avoided it because it was reputed to host the greatest concentration of water snakes. She had seen two herself. When she asked Tin Win if he was afraid of them, he laughed and said that he had never seen any.

On this day, Mi Mi watched Tin Win carefully. The wind picked up. It rippled the water, and Mi Mi heard tiny waves lapping at the stones at her feet. She was crouching on the bank of the little lake, her eyes upon him. He was no mean swimmer. He had developed a style all his own, lying sideways in the water and always keeping one hand in front of his body so that he would feel any obstacles. He was cautious and preferred to stay near the shore, where his feet could still touch bottom. But he had endurance, and he could dive very well.

Mi Mi loved the water. Even as a little girl she had gone with her brothers to the four lakes about an hour's hike from Kalaw. They had taken turns carrying her and quickly taught her to swim. These excursions were among Mi Mi's fondest memories. In the water she could vie with her brothers and play with the other children. She was quick and adroit, the best diver of them all. Feet were irrelevant in the water.

Tin Win had swum to the middle of the lake, where a stone large enough to sit on rose out of the water. He climbed atop and let the wind and sun dry him off. Mi Mi felt desire stealing over her. These afflictions vanished only when she found herself on his back again, putting her hands about his neck and feeling his shoulders. There was no place she felt safer or happier.

Mi Mi could not help but think of that afternoon when the storm raged over them and they had taken shelter in the shack. He had really touched her for the first time then, and that touch had awakened a desire in her that was sometimes stronger than all of her other emotions combined. She wondered whether everything she felt in such moments had been slumbering within her. Had Tin Win merely brought it to life? Or had it come from some other place? Was he enchanting her? What was it he had woken with his kiss? Whenever his lips touched her skin? Every time his fingers brushed across her neck, her breasts, her belly, her thighs, she felt as if he were revealing her own body to her for the first time. Tin Win reacted no differently to her hands, to her lips. She could arouse his body, caressing him and stroking him until he twitched and chafed with uninhibited desire. At moments like this she felt so alive that she did not know where to keep all her happiness. She seemed to float on the wind, and she was light and weightless as otherwise only in the water. She sensed a power she had never thought herself capable of. A power that only Tin Win could call to life.

He had taught her to trust, had given her the space to be weak. When she was with him, she had nothing to prove. He was the first and only one to whom she confessed that she found it humiliating to crawl on all fours. That she sometimes dreamed of walking through Kalaw on two sound feet and of jumping as high as she could into the air. Just because. He did not try to console her at such moments. He took her in his arms, said nothing. Mi Mi knew that he understood what she meant and how she felt. The more she spoke of her desire to walk on her own feet, the less frequently it tormented her. And she believed him when he said there was no more beautiful body in the world than hers.

There was no step that she would not venture with him.

Mi Mi looked over at him, and although he was little more than fifteen yards away, she could not bear the distance. She took off her shirt and her longyi, slipped into the water, and swam a few vigorous strokes. The sun had warmed the lake, but the water was still cool enough to refresh her. There would be room enough for both of them on the rock if she sat between his legs and leaned against him. She swam over to him. He reached out a hand and helped her out of the water. She leaned on him. He put his arms around her waist and held her tightly.

"I couldn't bear to be without you," she whispered.

"I've been here the whole time."

"I wanted to feel you. And I was sad."

"Why?"

"Because you were so far away, because I couldn't touch you," she answered, astonished at her own words. "Every hour we spend apart saddens me. Every place I go without you. Every step you take without me on your back. Every night that we don't fall asleep in each other's arms and every morning that we don't wake up side by side."

She turned around and knelt in front of him. She took his head in her hands, and he could hear the tears running down her cheeks. She kissed his brow and his eyes. She kissed his mouth and his neck. Her lips were soft and moist. She covered him with kisses. He drew her to himself, and she wrapped her legs around his hips. He held her tightly, very tightly. Otherwise she might fly away.

# Chapter 16

THE BEATS REMINDED him of a downspout's steady dripping. In recent days the silences between beats had grown ever longer. It was a wellspring that was gradually drying up.

Tin Win had heard it coming. Weeks ago. U May's heart had always sounded tired and weary to his ears, but recently the beats had been fainter even than usual. For the past two weeks a young monk had been instructing U May's pupils single-handedly while U May lay in his bed, too weak to lift himself. He ate nothing and drank little, in spite of the tropical temperatures.

Mi Mi and Tin Win had spent the past few days and nights by his bedside. Tin Win had read to him until his fingertips were sore. Mi Mi offered to sing for him, but U May declined. He said that he knew of her voice's magical powers and that he did not wish to lengthen his life by any artificial means. A brief smile graced his lips.

Now, having granted themselves a respite, the two were sitting in a teahouse on the main thoroughfare, drinking fresh sugarcane juice. It was hot. For the past two weeks Kalaw had been beleaguered by a heat wave that showed no signs of relenting. The air stood still. Neither said a word. Even the flies were suffering in this heat, thought Tin Win. Their buzzing sounded more sluggish and listless than usual. Beside them sat merchants and vendors; everyone was complaining continuously about the weather. To Tin Win it was incomprehensible. U May lay dying not two hundred yards away, and the people were just drinking their tea. Going about their business. Chatting about trivialities like weather.

He recognized the approaching monk immediately by his uneven gait. It was Zhaw, whose left leg was a hair shorter than his right and who limped because of it, though not visibly—no one besides Tin Win had ever noticed it. Zhaw had bad news—his heart sounded nearly as wretched as that of the wounded calf Mi Mi had found not long before and who had died in her hands.

"U May has lost consciousness," Zhaw rasped, completely out of breath.

Tin Win rose and knelt before Mi Mi, who clambered onto his back, and together they set off. He ran down the main street, Mi Mi directing him through the foot traffic and past carts. They turned onto the road leading to the monastery, hurried across the courtyard, up the steps.

All the monks and many of the townsfolk had gathered around U May. They sat on the floor and filled nearly half of the great meditation hall. At the sight of Tin Win and Mi Mi they cleared a narrow aisle to U May's bed. Mi Mi was shocked by the sight of him. His face had sunken further in the past hour. His eyes now sat so deeply they seemed to be vanishing into his skull. His nose protruded, and his lips had nearly disappeared. The skin stretched across his cheekbones was as pale and lifeless as a piece of leather. His hands lay folded on his abdomen.

They crouched beside his bed, Mi Mi somewhat behind Tin Win with her arms around his chest.

Tin Win knew it would not be much longer. U May's heart was scarcely louder than a butterfly's wing beats. How he had been dreading this moment. For some time now he had been unable to imagine a life without U May. Without his voice. Without his advice. Without his encouragement. U May was the first person he had opened himself up to. And U May had tried to release him from fear. "Every life contains the seed of death," he had explained to Tin Win repeatedly in those first years of their friendship. Death, like birth, was a part of life that no one could escape. It was senseless to resist it. Far better to accept it as natural than to fear it.

Tin Win appreciated the logic of the argument, but it had never really persuaded him. The fear still lingered. The fear of U May's death, but also of his own. It was not as if he was clinging to his own life or that he considered it especially worth living. Yet the fear had been there, verging at times on panic. It had an animal quality, and it put him in mind of the piglet he had once watched his father slaughter. It was a sight he would never forget. The eyes stretched wide. Those bloodcurdling squeals, the desperate struggling, the whole body twitching. The fear of death is presumably a survival instinct, Tin Win later thought. It must be an essential part of us, of every living creature. At the same time, we must transcend it to take our leave in peace. He found this an irresolvable contradiction. Not once in the past two years had he contemplated dying, and now that U May's impending death compelled him to, he found himself unexpectedly serene. Now that he finally had something to lose, he was no longer afraid. He would have loved to ask U May for an explanation, but it was too late. U May suddenly moved his lips.

"Tin Win, Mi Mi, are you there?" He was not speaking, but breathing the words.

"Yes," said Tin Win.

"Do you remember how I wished to die?"

"Free of fear and with a smile on your lips," answered Tin Win.

"I have no fear," whispered U May. "Mi Mi will tell you whether I am also managing to smile." Tin Win took U May's hand and implored him to say no more. "Spare yourself."

"For what?"

It sounded like his final word. Tin Win hoped he would say something else. No life should end with a question. For what?

It sounded like vain striving. Like doubt. Like something unfulfilled. Tin Win counted the seconds between heartbeats. Several breaths passed between each.

Again U May opened his mouth. Tin Win leaned forward.

Then it was quiet. Tin Win waited. Silence. A boundless silence, engulfing everything, drowning out every sound.

He heard Mi Mi's heart and then his own, their rhythms gradually converging, beat by beat, conforming to each other, and for a few seconds—it seemed to him a long time—he heard their two hearts beat as one.

# Chapter 17

THERE HAD BEEN certain powerful moments in her life Yadana would remember until her dying day. The first time she set eyes on Tin Win was one of them. She'd been sitting on the porch of her house, ready to weave some dried grass into a basket. It was late afternoon; she could already smell and hear the neighbors' fire, the clatter of their pots and tinware. She was alone. Her husband and sons were still in the field. Suddenly Tin Win was standing in the yard, carrying Mi Mi on his back. Even now she could not have articulated just what moved her so. It was the radiance in Tin Win's young face. It was his laughter when Mi Mi whispered something in his ear. It was the way he gingerly climbed the steps to the porch, feeling his way from one to the next, then squatting down to let Mi Mi slide gently off his back. It was simply the new light in her daughter's face, her eyes like two stars in the night.

After that, Tin Win brought Mi Mi home evening after evening. At first he was noticeably aloof, setting Mi Mi down and bidding them farewell shortly thereafter. Within a few weeks, though, he was helping Mi Mi with the cooking and staying for supper.

Yadana took to calling him her youngest son. The longer she knew him, the better she liked him. His tact, his thoughtfulness, the tenderness he showed Mi Mi. His humor and his modesty. His intuition. Often he seemed to know how Yadana and her family felt even before they had exchanged a single word. Nor did Yadana have the sense that he was particularly troubled by his loss of his vision, least of all with Mi Mi on his back. Sometimes the sight of the two of them walking up the mountain would move her to tears. Despite his burden, Tin Win walked perfectly upright. He was not lugging Mi Mi. He carried her like a gift, happily and proudly. She sat on his back, singing or whispering in his ear. Often Yadana would recognize the two of them by their laughter well before she saw them coming.

Her husband had dubbed them "brother and sister" after a few months and was still calling them that almost four years later. Was he just careless in his choice of words, or did he really fail to appreciate what was playing out right before his eyes? The longer she thought about it, the more she suspected that he meant what he said and that he, like many men, apparently lacked a feel for certain things, a sense that would have helped him to see beyond the superficial.

Obviously Mi Mi and Tin Win had been more than

brother and sister for a long time now. The joy Mi Mi radiated had nothing of a child's. Tin Win was still very quiet, polite, and respectful, but in his voice, his gestures, and his movements was now more than thoughtfulness and tenderness. These two young people enjoyed an intimacy of which Yadana was almost a bit envious. She herself had never experienced anything like it with her husband, and truth be told, she did not know any other two people so close to each other.

Yadana wondered whether it might be time, now that they were both eighteen, to broach the subject of marriage. But since Tin Win was obviously an orphan, it was unclear to whom she should turn. Perhaps, she thought, she should simply wait until Mi Mi or Tin Win asked her. What difference would a few months or even a year make? She was convinced that she need not worry about her daughter or Tin Win. They had discovered a secret of life that had eluded her, even if she had always sensed its existence.

# Chapter 18

IT WAS JUST after nightfall one summer evening when Tin Win got home from spending the afternoon at the lake with Mi Mi. The swimming and the long hike had left him pleasantly exhausted. It was a mild evening after a hot day. The air was dry and comfortably warm. The croaking of the frogs in the nearby pool was so loud that it drowned out all other sounds. Su Kyi would have supper waiting for him by now. Opening the garden gate, he suddenly noticed two unfamiliar voices—men talking with Su Kyi. They were sitting by the fire in front of the house. He heard Su Kyi stand up and come over to him. She took him by the hand and led him to the strangers. The men got right to the point. They had been waiting for Tin Win all afternoon. Su Kyi had made them very welcome, serving them tea and nuts. Now they were weary from their long journey and looking forward to their hotel. Especially since tomorrow would bring further strenuous traveling. They had come from Rangoon. His uncle, the venerable U Saw, had charged them with bringing him, Tin Win, to the capital by the fastest means possible. He would learn all further details personally from his uncle. They would take the early train the next morning to Thazi, where, a few hours later, they would board the night express from Mandalay to reach Rangoon the next morning. The tickets had already been purchased, seats reserved. The first train was leaving Kalaw at seven. They would come to get him. Would he please be waiting for them at six? Ready to leave.

At first Tin Win didn't understand what they were saying. As always with strangers, he had listened first to their hearts and their voices rather than to their words. The heartbeats had not revealed much. Their voices sounded oddly expressionless. Whatever they were doing in Kalaw, whatever they were telling him just now, it was of little importance to them.

Only Su Kyi's deep sigh put him on the alert. And her heart. It was beating more quickly than the occasion called for, as though she had just climbed a mountain. But Tin Win had learned with Mi Mi's help that not only physical exertion could set a heart to pounding like that. People might be sitting quietly on the ground, externally at peace, all while their hearts were racing in their chests like animals running for their lives. He knew from personal experience that dreams and fantasies often worried and threatened people more than reality did, that the head could tax the heart infinitely more than even the hardest labor.

What was Su Kyi so worried about? Now that the men had left, and she was repeating sentence for sentence what they had said, the words very gradually sank in. By train. To the capital. Alone.

"Why? What does my uncle want from me?" asked Tin Win when he finally understood.

"I don't know," she answered. "People in town say he's very wealthy, that he has good and influential friends among the English. Supposedly even the governor. I'm sure he can help you."

"I don't need any help." Tin Win scoffed at the thought that anyone, out of pity, might offer him help.

"Maybe he's heard of the trouble with your eyes and would like to have a British doctor examine you. At any rate, we've got to sort out now what you're going to take with you tomorrow." She turned to go into the house.

"Su Kyi." Her heartbeat was out of step with the words she meant to comfort him. "What do you really think?"

"Oh, Tin Win. It's just that I'm going to miss you. But what am I saying, me, a selfish old crone. I ought to be happy for you."

"Su Kyi!" His voice was reproving. He heard quite distinctly that she was concealing her true thoughts.

"Besides, you won't be gone for more than a few weeks, at most," she went on, as if she hadn't heard him at all.

He was taken aback. Until now the idea of the journey had been something abstract. He had never traveled and had no concept of what it involved. He would have to leave Kalaw. He would arrive in a new place, strange and therefore threatening, and he did not know what to expect there. He would have to do without Su Kyi, without the monastery or the monks, without his home, without the familiar noises or smells. Without Mi Mi.

The idea was so preposterous that it had not registered until that moment. Now he was expected to set off in a few hours without even knowing when he would be able to return. In a few weeks? A couple of months? Ever? He felt the demons and phantoms stir in his breast.

Tin Win took the bumpy path over the mountain ridge. He knew every stone, every pit along the way. He walked faster, started to run. At first warily, then with increasing strides until he was bounding along at top speed. Some power was driving him forward, some power that had no thought of falling. He raced past the pool and turned at the bamboo grove. He sped down the meadow and back up the other side. He ran without stumbling, barely feeling the earth beneath his feet. Was it memory, instinct, or longing that guided him so confidently to Mi Mi's house?

He took the last few yards more slowly and caught his breath for a moment behind the hibiscus hedge that sheltered the house from the road. He stepped into the yard.

The dog ran over and leapt on him. Tin Win patted and calmed him. The pig was snoring under the porch. All was quiet in the house. He climbed the steps slowly. The door was unlocked. It creaked when he opened it. He could tell by her heartbeat where Mi Mi lay sleeping, and he felt his way carefully through the room to her mat. He nearly fell over a tin pot sitting in the middle of the floor. He knelt beside her and laid a hand on her face.

She woke with a start. "Tin Win, what are you doing here?"

"There's something I've got to tell you," he whispered. Tin Win pushed one arm under her neck, the other under her knee, and lifted her. Their faces nearly touched. He had never carried her in his arms. They went to the stairs, down the steps, and across the yard.

She caressed his face and neck. "You're sweating."

"I ran the whole way. I had to see you."

"Where should we go?" she asked.

"I don't know. Somewhere we can be alone without waking anyone."

Mi Mi thought a moment. The fields began a few houses down, and there was a rain shelter in one of them. She directed him there, and a few minutes later they reached the refuge and crawled inside. The walls were woven grass, and through the holes in the roof Mi Mi could see the sky. It was a clear night, full of stars, unusually warm. Mi Mi felt her heart beat quickly, expectantly. She took his hand and laid it on her belly.

"Mi Mi, I'm leaving for Rangoon tomorrow morning. An uncle of mine who lives there sent two men to take me there."

Decades later that sentence would still ring in her ears. Only hours earlier, at the lake, she had been dreaming of their future, of a wedding. She had imagined herself and Tin Win living in a house with children in the yard, children with feet for walking and eyes for seeing. She had lain in his arms, describing the scene to him. They had determined to raise the issue of marriage with Mi Mi's parents in the coming weeks. And now he would be going to the capital. Mi Mi knew what that meant. Rangoon was the other end of the world. Few people ever went there and even fewer returned. She wanted to ask what his uncle wanted with him and how long he would be away and why they had to be apart, but at the same time she sensed that words could not help her, not now, when she longed with her whole body for Tin Win. She took his hands and pulled him down to her. Their lips met. She pulled her shirt over her head, and he kissed her breasts. His warm breath on her skin. His mouth dancing downward along her body. He loosened her longyi. They were both naked. He kissed her legs and thighs. He teased her with his tongue. She felt him now as never before. And she felt herself. More and more deeply, more beautifully than ever. He was giving her a new body with every movement. She pictured herself flying over Kalaw, over the forests and mountains and valleys, from one peak to the next. The earth receded to a miniature ball on which

Rangoon and Kalaw and all the other cities and countries lay no more than a finger's breadth apart. She lost all control over her body. It was as if every one of her emotions had suddenly exploded, the rage and the fear and the doubt, the longing, the tenderness, and the desire. For one moment, for the duration of a few heartbeats, every one of the world's promises was fulfilled, and nothing could contain her.

# Chapter 19

THERE WASN'T MUCH to pack. Tin Win owned little more than a few undergarments, three longyis, four shirts, and a pullover, and he wouldn't even need all of those. It was hot and humid all year round in the capital. Su Kyi packed the things in an old cloth bag she had found long ago outside one of the British clubs. For the journey she had made him rice and his favorite curry of dried fish. She put the food into a tin with a sealable lid and tucked it between the longyis. At the very bottom she put the tiger bone from Tin Win's father. And the snail shell and the bird's feather Mi Mi had given him a few months earlier. Su Kyi looked out the window. It had to be just after five-thirty. It was still dark, but the birds were already at it and dawn was coming. Tin Win had come home only a few minutes ago. He was sitting in front of the kitchen.

For the first time in a long while Su Kyi was worried again about Tin Win. Since the beginning of his friendship with Mi Mi he had changed in a way she would not have thought possible. He had discovered life, and when they ate together in the morning, she often had the feeling of sitting beside a child, he was so brimming with joy and energy. As if he was making up for all the lost years. She couldn't imagine he'd find his way in a strange environment without Mi Mi's help. She had never witnessed such a symbiosis between two people, and there were moments when the sight of them made her wonder whether, in the end, a person maybe wasn't alone after all, whether in some cases, the smallest human unit was two rather than one. Perhaps the uncle really did have his nephew's best interests at heart. Perhaps the doctors in the capital could cure him. Perhaps he'd be back in a matter of months.

She stepped out of the house and looked him full in the face. She'd seen people die, and she'd seen bereft mourners, but she couldn't recall ever having seen a face so clouded with pain. She held him by the arm and he wept inconsolably. He wept until the two men stepped through the garden gate. She wiped his tears away and asked if she might see them to the train. Of course, one man said. The other took the bag.

They spoke not a word the entire way. Su Kyi took Tin Win's hand. He was shivering. His gait was tentative and clumsy. He felt his way along, fearfully, stumbling more than walking as if only recently stricken blind. Su Kyi's legs grew heavier with every step. She fell into a kind of trance, taking in only fragments of what was happening around her. She heard the wheezing of the locomotive that was already waiting at the station. She saw white clouds rising from a black tower. The place was crawling with people bellowing in her ears. A child screamed. A woman fell. Tomatoes rolled onto the track. Tin Win's fingers slipped from hers. The men led him away. He disappeared behind a door.

The last image ran together in a blur of tears. Tin Win sat at an open window, his head buried in his hands. She called his name, but he did not react. With a shrill whistle blast, the engine started to move. Su Kyi walked along beside the window. The train picked up speed. The wheezing grew louder and stronger. She started to run. Stumbled. Bowled into a man, jumped over a basket of fruit. Then the platform came to an end. The two rear lights shone like tiger's eyes in the night. Slowly they vanished behind a gentle curve. When Su Kyi turned around the platform was empty.

# Chapter 20

U BA HAD been talking for hours without pause. His mouth hung half open. His eyes looked right through me. He was motionless but for the steady rise and fall of his chest. I heard my own breath, the bees. I was clutching the arms of the chair. Only in airplanes did I sit so tensely, and even then only when they strayed into turbulence or began their landing approach. Slowly I let go and sank back into the soft cushions.

As our silence persisted, so the house slowly filled with disturbing noises. The wood creaked. There was rustling at my feet. Something was cooing under the eaves. Somewhere the wind was rattling a shutter. The kitchen faucet was dripping—or was I imagining that I heard U Ba's heart beating?

I tried to picture my father. The solitude in which he had lived, his deprivation, the darkness that had surrounded him until he met Mi Mi. How must he have felt at the prospect of losing everything she had given him? My eyes filled with tears. I strained to hold them back, but that only made everything worse. So I just wept—wept as if I myself had brought him to the train for Rangoon. U Ba rose and came over to me. He put a hand on my head. I was disconsolate. Perhaps this was the first time I had ever really cried about my father. There were days after his disappearance when I missed him terribly. I would be downcast, despondent. I suppose I even cried, yes. But I don't remember for certain. Besides, whom would those tears have been for? For him? For myself because I had lost my father? Or were they tears of rage and disappointment because he had skipped out on us?

To be sure, he had never told us anything about those first twenty years and therefore had never given us the chance to mourn with or for him. But would I have wanted to hear it? Was I in any position to empathize with him? Do children want to know their parents as independent individuals? Can we see them as they were before we came into the world?

I took a handkerchief from my backpack and dried my face.

"Are you hungry?" asked U Ba.

I shook my head.

"Thirsty?"

"A little."

He disappeared into the kitchen and came back with a mug of cold tea. It tasted of ginger and lime and soothed me.

"Are you tired? Should I take you back to your hotel?"

I was exhausted, but I did not want to be alone. The mere thought of that room unsettled me. In my mind's eye it loomed larger even than the empty dining hall, and the bed seemed wider than the hotel lawn. I saw myself lying on it, alone and lost. "I'd like to rest a bit. Would you mind terribly if I . . . just for a few minutes, if I . . . ?"

U Ba interrupted me: "By all means, Julia. Lie down on the sofa. I'll bring a blanket."

I could hardly lift myself out of the armchair, I was so weak. The couch was more comfortable than it looked. I curled up on the cushions and was only vaguely aware of U Ba spreading a light blanket over me. I fell almost immediately into a half sleep. I heard the bees. Their unvarying drone lulled me. U Ba passed through the room. Dogs barked. A rooster crowed. Pigs grunted. Saliva ran out of the corner of my mouth.

When I woke again it was dark and still. It took a few moments for me to realize where I was. It was cool. U Ba had draped a second, heavier blanket over me and tucked a pillow under my head. On the table in front of me were a glass of tea, a plate of pastries, and a vase with fresh jasmine blossoms. I heard a heavy old wooden door clicking shut, turned on my side, pulled my knees very close to my body, the blankets up to my chin, and fell back asleep.

# Chapter 21

IT WAS LIGHT when I opened my eyes. In front of me hot steam rose from a glass of water. Beside it a packet of Nescafé, a sugar cube, condensed milk, and fresh pastries. Sunbeams fell through one of the two windows, and from the couch I could see a bit of sky. Its blue was darker and more intense than I had known it in New York. It smelled like morning, and suddenly I couldn't help but think of our summer weekends in the Hamptons, when I would lie awake in bed in the early morning, a little girl listening to the roar of the sea through open windows, smelling the cool air in the room, air which—in spite of the cold—already foreshadowed the heat of the day.

I rose and stretched. Astonishingly, I had none of the back pain I usually suffered after spending the night in a strange bed. I must have slept well on that old couch with its threadbare upholstery. I walked over to one of the windows. A thick hedge of bougainvillea grew around the house. The courtyard was swept clean. Firewood was piled neatly between two trees, a stack of kindling beside it. A dog of indeterminate breed was roaming about, and the pig was wallowing below me.

I went into the kitchen. A small fire smoldered in one corner, above it a kettle. The smoke drafted straight upward and disappeared through a hole in the roof. Still, my eyes burned. Against the wall stood an open cupboard with a pair of white enameled tin bowls and plates, glasses, and sooty pots. On the lowest shelf were eggs, tomatoes, a huge bunch of scallions, ginger root, and limes.

"Julia?" His voice came from the next room.

U Ba sat at a table, surrounded by books. The whole room was full of them. It looked like a library gone to seed. The books filled shelves from floor to ceiling. They lay in piles on the wooden floorboards and in an armchair. They towered on a second table. Some were finger-thin, others the size of dictionaries. There were paperbacks among them, but most were hardcovers, a few even bound in leather. U Ba sat hunched over an open book whose yellowed pages resembled a punch card. Beside it an assemblage of various tweezers and scissors, and a jar of viscous white glue. Two oil lamps on the table offered additional light. U Ba looked at me over the rim of his thick glasses.

"What are you working on, U Ba?"

"Just passing the time."

"Doing what?"

He picked up a tiny scrap of paper with a long, thin pair of tweezers, dipped it briefly in the glue, then positioned it over one of the tiny holes in the book. With a fine black pen he then inked in the upper half of an *o*. I tried to read the text to which the letter belonged.

> *We s al not cease fr m exp orati n*
> *and t e end of al our expl ring*
> *wi l b to a rive w er we starte*
> *and kno the pl ce fo he fir t im .*

U Ba looked at me and recited the complete lines by heart.

"From a collection of Eliot poems," he said. "T. S. Eliot. I hold him in high regard." He smiled, satisfied, and showed me the first pages of the book. They were studded with bits of glued-on paper. "Not as good as new, perhaps, but at least it is legible once again."

I looked from him to the book and back. Was he serious? That volume must have contained at least two hundred hole-ridden pages. "How long does a book like that take you?"

"These days, a few months. I used to be faster. Now my eyes no longer fully cooperate, and my back objects after only a few hours of hunching over. On other days my hands tremble too severely." He leafed through the remaining pages and sighed. "This particular book is in a truly pitiful state. Even the worms seem to fancy Eliot."

"But surely there's some more efficient method of restoring books. You'll never manage it like this."

"No method within my power, I fear."

"I could send you new editions from New York of the ones that mean the most to you," I suggested.

"Don't go to the trouble. I read the most important ones while they were still in better condition."

"Then why are you restoring them?"

He smiled.

Neither of us spoke, and I looked around. Here I stood, in a wooden house without electricity or running water, surrounded by thousands of books. "Where did you get them all?" I asked.

"From the English. I was enamored of books even as a boy. Many of the British never returned after the war, and after independence more of them left every year. Whatever books they did not wish to take they left to me." He rose, walked over to a bookcase, pulled out a leather-bound tome, and leafed through it. The pages looked perforated. "You see, many have shared the same sad fate as the Eliot volume. The climate. The worms and insects." U Ba walked over to a little cupboard behind his desk. "These are the ones I've finished." He pointed to a couple of dozen books, took one of them, and handed it to me. It had a sturdy leather binding and a lovely feel. I opened it. Even the title page was dotted with paper bits. THE SOUL OF A PEOPLE, it read in a large font. London, 1902.

"Should you care to learn more about our country, this is a good place to start."

"It's not exactly current," I said, slightly irritated.

"The soul of a people does not change overnight."

U Ba pulled at his earlobes and glanced around, looking for something. He took a few books from a lower shelf. He had shelved them one row behind the other. Taking a key from a red lacquer box on his desk, he opened a drawer. "Just as I thought—I've locked it away," he said, taking a book out. "It's in Braille. Su Kyi gave it to me just before she died. It's the first volume of one of Tin Win's favorites. She forgot to pack it when he set off for Rangoon."

It was heavy and awkward. Several pieces of tape just barely held the spine together. "You should sit down. Come with me. We'll have a cup of coffee, and you can examine it at your leisure."

We moved into the living room. U Ba poured hot water from a thermos into a glass and made me a coffee. I set the book on my lap and opened it. The pages were as riddled with holes as those of the other books. I brushed my index finger across one page, casually, as if inspecting my cleaning lady's attention to detail on a dusty shelf. The book unsettled me. I snapped it shut and put it on the table. In the distance I heard singing. Several voices, faint and barely audible, so soft that they threatened to fade away before reaching my ear. A wave melting into the sand before ever washing over my feet.

I listened hard into the silence, but heard nothing, picked up the song again, then lost it, held my breath and sat stock still until I heard the notes again, somewhat louder now. Loud enough that I would not lose track of them again. It could only be a children's choir untiringly repeating a melodic mantra.

"Is it the children from the monastery?" I asked.

"Not the ones from the monastery in the town, though. There's another in the mountains, and when the wind is right, their song drifts down to us in the morning. You are hearing what Tin Win and Mi Mi heard. It sounded no different fifty years ago."

I closed my eyes and shuddered. The children's voices seemed to pass through my ears into my body and to touch me where no word, no thought, and no person had ever done before.

Whence this magic? I could not understand a single word they sang. What was it that affected me so? How can a person be moved to tears by something she can neither see, understand, nor hold on to, a mere sound that vanishes almost the moment it comes into being?

Music, my father often said, was the only reason he could sometimes believe in a god or in any heavenly power.

Every evening before going to bed he would sit in the living room, eyes closed, listening to music on headphones. How else will my soul find rest for the night, he had said quietly.

I cannot remember a single concert or opera at which he did not weep. Tears poured down his face like water from a lake silently but forcefully spilling over its banks. He would smile the whole time.

Once I asked him which he would take to a desert island, given the choice between music and books.

I wished the children's chanting might never end. It should accompany me through my day. Through my life. And after that. Had I ever felt so close to my father? Perhaps U Ba was right. Perhaps he was nearby, and I had only to look for him.

# Part Three

# Chapter 1

I WANTED TO see the house where my father spent his childhood and youth. Maybe he and Mi Mi were hiding there? U Ba hesitated.

"The buildings are in dismal condition. You will need a lot of imagination to find traces of his childhood there," he warned me.

But already I could hear my father's breath just a few yards ahead of me. He was panting from lugging her up the mountain. She was heavier, and he was older. I heard them whispering. Their voices. A few steps more and I would overtake them.

Just a few steps more.

"There's something I need to take care of," U Ba told me. "Will you go on ahead?" He pointed out the way and said he would catch up with me.

So I trudged over the mountain ridge alone. U Ba had described it in precise detail, the mud path with the deep pits and ruts. It was oddly familiar to me. I closed my eyes and tried to imagine my father walking along the road. I was startled by the many and varied noises I suddenly heard. Birds. Grasshoppers. Cicadas. An unpleasantly loud buzzing of flies, the distant barking of a dog. My feet got mired in the holes and ruts in the earth. I stumbled but did not fall. It smelled of eucalyptus and jasmine. An ox-cart overtook me. The animals were truly wretched. The skin clung to their ribs, and their eyes protruded from their skulls as if they were about to burst from the strain.

Beyond the summit I saw the house. I slackened my pace. At the garden gate I halted, dispirited.

The gate hung askew, its lower hinge broken off. Grass grew out of cracks in the masonry pillars. The wooden fence was overgrown with shrubbery. Every second or third slat was missing. The grass in the yard was grayish brown, scorched by the sun. The main building, a yellow two-story Tudor villa, had a grand balcony on the second floor from which one must have had a view of the town and the mountains. Its supports, the eaves, and the window frames were ornamented with wood carving. There was a conservatory, and several bay windows. A tree was growing out of the chimney. The thin framing of the roof was partly exposed where several tiles were missing. The balcony railing had lost nearly half its uprights, and the rain had bleached the color of the façade. Most of the windows were broken in.

Vacant buildings depressed me, even in New York. As a child I had always given them a wide berth, crossing the street whenever I came upon one. They were haunted. Behind their boarded-up windows ghosts lay in wait just for me. I dared to walk past them only when my father was with me, and even then I had to take the street side.

This villa had that same eerie quality. Why wasn't anyone maintaining it? Its former grandeur was still plain to see. Anyone could have kept it up without much effort. Could have.

What might have been, if? What lurked within? Phantoms? Two unlived lives?

Somewhat below the house was the ruined shack in which Su Kyi and my father must have lived. It was smaller than our living room in New York. I could see no window and only one empty doorframe. The brown corrugated tin roof was destroyed by rust, the clay crumbling out of the walls. I spotted the fire pit, a stack of weathered kindling, and the wooden bench. Two young women were sitting on it with babies on their laps. They looked at me and smiled. Beside the hut, four longyis hung in the sun. Two young dogs roamed about the yard. A third arched its back to shit, then cast me a mournful expression.

I drew two deep, even breaths and stepped through the gate. Ahead of me on the lawn was the tree stump. It must have come from a very old and large pine. Ants streamed over its thick bark. The wood was soft and eaten away in several places, but the heartwood was still sound, even after all the years. I climbed onto it without difficulty. It was damp and firm. The view into the valley was obstructed by several large bushes. I knew now why I had wanted to see this place at all costs and yet had dreaded it. Here was the key to U Ba's narrative. Ever since I had heard the children singing in the monastery this morning, his story had ceased to be a fable. It reverberated in my ears, and I could smell it and touch it with my hands. This was the tree stump where my father had waited in vain for his mother, my grandmother. Where he had nearly starved himself to death. In this yard he had lost his eyesight, and he had lived in this odd town where little had changed over the past fifty years. He and Mi Mi. U Ba was leading me to them. I heard their whispering. Their voices. Just a few steps more.

What if the next thing I knew they were standing right in front of me? I was panic-stricken at the thought. Perhaps Mi Mi and my father were holed up in this derelict villa. Might they already have spotted me from a window? Would they hide from me, run away, or come out of the house and approach me? What would I say? Hi, Dad? Why'd you ditch us? How come you never told me about Mi Mi? I missed you?

How would he react? Would he be angry with me for seeking him out and for finding him when he had so obviously intended to disappear without a trace? Ought I not to have respected his wishes and stayed in New York? Would he take me in his arms in spite of it all? Would I see that light in his eyes, the light I so missed? It hurt to be so uncertain of his reaction. Why did I doubt that he would be happy to see me?

"Mi Mi and your father don't live here." It was U Ba. I hadn't seen him coming.

"U Ba, you frightened me."

"I'm sorry. I didn't mean to."

"How did you know what I was thinking?"

"What else would you be thinking?"

He smiled and bent his head to one side. It was an affectionate look he gave me then, a look that inspired daring. I wanted to reach out my hand to him. He ought to shepherd me past this haunted house, take me home. To safety.

"What are you afraid of?"

"I don't know."

"You would have no reason to worry. You are his daughter. Why do you doubt his love?"

"He left us."

"Does one thing exclude the other?"

"Yes."

"Why? Love has so many different faces that our imagination is not prepared to see them all."

"Why does it have to be so difficult?"

"Because we see only what we already know. We project our own capacities—for good as well as evil—onto the other person. Then we acknowledge as love primarily those things that correspond to our own image thereof. We wish to be loved as we ourselves would love. Any other way makes us uncomfortable. We respond with doubt and suspicion. We misinterpret the signs. We do not understand the language. We accuse. We assert that the other person does not love us. But perhaps he merely loves us in some idiosyncratic way that we fail to recognize. I hope you will understand what I mean once I have finished my story."

I didn't understand. But I trusted him.

"I bought some fruit at the market. If you like, we could sit under the avocado tree, and I could go on with our tale." He hastened ahead with his brisk steps, over to the two young women, who apparently knew him well. They laughed together, looked over at me, nodded, and stood up. U Ba took the wooden bench under his arm and brought it to the tree in whose shadow I stood waiting.

"Unless I'm mistaken, it was your grandfather who built this. Teak. It will last a hundred years, at least. We only ever had to repair it once." He drew a thermos and two little glasses from a bag and poured tea.

I closed my eyes. My father was on his way to Rangoon, and I sensed it would turn out to be a harrowing trip.

# Chapter 2

PLAY DEAD. DON'T move. Hope the time will pass. Don't make a sound. Refuse food and drink. Take shallow breaths. Hope it's not real.

Tin Win sat cowering in the train, unresponsive. He ignored the men's questions until they gave up and left him in peace. The conversations, the heartbeats, of his fellow travelers flew past him unremarked, much as the night landscape flew past the eyes of the other passengers.

The quiet atmosphere in his uncle's house made things easier. No need to change trains or ignore questions. He was alone. He lay motionless on a bed, arms and legs spread wide.

Play dead. He didn't always manage it.

He would weep. He would succumb to convulsions that lasted a few minutes, then slowly ebbed away. Like water draining through sand.

"Please," he said in a half whisper, as if to someone in the room, "please, let it not be so. Please, let me wake up." He imagined himself lying on his straw mat in Kalaw with Su Kyi sleeping next to him. He stayed in bed while she rose. He heard her rattling about in the kitchen. He caught the bittersweet scent of fresh papayas. He heard Mi Mi sitting in front of him sucking on a mango pit. Rangoon was a bad dream. A misunderstanding. Far, far away, like thunderclouds on the horizon, moving in some other direction.

He felt the immeasurable relief it would bring. But already it was gone, flown like smoke before the wind.

There was a knock at the door. When Tin Win failed to answer, there came another. The door opened and someone entered. A boy, thought Tin Win. He could tell by the gait. Men and women walked differently. Men were clumsier, making louder entrances, landing flat on their feet, whereas women often stepped heel to toe, making softer sounds. They caressed the floor with their soles. The boy's steps were very brisk. He set a tray on a table beside the bed. Aroma of rice and vegetables. From a pitcher the boy poured water into a glass. Tin Win ought to drink a lot, he said. After all, he came from the mountains and was unaccustomed to the heat of the capital. After a few weeks of acclimation, he would get along better. Tin Win ought to rest as much as he wished and to call if he needed anything. His uncle was out of the house but would be back for supper.

Tin Win, alone again, sat up in bed and took the tray. He ate a few spoonfuls. The curry was tasty, but he had no appetite. The water refreshed him.

A few weeks of acclimation. Those words, meant to reassure him, sounded instead like a curse. He could not imagine spending even one more day without Mi Mi.

Something was buzzing overhead, a thoroughly and utterly objectionable noise with no rhythm at all, repulsively monotonous. It never relented, grew neither quieter nor louder, nor even weaker. At the same time he felt a faint draft from above. Only then did he notice how hot it was. The gentle breeze did not cool him. The air was too hot for that. Any hotter and it would have burned his skin.

He stood up in order to explore his quarters. He held his breath and listened. A couple of ants were walking on the wall in front of him. Beneath the bed lurked a spider in whose web a fly had just become entangled. He heard it flailing, heard its desperate buzzing trailing off. The spider crept toward its prey. Two geckos clung to the ceiling, flicking their tongues in turn. None of these noises was particularly edifying. He waved his arms and took a step.

Chairs make no noise and have no scent. The back of his hand struck the edge of the wood, and he cried out briefly. The pain shot right up to his shoulder. He got down on his knees and crept through the room on all fours. Tables make no noise and have no scent. There'd be a nasty bruise on his forehead.

Like a surveyor charting new terrain, Tin Win felt his way around every corner of the room, so that he would not injure himself again. Besides the table and chair, there was a large cupboard against the wall. Next to the bed stood two tables, high but small, a lamp on each. Above the table a picture. The two tall, half-opened windows reached nearly to the floor. The shutters were closed. Tin Win tapped on the floor. Seasoned teak. It had that unmistakable resonance. He considered exploring the entire house, but lay down instead to await his uncle's return.

A knocking at the door roused him. It was the same boy as at midday. His uncle was expecting him for supper.

Tin Win set one foot hesitantly in front of the other as he descended the staircase that circled in a broad arc down to the first floor. The reverberation of his steps betrayed to him the dimensions of the room. It had to be vast, a kind of atrium that extended right up to the top of the house. Tin Win heard the boy walking beside him. On the last step he took Tin Win's arm and led him through two more large rooms into the dining room.

While waiting for his nephew, U Saw had mixed himself a soda water with lime juice and stepped onto the terrace to inspect the garden behind the house. A great brown leaf hung from one of the palms. One of the gardeners must have overlooked it, a carelessness that U Saw could not tolerate. He wondered if it was already time again to sack one of the servants. There was no surer way to cure the others of their indolence—at least for a few months. He stepped onto the lawn, bent over, and checked to see whether the grass was evenly mown. A few blades protruded noticeably above the others. He would make the necessary arrangements tomorrow.

U Saw belonged to the few Burmese who had achieved more than modest affluence under British rule. If one counted his business ventures, his foreign real estate, and his disposable cash, he was one of the richest men in the country, aside—of course—from certain Englishmen and a few other Europeans who lived in a world apart, a world that had little to do with the rest of Burma and therefore did not invite comparison. His estate on Halpin Road could hold its own against the most splendid villas of the colonial lords. A house with more than two dozen rooms, a swimming pool, and a tennis court was not to be found on every street corner, not even in the white neighborhoods. Since U Saw himself didn't play tennis, he insisted that his servants do so. Every morning just after sunrise, two of the five gardeners would hit the ball back and forth for an hour, creating the impression that the owner himself used the court regularly. Hence his neighbors and visitors considered him extraordinarily athletic. Besides the gardeners, U Saw employed two cooks, two drivers, several cleaning women, three night watchmen, a houseboy, a butler, and a kind of financial coordinator responsible for the shopping.

Years ago there had been ample speculation about the source of his wealth, but the rumors had died down even as his fortune had increased. There is a certain social status that insulates one from idle speculation.

Of his story, all anyone in the capital knew was that as a young man at the beginning of the century he had moved in Rangoon's German circles. He spoke the language fluently and had risen early on to be manager of a large German-owned rice mill. The First World War had driven the owner and most of his compatriots to abandon the British colony. He had signed his business over to U Saw, ostensibly on the condition that it revert to his ownership upon his return at the end of the war. Two rice moguls had supposedly cast their lots with his, selling their enterprises to U Saw for the symbolic price of a few rupees. None of them was ever seen in Rangoon again. U Saw himself had never uttered a word about this felicitous turn of fate.

U Saw's business ventures expanded in the twenties, and he cleverly turned the Great Depression at the beginning of the thirties—even Southeast Asia felt its effects—to his own advantage. He bought up paddy fields and financially stricken mills, then took over the business of an Indian rice baron, so that he soon controlled the rice traffic from seed to export. He cultivated good relationships not only with his Indian competitors but also with the English and with the Chinese minority. He had learned early that connections hurt only the man who did not have them. As befit a personage of his stature, he made generous donations to the two largest monasteries in Rangoon. He had already commissioned three pagodas in his name, and in the entrance hall to his house stood an imposing Buddhist altar.

In short, U Saw, at fifty, was more than satisfied with himself and his lot. Even the tragic death of his wife two years earlier had not detracted from that. For him, their childless marriage had been nothing more than a partnership of convenience. His wife was the daughter of a shipping magnate, and U Saw had expected the match to lower his transportation costs. How could he have known that the prestigious shipper was on the brink of bankruptcy? The marriage was official but seldom consummated.

U Saw could not claim to have missed his wife particularly. More troubling to him were the circumstances under which she met her death. An astrologer had advised him fervently against a certain business trip to Calcutta. Were he to make the journey, a great calamity would befall his family. U Saw had gone anyway. Two days later, his wife was found in her bed. A cobra lay coiled and sleeping on the sheet. It must have crawled through the open window into the bedroom.

Since then U Saw made no important decisions without first consulting astrologers or fortune tellers. Only two weeks earlier an astrologer had prophesied a personal and commercial catastrophe—U Saw had not really understood the difference, but neither had he asked the man to elaborate—that could be avoided only by assisting a family member in great distress. This admonition had cost him a few sleepless nights. He was unaware of any relations in particular distress. All of them were poor. They always wanted money—that's why he had broken ties with them years ago. But great distress? Eventually he dimly recalled having heard the sad fate of one of his wife's distant relatives, a boy whose father had died. The young man himself had lost his eyesight overnight and his mother had abandoned him. Rumor had it he was living with a neighbor woman who also looked after his, U Saw's, villa in Kalaw. How better to appease the stars than to help a blind boy? He had tactfully inquired of the astrologer whether a donation to a monastery—a generous one, mind you—might not also forestall said catastrophe. It would have involved fewer complications. No? The erection of a further pagoda, perhaps? Or two? No. The stars were unequivocal.

The very next day U Saw had dispatched two of his most trusted assistants to Kalaw.

Hearing voices in the dining room, U Saw went back into the house. He stood thunderstruck at the sight of Tin Win. He had been expecting a cripple, a physically and mentally underdeveloped boy whose plight would evoke pity. But this nephew was a robust, good-looking young man at least two heads taller than his uncle and radiating a curious self-confidence. He wore a white shirt and a clean green longyi. He hardly appeared to be in need. U Saw was disappointed.

"My dear nephew, welcome to Rangoon. It's a pleasure to have you here with me at last."

U Saw's voice irritated Tin Win from the very first sentence. He could not interpret it. It struck no chord in him. It was friendly, neither too loud nor too deep, but it was missing something that Tin Win could not quite put his finger on. It reminded him of the buzzing from his ceiling. And the beat of his uncle's heart was odder yet—expressionless and monotonous, like the ticking of the clock on the wall in the corridor.

"I trust the long journey was not too arduous," U Saw continued.

"No."

"How are your eyes?"

"They're fine."

"I thought you were blind."

Tin Win heard the confusion in his voice. He sensed that it was not the right moment to embark on a discussion of blindness and the capacity to see.

"I only meant to say that they don't hurt."

"That's lovely. Alas, I learned of your affliction only recently, through an acquaintance in Kalaw. Naturally I would otherwise have tried to help you sooner. A good friend of mine, Dr. Stuart McCrae, is head physician at Rangoon's biggest hospital. He directs the ophthalmology department. I have arranged for him to examine you in the coming weeks."

"I am humbled by your generosity," said Tin Win. "I do not know how to thank you."

"Don't give it a second thought. Medicine is making great strides. Perhaps spectacles or an operation can help you," said U Saw, whose mood was improving perceptibly. He appreciated his nephew's obsequious tone. Already it rang with fitting gratitude. "Would you care for something to drink?"

"A bit of water, perhaps."

U Saw poured water into a glass and set it—uncertain how he ought to give it to his nephew—with a loud noise on the table standing beside them. Tin Win felt for the glass and drank a sip.

"I have asked my cook to prepare chicken soup and fish curry with rice for you. I trust they will be to your liking."

"Most certainly."

"Do you require assistance to eat?"

"No, thank you."

U Saw clapped his hands and called a name. The boy returned and led Tin Win to his chair. He sat down and felt the objects on the table in front of him—a flat plate with a deep bowl, beside it a napkin, a spoon, a knife, and a fork. At the monastery U May had once pressed these utensils into his hand and explained that the English ate with such things and not with their fingers. Having already sampled his noontime curry with a spoon, Tin Win had discovered to his astonishment how easy it was to use.

U Saw observed with relief that Tin Win could handle cutlery and that his blindness did not prevent him from eating decorously. Not even the soup gave him any trouble. U Saw had imagined, full of dread, that his nephew might need to be fed every evening, that he might drool, perhaps, or spill his food on the table.

Neither of them spoke. Tin Win was thinking of Mi Mi. He wondered how she would describe his uncle. Did he have chubby fingers? Was he overweight? Did he have a double chin like the sugarcane merchant in Kalaw whose heartbeat sounded similarly flat? Did his eyes sparkle? Or was his gaze as expressionless as the thumping in his chest? Who would help him, Tin Win, decipher this new world he had entered? The doctors? What would his uncle's friend do with him? And would he be allowed to return to Kalaw once they realized there was nothing to be done? With a bit of luck he might be back with Mi Mi by the end of next week.

And if the doctors restored his eyesight? Tin Win had not considered this possibility until now. Neither in the preceding years nor since coming to Rangoon. And why should he have? He already had everything he needed.

Tin Win tried to imagine the consequences of a successful operation. Eyes to see with. Sharp contours. Faces. Would he retain the art of hearing? He pictured himself looking at Mi Mi. She lay naked in front of him. Her lean body, her small, firm breasts. He saw her flat belly and her pubic hair. Her tender thighs, her genitalia. It was odd, but the image did not excite him. There could be nothing lovelier than to caress her skin with his tongue, to touch her breasts with his lips, and to hear her heart dancing ever more wildly.

His uncle's voice interrupted this train of thought. "I have much to do in the coming days and will have little time to spend with you." He set down his eating utensils. "One of the houseboys, though, Hla Taw, will be at your permanent disposal. He can show you around in the garden or even in the city, if you like. Tell him whatever you need. If I can arrange it, we will dine together on the weekend. The appointment with Dr. McCrae is on Tuesday." U Saw hesitated. Had the astrologer prescribed how much time he ought to spend with the family member in distress? He could not recall anything of the kind. To make certain, he would call on him again tomorrow afternoon.

"I thank you, U Saw," replied Tin Win. "I do not deserve your generosity."

U Saw rose. He was exceedingly pleased. His nephew understood propriety. The thought that he, U Saw, might restore the boy's eyesight delighted him. Such a gesture of magnanimity, a generosity that could hardly be taken for granted, would surely not go unrewarded.

# Chapter 3

TIN WIN LAY awake at night and slept during the day. He had come down with diarrhea. The bathroom seemed farther and farther away, and he spent hours on the tiles in front of the toilet for fear he might not manage the trip.

Strange noises mocked or frightened him at every turn. Something was rattling and gurgling behind the walls and under the floor in the bathroom. The spider under his bed had turned ravenous. The flies in their death throes, the breaking of their legs, the sucking and chewing sounds of the spider—it all disgusted him. One morning he heard a snake slithering silently across the floor of his room. Her heartbeat betrayed her. He heard her approaching. Crawling into his bed. Across his legs. He felt her cold, moist body through the thin sheet. She hissed beside his head as if she wanted to tell him a story. Hours later she disappeared through the half-open window. The geckos on the walls were having a laugh at his expense. More than once he covered his ears and cried out for help.

Hla Taw blamed it on the unfamiliar food and the heat. Tin Win knew better. He was sitting on a tree stump. Waiting. Soon, she had said.

He drew a deep breath and held it. Counted the seconds. Forty. Sixty. The pressure in his chest increased. Ninety. One hundred twenty. He started getting dizzy. His body screamed for oxygen. Tin Win did not give in. He heard his own heart stutter. He knew he had the power to bring it to a standstill. Good.

Death appeared in the distance, approaching with long strides, looming ever larger until he stood right in front of Tin Win.

"You summoned me."

Tin Win was afraid of himself. He had summoned death, but didn't yet want to die. Not yet. Not here. He needed to be with Mi Mi again, to feel her again, her breath on his skin, her lips at his ear, the song of her heart.

He inhaled deeply.

He would find out what his uncle wanted from him. He would do what was asked of him and then return to Kalaw as quickly as possible.


Four days later Tin Win stood in the doorway to the terrace, listening hard. It was raining. Not a downpour, but more of a steady, slow rustling and pattering. Tin Win liked rain, it was an ally. In it he heard Mi Mi's whispering, that voice capable of such tenderness. It gave shape to the garden and the house, lifted a veil from his uncle's estate. Drew pictures. The rainfall sounded different in every part of the yard. Beside him the water crashed on the tin roof connecting the kitchen to the house. In front of him it crackled on the stones of the terrace, whose size he could now precisely determine, thanks to the rain. The drops fell more softly on the grass. He could hear the path between the flowerbeds, the bushes, and the lawn. The sandy ground swallowed the water almost without a sound. It struck the large palm leaves, then ran down the stems; it gushed over the flowers, plucking and tearing at the blossoms. He noted that the yard was not flat, that water flowed, barely audibly, away toward the street. He felt as if he had gone to the window in his room, had opened the shutters and seen the grounds for the first time.

As the rain fell harder the drumming on the tin roof surged, and Tin Win stepped out onto the terrace. The water was much warmer than in Kalaw. He stretched out his arms. The drops were big and fat. He felt Mi Mi on his back. He wanted to show her the garden. He took a few steps, then broke into a run. He tore across the terrace onto the lawn, dodged a palm, ran around the tennis court, hopped over two small bushes, raced in a broad arc to the hedge that bordered the property and then back to the terrace. A second time. A third. Running set him free. It released energies that had atrophied in recent days.

The rain wrenched him out of his anxiety; he was more alive with every drop. Mi Mi was with him. Because it was she who had opened his eyes, because it was she, in a very real sense, seeing for him, she would always be with him. All that came between them were his fear and sorrow. U May had told him: Fear blinds and deafens. Rage blinds and deafens. So, too, envy and suspicion. There was only one force stronger than fear.

Tin Win ran to the terrace. Out of breath, dripping with joy.

"Tin Win." His uncle's voice. Why had he left the office early?

"Doctor McCrae has sent word. We should go today. Right now." U Saw observed his nephew quietly for a moment. "I saw you running. Are you really blind?"

So close to the truth, and yet so far.

The examination took only a few minutes. A nurse held his head. A doctor with powerful hands pulled at the skin around his eyes. Stuart McCrae leaned forward right in front of him. His breath smelled of tobacco.

McCrae did not say a word during the exam. Tin Win focused on the beating of his heart and wondered whether he might even infer the diagnosis from it. Its rhythm never varied. It was not unpleasant, merely alien. It sounded even, reliable. As did the voice. McCrae spoke in short sentences that started anywhere and ended just as abruptly, uninflected by rises or dips. Not unpleasant, merely devoid of emotion.

The diagnosis was quick and simple. Tin Win was blind. Cataracts. Highly unusual at his age. Presumably a genetic disorder. Operable. Tomorrow, if they liked.

T he injections were the worst part. They stuck him with long, fat needles above and below his eyes and near his ears. The cold metal penetrated deeper and deeper into his flesh, as if they were trying to skewer him. Then they removed the lenses. Tin Win felt the incisions but experienced no pain. They called for needle and thread and stitched his skin back together. Like a piece of cloth. He wore a bandage around his head for the next two days.

Now doctors and nurses were clattering about with scissors and tweezers, giving one another instructions Tin Win did not understand. They were going to restore his sight, they said. He would feel like a newborn. They would remove his bandages, and he would perceive light—warm, glowing light. He would recognize outlines and shapes, and in a few days, when his glasses were ready, he would be able to see again. Better than before he was blind.

Tin Win was not sure whether to believe them. Not that he mistrusted them or suspected they would knowingly mislead him. They meant what they said, but they seemed to be talking about something else. "What is more precious than our eyes?" Stuart McCrae asked before the

operation and also immediately answered: "Nothing. Seeing is believing."

They acted as if they were liberating him from a prison.
As if there were but one truth. The nurses bade him be
patient but Tin Win wanted to tell them no one need hurry
on his account. If he was impatient, it was only because he
wanted to be with a young woman who moved about on
hands and knees. She knew that one saw with more than
eyes and that distances were measured not only in steps. To
the doctor and nurses, however, Tin Win thought it best to
say nothing.

"There we are." McCrae undid the bandage. He rolled
it up, and with each turn the tension in the room increased.
Even McCrae's heart was beating a tick faster than usual.

Tin Win opened his eyes. It hit him with the force of a
blow. Light. Glaring, blazing light. Not dim, not milky, but
white and bright. Truly bright.

The light hurt. It hurt. It burned his eyes. He felt a stab-
bing pain in his head. He pinched his eyes shut, retreating
back into darkness.

"Can you see me?" his uncle cried. "Can you see me?"

No, he did not. Nor did he need to. The heartbeat was
quite sufficient. It sounded as if U Saw were applauding
himself.

"Can you see me?" U Saw repeated.

Tin Win squinted. As if squinting might filter the pain
out of the light.

As if there were any going back.

# Chapter 4

THE GLASSES FIT straightaway—on his nose, behind his ears.

He was supposed to open his eyes. As if it were that simple. After eight years.

He wanted to wait until Mi Mi was sitting before him. He wanted her, and only her, to be the first thing he saw. He granted them a crack. He peered through them as if out of a hiding place.

The veil was gone. Just like that, the milky gray fog had disappeared.

Everything he saw was sharp and clear. The acuity sent a pang from his eyeballs across his brow all the way to the back of his neck. Doctor McCrae and U Saw were standing in front of him. They were staring at him, proud and anxious, as though they had created the world afresh, just for him.

His uncle's face. Yes, there it was. He saw it.

His eyes closed again. No, it didn't hurt. No, he was not dizzy. No, he did not wish to lie down. It was just too much. Too much light. Too many eyes staring at him. Too many expectations. Too many colors. They irritated him. The creamy white of U Saw's teeth with their brown edges. The silvery glint of the chrome lamp on the doctor's desk. His reddish hair and eyebrows. The nurses' dark-red lips. Tin Win had lived in a black-and-white world. Colors make no sound. They neither bubble, nor chirp, nor croak. His memory of them had faded over the years, like symbols written on a page.

Please open your eyes again. Tin Win shook his head.

"Something is wrong with him," U Saw said.

"I don't think so. It's the shock. He'll get used to it."

Both were right.


T in Win sat on a redbrick wall on the banks of the Rangoon River, the harbor spread out before him.

Open your eyes. He had to remind himself. Ten light-filled days. Ten days crammed with images. Needle sharp. Multicolored. He still wasn't used to it.

Downstream stood leafless trees of steel rattling back and forth on rails. Their hooks vanished into the bellies of freighters to reemerge carrying dozens of bound sacks. Yesterday they hoisted an elephant on board. He was hanging from ropes in a red tarpaulin, waving his legs about. Helpless, like a beetle on its back. In front of the warehouses were piles of crates and casks, destinations spelled out in black. Calcutta. Colombo. Liverpool. Marseilles. Port Said. New York.

Hundreds of boats cruised the harbor. Some under sail, others motorized. In many sat a lone rower. Several ships were so brimming with people, baskets, and bicycles that every swell brought water on board. Upstream, houseboats were homes to entire families. Between the masts the laundry hung to dry. Children scampered on deck. An old man napped in a hammock.

Tin Win watched seagulls glide without a wing beat through the air. He had never seen such elegant birds. It was damp and hot, despite the light breeze that flitted across the water.

Again he shut his eyes. He heard the piston beats of a ship's motor. The wood worms in the wall of the warehouse next to him. The faltering heartbeats of the fish in a basket at his feet. The slap of waves against the hulls. He could tell by the tone whether a boat was built of metal or wood. He could even distinguish different types of wooden planks. These noises portrayed the harbor more vividly than anything his eyes might have taken in. Eyes registered images, a torrent of them. Every second, every movement of his pupils, every turn of his head resulted in new ones. He watched these images, but they did not engage him. He was a curious observer, nothing more.

For minutes at a time his eyes might fixate on the same spot, on a sail, an anchor, a cutter, or a blossom in his uncle's garden. He would touch the object with his gaze, get the feel of it, every crook, every edge, every shadow, as if he could take it apart and put it back together in order to look behind the surfaces, the façade. Bring it to life. It did not work. Seeing something—a bird, a person, a fishing boat— neither made that object more real nor brought it any closer to him. The images before him would lapse into motion, yet images they remained. Tin Win felt an odd distance between himself and everything he saw. The glasses were a poor substitute for Mi Mi's eyes.

He climbed off the wall and walked along the harbor. Was he an ingrate? What had he expected? His eyes were indeed practical in everyday life. He got around more easily, didn't need to worry about running into chairs or walls, or about tripping over sleeping dogs or tree roots. They were tools he would soon master. They would make his life safer, simpler, and more comfortable.

Perhaps the distance they created was the price one had to pay. The essence of a thing is invisible to the eye, U May said. Learn to perceive the essence of a thing. Eyes are more likely to hinder you in that regard. They distract us. We love to be dazzled. Tin Win remembered every word.

He walked along the Rangoon River, past boats and cranes. Around him men carried sacks of rice from the pier into a warehouse. They walked bent, carrying their burdens on their backs. They had tied their longyis up above their knees. The sweat made their eyes sticky. Their dark legs were slender as sticks and their muscles tensed with every step under the weight. Coolies at work. Only when Tin Win closed his eyes did the scene move him. They were groaning. Softly but woefully. Their stomachs growled with hunger. Their lungs were gasping for breath. Their hearts were spent and feeble.

So. He had retained the capacity to hear. He would think of vision as an auxiliary sense. It would do no harm, provided he took U May's warning to heart.

He walked farther downstream, then turned into an alley. The air in it was nearly unbearable. No breeze from the harbor, none of the openness of the avenues where Europeans strolled. Most of the closely packed houses were of wood, with windows wide open. He felt he had descended into the cellar of the city. It was filthy, narrow, loud. It stank of sweat and urine. In the gutters lay rotten fruit, scraps of food, rags, and paper. On all sides people squatted on stools, and benches packed the far-too-slim sidewalk. Many edged into the street. The single-story shops were crammed to the ceiling with goods: bolts of cloth, tea, herbs, vegetables, noodles, and above all rice. Tin Win had not known there were so many varieties, each with its distinctive bouquet. The passersby laughed and chatted in a language he did not understand. Many stared at him as if he was an intruder.

Tin Win wondered if he ought to turn around. He closed his eyes. There was nothing threatening in the sounds he heard. Fat sizzled in the kitchens. Women kneaded dough or chopped meat and vegetables. In the upper stories children were laughing and shrieking. The voices on the street were not hostile.

Nor the hearts.

He walked on, taking in the sounds, the scents, the sights, putting everything in its place, wrapping up the impressions and tucking them away to share them later with Mi Mi.

He wandered from a Chinese quarter into an Indian one. The people were taller, their skin darker, but the air was no better, the streets no less crowded. Another room in the cellar. The cooking smells were more familiar. Curry. Ginger. Lemongrass. Red pepper. The people he passed paid him no heed. Tin Win could not determine from the heartbeats whether he was walking down a Chinese or an Indian street, whether he was among the English or the Burmese. Hearts sounded different from person to person, betraying age or youth, joy, sorrow, fear, or courage, but that was all.

The driver was waiting for him, as agreed, in the early evening near the Sule Pagoda. They drove past lakes reflecting clouds of dusk in light pink.

At home U Saw was waiting for him. Uncle and nephew had dined together every evening since the operation. On that first occasion Tin Win had felt so ill at ease that he had touched neither his rice nor his curry. He had excused himself, blaming the heat. U Saw did not notice his lack of appetite. He had wanted to know what his nephew had done that first day with his—U Saw's—gift. What did you see? Where did you go?

The questions made Tin Win uncomfortable. He did not wish to share his experiences with U Saw. He was saving them for Mi Mi. At the same time, he did not wish to appear impolite or altogether unappreciative. He outlined skeletal impressions as succinctly as possible. On the fifth evening Tin Win noticed that his uncle did not react at all when he repeated the stories from the previous evening. U Saw was not listening. Or he was not interested. Probably both. That made things easier. Same questions, same answers. And thus arose evening after evening a conversation that his uncle invariably cut short in mid-sentence after exactly twenty minutes. Just as he was taking his last bite, he would stand up and explain that he still had work to do. Bidding Tin Win a good night and a pleasant morrow, he would disappear.

Today was different. U Saw was standing in the corridor, welcoming a visitor. They bowed repeatedly and spoke in a language Tin Win did not know. When his uncle saw him coming, he waved him through into his office. Tin Win sat waiting on the edge of a leather armchair. The room was dark. Against the walls books were piled up to the ceiling. On the leather-upholstered desk a fan was blowing hot air. U Saw came in a few minutes later. He sat down behind the desk and looked at Tin Win.

"You attended the monastery school in Kalaw, did you not?"

"I did."

"You know how to count?"

"Yes."

"And to read?"

"Yes. Braille. I used to . . ."

"And to write?"

"Before I went blind I could write."

"It will come back quickly. I would like you to go to school in Rangoon."

Tin Win had been hoping for the train ticket to Kalaw. Perhaps not tomorrow, but in the coming days. The prospect had given him the strength to weather those days and to explore the city. Now he was supposed to go to school. In Rangoon. Stay. U Saw did not make suggestions. He simply announced what was to be done. Tin Win's respect for an older family member prevented him from doing anything but showing humility and gratitude. Only one person in this house asked questions.

"I am not worthy of your generosity, Uncle."

"It's nothing, really. I know the director of St. Paul's High School. You will visit him first thing tomorrow morning. The driver will take you. Actually, you are too old, but he has agreed to test you. I am certain he can help us."

U Saw rose. "Now I must attend to my guest. Tomorrow evening you will report to me about St. Paul's."

U Saw went into the parlor, where the Japanese consul sat waiting for him. He wondered briefly whether Tin Win's gratitude was genuine. Did it matter? The astrologer had left him no choice, anyway. A generous donation to the hospital in Rangoon would not help. It had to be a relative, and it must be a long-term commitment. He had to take the boy under his wing. Besides, had not the astrologer's warnings and U Saw's generosity already borne fruit? Had he not, only two days after the operation, signed his name to the long-coveted contract for the sale of rice to the government? Would not all British garrisons in the capital soon be eating his rice? Even the negotiations for the purchase of the cotton fields on the banks of the Irrawaddy had shown surprising promise since Tin Win's arrival.

Perhaps, U Saw thought, I have brought a lucky charm into the house. He ought to remain in Rangoon at least for the next two years. U Saw might even find a use for him in his expanding business. Why should Tin Win not make a valuable assistant? It was no imposition to keep him in the household. What's more, he always told such novel and entertaining tales at table.

# Chapter 5

Did you hear the birds this morning, Mi Mi? Were they louder or quieter? Did they sing any differently? Did they deliver my message? Last evening I walked through the garden telling them in whispers, and they promised to pass the word along from bush to bush and tree to tree all night long, across the delta and up the Sittang, up into the mountains all the way to Kalaw. They said they would perch in the trees in front of your house and tell you.

And you, Mi Mi? I wish nothing so passionately as that you are well. I often picture you going about your daily business. I see you sitting at the market, passing through Kalaw on one of your brothers' backs, or preparing food at home in the kitchen. I hear you laughing, and I hear the beat of your heart, the loveliest sound I have ever heard. I see you suffering but not discouraged. I see you sad, but not without joy and happiness. I hope I am not deluding myself. Something inside me tells me you feel the same way I do.

Do not be angry, but I must stop for now. Hla Taw is waiting. He takes my letters to the post office every morning, and I would not wish for one day to pass without your hearing from me. Please give my best to Su Kyi, your parents, and your brothers. I think of them often.

I embrace you and kiss you,

The one who loves you above all else,

Tin Win

Beloved Mi Mi,

When I look at night into the sky over Rangoon I see thousands of stars, and I am comforted by the thought that there is something we can share every evening. We see the same stars. I imagine that each of our kisses has turned into a star. Now from on high they are watching over us. They illuminate my path through the darkness. And you are the brightest of all planets, my sun . . .

U Saw read no further. He shook his head, set the letter aside, and pulled a handful of new envelopes out of the stack in front of him.

Beloved Mi Mi,

Why does time stand still when you are not with me? The days are endless. Even the nights have conspired against me. I cannot sleep. I lie awake and count the hours. I feel as if I am gradually unlearning the art of hearing. Now that I see again with my eyes, my ears are losing their edge.

Hearing for seeing? An appalling thought. It would be a miserable exchange. I trust my ears more than my eyes. Even now my eyes are foreign to me. Perhaps I am disappointed with them. I have never seen the world as clearly and vividly, as beautifully and intensively through them as through yours. To my eyes, the half moon is but a half moon, not a melon of which you have eaten half. To my eyes a stone is but a stone and not an enchanted fish, and in the sky there are no water buffalo, no hearts, no flowers. Only clouds.

But I do not wish to complain. U Saw is good to me. I concentrate on school and believe that I can be with you again at the end of the school year.

Do not forget to give my love to Su Kyi, the good woman. I kiss and hug you.

Yours forever,
Tin Win

Beloved Mi Mi,

It is seven months now since U Saw sent me to that school. Yesterday, for the third time, they promoted me to a higher class. They say now that I have landed where I ought to be for my age. No one understands how a blind boy at a monastery school in Kalaw could have learned so much. They did not know U May . . .

Beloved Mi Mi,

Forgive me if my letters in recent weeks have sounded so melancholy. I would not wish to burden you with my longing. Please do not worry about me. Sometimes it is simply difficult not to know how much longer I must be strong before I finally see you again. But it is not longing or fear that I feel when I think of you. It is a boundless gratitude. You opened the world for me, and you have become a part of me. I see the world through your eyes. You helped me to overcome my fear. With your help I learned to face it. My phantoms no longer overpower me. They diminished every time you touched me, every hour I was privileged to feel your body against my back, your breasts against my skin, your breath against my neck. Diminished. Tamed. I dare to look them in the eye. You have freed me. I am yours.

In love and gratitude,

Tin Win

U Saw refolded the letters. He had read enough. Where does love end and madness begin, he asked himself while tucking the papers back into their envelopes.

Why did Tin Win continue to write of the gratitude and admiration he felt for this woman? Even after long reflection U Saw could not think of a single person he particularly admired. To be sure, he respected a few of the rice barons. Especially those more successful than he. He had respect, too, for a number of the English, though recently it had been on the wane. And gratitude? He knew no one to whom he owed gratitude. He had been grateful to his wife whenever she held her tongue long enough for him to eat his dinner in peace.

He looked at the stack of letters sitting on the desk in front of him. His nephew had written a letter to this Mi Mi in Kalaw every day for the past year. A whole year. Every day. Without fail. And all in spite of the fact that he had never yet received a single response. Of course, he also sorted out the letters that came from Mi Mi every day with the afternoon post. They hear and read nothing of each other, and still they never fail to write. U Saw had to laugh out loud at so much lunacy. He tried to contain himself, but snorted, choked, coughed, and gasped for breath. When he had calmed himself, he put the envelopes back in the top drawer and opened the bottom one, where he had been keeping Mi Mi's letters, unread until now. He selected a few at random.

. . . I hope you have found someone to read my letters
out to you. Yesterday my mother came and sat by me
on the porch. She took my hands, looked at me, and

asked if I was feeling well. She looked as if she were
coming to tell me of her own impending death. Thank
you, Mama, I'm doing fine, I answered. How are you
managing without Tin Win, she wanted to know.
He's already been away more than a month. I tried to
explain that I am not without you, that you are with
me from the moment I wake until the moment I fall
asleep, that it's you I feel when the wind caresses me,
that it's your voice I hear in the silence, you whom I
see when I close my eyes, you who makes me laugh
and sing when I know no one else is around. I have
seen the pity in her eyes and said nothing. It was one
of those misunderstandings where words are of little
use.

It's sweet the way my entire family watches out
for me. My brothers ask me all the time if I want to go
anywhere, and they carry me all over Kalaw. I think
of you and hum to myself on their backs. They find
my joy puzzling, sometimes even disturbing. How can
I explain to them that what you mean to me, what
you give me, does not depend on where you are in
the world? That one need not feel the other's hand in
order to be in touch?

Yesterday we paid a visit to Su Kyi. She is doing
well. She would be glad if you would send some
word. I've told her we'll hear from you, we'll see you
again, when the time comes. But you know her. She's
worried . . .

My big and strong, my little beloved Tin Win,

A few weeks ago I started rolling cheroots. My mother thought I ought to learn some craft so that I can one day earn money to look after myself. I get the feeling she doesn't expect you to return. She never says as much, though. Neither she nor my father is doing particularly well. Both have pain in their legs and backs, and my father is getting shorter and shorter of breath. He hardly works in the field anymore. His hearing is also deteriorating. It's touching to see how they're growing old. Both of them are well over fifty, an age that few people in Kalaw ever attain. My parents are very fortunate. They are even growing old together. What a gift! If I have a single wish then it is this: that you and I will enjoy that same good fortune. I want to grow old with you. I dream of it while rolling cheroots. Of you and our life.

The work is much easier than I expected. Several times a week a man comes from town with a stack of dried thanat leaves, old newspapers and corn husks (I use these as filters), and a bag with the tobacco blend. Every afternoon I sit for a couple of hours on the porch, lay a handful of tobacco in a leaf, press it a bit, roll it back and forth between my palms until it is firm but not too hard, stick the filter in, fold the leaf, and cut off the end. The man says he has never seen a woman who can roll cheroots so quickly and effortlessly. His customers are quite enthusiastic and claim that my cheroots have a particular flavor that distinguishes them from other women's cigars. Should they continue to sell so well, we need not have any worries about our future.

It has just started to rain. Cloudbursts always give me goose bumps now . . .

My sweet little Tiger,

I found this butterfly dead on our porch a few weeks ago. I have pressed it. It's one of those whose wing beats you loved best. You once said it reminded you of my heartbeat. None sounded sweeter . . .

U Saw dropped the letter. He stood up and went to the window. It was raining. On the puddles the drops formed fat bubbles that quickly popped.

Tin Win and Mi Mi were out of their minds. Not one bitter word, not even after a year of silence. No hint of an accusation. Why aren't you writing to me? Where are your responses? I'm writing every day, what about you? Don't you love me anymore? Is there someone else?

He was happy that love was not a contagious disease. Otherwise he would have had to fire all his servants and thoroughly sanitize the villa and the garden. He might even have already contracted it himself, might have fallen for one of his female servants—a notion that he refused to entertain further.

U Saw considered whether the letters changed his plans in any way. He was convinced the infatuation would pass. There was no emotion strong enough to withstand the corrosive power of time. Given distance and the passage of years, this love, too, would eventually fall to pieces.

In all other ways Tin Win proved to be extraordinarily competent and useful. He seemed to have deflected the catastrophe foretold by the astrologer. Business was running more smoothly than ever, and that even while the general business climate was deteriorating. On top of everything else, the teachers at St. Paul's High School—far and away the most prestigious school in Burma, incidentally—regarded Tin Win as extraordinarily talented. Everyone was predicting an illustrious future for him. After his graduation in one year he would be accepted at any university in England and would certainly be offered a scholarship, the director thought. The country would need native talent down the road.

U Saw had been flattered, but the war in Europe had him worried. It was going to escalate. The Japanese were advancing in Asia, and it could be only a matter of months, perhaps weeks, before they would be attacking the British colonial government. How long would the English then be able to resist the Germans in Europe? For him it was only a question of time before the German flag was fluttering atop Big Ben. The era of London as the capital of the world was coming to its inevitable close.

U Saw had other plans.

# Chapter 6

TIN WIN HAD imagined the departure of a passenger steamer as something quite festive. The crew on board in white uniforms. Music. Pennants and banners in the wind. A few words from the captain perhaps. Instead, the sailors walked past him in oil-smeared uniforms. There was no band. No streamers, no confetti. He leaned on the railing, looking down at the quay. In the shadow of a warehouse stood a horse cart and several rickshaws whose drivers lay sleeping in their vehicles. The gangplank had long since been drawn up. In front of the ship a few uniformed men from the port authority were still waiting around. Some passengers' relatives were gazing at the black hull of the ship and waving, craning their necks like baby birds. Tin Win did not see anyone he knew. At U Saw's behest, Hla Taw had remained at home. A driver brought Tin Win to the harbor. Two porters took his trunk and lugged it on board for him. They were long gone now.

He and U Saw had dined together the night before, after which U Saw had given him the travel documents. The passport with the visa for the United States of America. One ticket for the journey to Liverpool, a second for the Atlantic crossing. A letter to his business partner, an Indian rice importer in New York who was supposed to look after Tin Win for the first few months. An envelope with money. Once more he had explained what he was expecting of him. At least six letters a year with detailed reports. A college degree. With honors. He had spelled out once again the future that awaited him on his return. He would make him into a manager, then into a partner. He would be among the most influential men in the city. He would want for nothing.

U Saw wished him every success. On his journey, with his studies. Then he turned and walked into his study. There was no physical contact between them. They never saw each other again.

Watching him go, Tin Win wondered how long it took a young tree to establish roots after being transplanted. A few months? A year? Two? Three? He had lived in Rangoon for two years now and had felt out of place the entire time. He had remained a stranger in the city. A tree that might be lifted and carried off by a gust of wind.

At school the teachers respected him for his accomplishments. His fellow students appreciated his readiness to help.

Friends he had none. There was no one keeping Tin Win in Rangoon.

He looked out over the harbor and the city. The golden spire of the Shwedagon Pagoda glinted far off in the late-afternoon sun. The sky was blue, without a cloud. In the weeks preceding his departure, Tin Win had spent many evenings wandering through the city. Along the way he had picked up on the rumors that were sweeping the city like a swarm of locusts in a paddy field. Every lowered voice at every soup stand offered a new one. As if people were living off nothing else. In the Bay of Bengal, the typhoon of the century was brewing, ran one theory. A tiger had swum across the harbor basin and helped himself to a family of five, along with the pet pig. Which, on top of everything else—as if it were not tragic enough in and of itself—was a clear sign of an impending earthquake, as anyone with even a modest confidence in fortune-tellers knew. German warships were blockading English ports, it was said, and, worse yet, the Japanese were preparing to attack Burma. The stars were not favorable for the British, neither in Europe nor in Asia. Burma was as good as lost if the invasion were to fall on a Wednesday or a Sunday.

Tin Win noticed these rumors and in a humble way even contributed to their dissemination. Not because he lent them any credence, but rather out of a sense of civic duty. The prattle meant nothing to him. True, his journey would take him through the Bay of Bengal and into English ports, but he was not afraid. Not of earthquakes, and not of the Japanese. Not of typhoons. Not of German U-boats.

His fear had dissipated gradually. Tin Win did not know when or how it had started. It was a lengthy process. A mango does not ripen overnight. He first noticed it on one of those unbearably hot summer days. He sat bathed in sweat in the park at the Royal Lake. A pair of doves perched in front of him, their heads drawn in, too exhausted to bill and coo. He gazed at the water and dreamt of Mi Mi. For the first time, the thought of her did not evoke in him that crippling, all-consuming longing that would sap him of all vigor. No fear. Not even sorrow. He loved Mi Mi more than ever, but his love was not devouring him. It no longer chained him. Not to his bed, not to a tree stump.

When it started to pour, he closed his eyes. A brief but intense shower. When he opened his eyes again, dusk had fallen. He straightened, walked a few paces, and felt with his whole body that something had changed. A burden had fallen away from him. He was free. He expected nothing more from life. Not because he was disappointed or embittered. He expected nothing because there was nothing of importance he had not already experienced. He possessed all the happiness a person could find. He loved and was loved. Unconditionally. He spoke a sentence aloud, softly, barely moving his lips.

As long as he breathed, he would love her and be loved by her. Even if she lived two days' journey away. Even if she did not answer his letters and he had given up all hope of seeing her again anytime in the next few years. He would live every day as if he had woken up next to Mi Mi and would fall asleep beside her.

"Cast off." The voice of a young officer on the bridge wrenched Tin Win out of his reverie.

"Cast off," repeated two men on the pier. With a splash the lines fell into the water. Black smoke billowed from the stacks. The ship vibrated. The blast of the horn was loud and deep. Tin Win turned around. An old man beside him gazed at Rangoon and briefly tipped his hat, a curious melancholy in his eyes. As if he was taking leave of more than just a city full of people. Beyond him two young Englishwomen waved white handkerchiefs and wept.

# Chapter 7

I REALIZED NOW that weariness had stolen over U Ba's face while he spoke. The creases around his mouth and on his forehead had deepened. His cheeks looked sunken. U Ba sat perfectly still, looking right through me.

I waited.

After a few silent minutes he reached into his pocket and, without a word, produced an old envelope. It was creased and torn, having apparently been opened and closed many times in its life. It was postmarked Rangoon and was addressed to Mi Mi. The address had faded a little, but the blue ink, the large letters, and the oddly extravagant handwriting were still plainly legible. On the reverse of the envelope, the return address: 7 Halpin Road, Rangoon.

There was no way it was my father's hand. I opened the envelope.

Rangoon
14 December 1941

Dear Mi Mi,

My nephew Tin Win bids me inform you that he left the country a few days ago. Even as I write, he is en route to America, where, after his arrival in New York, he will be enrolling in law school.

Occupied as he was with travel preparations during the weeks preceding his departure, it is no wonder he found it impossible to communicate with you personally or even to write you a few lines. I am sure you will understand. He has asked me to thank you on his behalf for the countless letters you wrote him over the past two years. His scholastic and personal responsibilities in Rangoon regrettably left him no time to reply.

Since he does not expect to return before completing his degree a few years down the road, he asks that you henceforth refrain from any further correspondence.

He wishes you all the best.

Respectfully,
U Saw

I read the letter a second time and a third. U Ba looked at me expectantly. He seemed alert and relaxed again. As if the recollection had cast only a momentary shadow across his face.

I had no idea what to say. Unfathomable, how the letter must have hurt Mi Mi. How betrayed and abandoned she must have felt. For more than two years she had heard nothing from my father. She had written hundreds of letters, and these lines were the only answer she ever got. Out there in Kalaw, rolling cigars, dreaming of my father, of a life with him, not even knowing if she would ever see him again, dependent on brothers who did not really understand her. Her loneliness aggrieved me. It was the first time I felt anything for her.

At the start of my journey she had been a name, a first stop on the quest for my father, nothing more. Over time she had acquired a face and a body. She was a cripple who had stolen my father from me. And now? She had been duped and deceived. U Saw's letter infuriated me.

"How did she take the letter?" I asked.

Out of his pocket U Ba drew a second missive, more heavily creased even than the first. Postmark: Kalaw 26-DEC-1941.

Addressee: U Saw, 7 Halpin Road, Rangoon.
From: Mi Mi

Honorable U Saw,
    How can I thank you for taking the trouble to write to me? I am humbled by your efforts. You really needn't have gone to such lengths.

Your letter has filled me with a joy I find difficult
to describe. Tin Win is on his way to America. He
is doing well. You could hardly have sent happier
news. In spite of all his responsibilities and the very
demanding travel preparations, still he found the
time to ask you to write to me. If only you knew how
happy that makes me. Once again I want you to know
how grateful I am that you have honored his wish.

Of course, I will likewise honor his request.

Yours with unfailing respect,<br>Mi Mi

U Ba folded the letter back into its envelope. We smiled
at each other. I had underestimated her. I'd seen her as a
helpless victim, powerless to defend herself against U Saw's
machinations. She was smarter and stronger than I had
given her credit for. And still I felt sorry for her. How lonesome she must have felt. How was she going to get by without Tin Win? How did she survive the long separation from
my father?

"It was not easy in the beginning," said U Ba without my
having asked. "Her parents died the following year. First her
father, her mother two months later. Her youngest brother
joined the independence movement and wound up fighting as
a guerrilla in the jungle. She never saw him again. The Japanese are said to have tortured him to death. Her eldest brother's family perished in an English air raid in 1945. Those were
difficult times. And still—it leaves me almost speechless,

Julia—still she grew more beautiful with each passing year. She mourned her family, no doubt. She longed for Tin Win, too, but she did not suffer from a broken heart. It marks a face forever, that pain, but Mi Mi never experienced it. Her features never hardened, not even in old age. It may seem difficult to understand, Julia, but physical distance or proximity were really irrelevant to her.

"I have often wondered what was the source of her beauty, her radiance. It's not the size of one's nose, the color of one's skin, the shape of one's lips or eyes that make one beautiful or ugly. So what is it? Can you, as a woman, tell me?"

I shook my head.

"I will tell you: It's love. Love makes us beautiful. Do you know a single person who loves and is loved, who is loved unconditionally and who, at the same time, is ugly? There's no need to ponder the question. There is no such person." He poured tea and took a sip.

"I don't think there was a single man in all of Kalaw in those days who would not have taken her for his wife. I'm not exaggerating. After the war, suitors turned up from all corners of Shan State, several supposedly even from Rangoon and Mandalay. Word of her beauty had spread that far. They brought gifts, silver and gold jewelry, precious stones, and sumptuous fabrics that Mi Mi would later redistribute around the village. She turned down all proposals. Even later on, when Tin Win had already been gone ten, twenty, thirty years.

"There were men prepared to die in hopes of coming back into the world as one of her animals, a pig, a chicken, or a dog.

"Mi Mi lived in her parents' house with relatives who looked after her. She tended the stock: the chickens, the two pigs, the scrawny old water buffalo, and the dog. She rarely ventured off the property. She spent every afternoon on the porch rolling cheroots, rocking gently to and fro, eyes closed. Her lips moved as if she was telling a story. Anyone privileged enough to have seen her at this task will never forget the graceful elegance of her movements.

"Her cheroots really did have an entirely distinctive flavor. They were sweeter, with a trace of vanilla that lingered in the mouth. A rumor arose a few years after independence that her cigars not only tasted extraordinary, but also possessed supernatural powers. That will not surprise you, Julia. You've seen how superstitious we Burmese are.

"One evening a widower smoked one of her cheroots. That night his dead wife appeared to him and gave her blessing to the marriage with the neighbor's daughter he had long wished for. Until then, the girl in question had scrupulously rebuffed his every overture, yet when he sat by her porch the next morning to serenade her, just as he had done every other day, she came out of the house, sat down beside him, and spent that whole day and evening with him. Beside himself with joy, the man smoked another of Mi Mi's cigars the next night, only to behold his wife's face smiling encouragingly at him amid the twisting smoke. The next morning, again, the young woman sat with him, and a week later she consented to his proposal. The widower attributed his good fortune to Mi Mi's cheroots, and since then there has not been a single man in Kalaw who has failed to smoke at least one of her cheroots before taking a stroll with his heart's desire. These cigars were quickly adopted as a remedy for all sorts of ailments, particularly for hair loss, constipation, diarrhea, headaches, stomachaches, and in fact for any kind of complaint.

"Over the years Mi Mi became something of a wise woman of Kalaw, held in higher regard than the mayor, the astrologers, and the medicine men put together. People disdainful of astrologers would seek her counsel when settling disputes between spouses, siblings, and neighbors."

U Ba stood up, folded the envelopes carefully, and tucked them into the waistband of his longyi. How had they fallen into his hands? Where did he learn of the contents of the correspondence between Mi Mi and Tin Win? Not from my father, who, after all, knew nothing of Mi Mi's letters. There were many details in U Ba's portrayal of events that my father could not have provided.

"Do you mind if I ask you a question?" I said.

He waited.

"Who told you the story of Mi Mi and Tin Win in such elaborate detail?"

"Your father."

"He can't have been the only one. You describe so many impressions and feelings that my father could not have known about."

"Once you've heard the whole story, you will have no more questions."

"Where did you get the two letters?" I insisted.

"Su Kyi. U Saw visited Kalaw in the early fifties. Fortune turned against him after the war. Or should I say his luck ran dry, which isn't quite the same thing. During the occupation he had collaborated with the Japanese, a fact that endeared him neither to the English nor to the Burmese independence movement. Once the British had retaken the country, a couple of his rice mills went up in flames. The cause of the fires was never determined. In the years following independence there were several assassinations in this country and endless factional violence. More often than not, U Saw found himself on the losing side, a circumstance that cost him a great part of his fortune. He allegedly tried to buy himself an appointment as minister. He came to Kalaw twice for a few days. We suspected things had got too hot for him in the capital. He brought a lot of luggage both times, mostly documents, folders, and files that he left in the house. He did not survive his third visit. Su Kyi found the letters among his effects."

"How did he die? Was he murdered?"

"Some who knew him have said so in retrospect. He was struck by lightening while playing golf."

"Did you know him personally?"

"I met him once briefly in Rangoon."

"You've been to Rangoon?"

"I attended school there for a while. I was a very good pupil. A friend of our family was generous enough to cover my tuition at St. Paul's High School for a few years. I even won a scholarship to study physics at a university in Great Britain. I had a knack for natural sciences."

"You studied in England?"

"No. I had to return to Kalaw."

"Why?"

"My mother took ill."

"Something serious?"

"Old age. She was in no pain, but everyday life became increasingly difficult for her."

"Don't you have any brothers or sisters?"

"None."

"Weren't there other relatives?"

"There were."

I shook my head perplexed. "So why didn't they take care of your mother?"

"It was my responsibility. I was her son."

"But U Ba! Your mother was not seriously ill. You might have brought her over to England after finishing your degree."

"My mother needed me right away."

"Was she an invalid?"

"No, what makes you say that?"

We were talking circles around each other. Each answer upset me more than the last, and at the same time it was clear I was not going to get anywhere pursuing my logic.

"How long did you take care of your mother?"

"Thirty years."

"What?"

"Thirty years," he said again. "She lived to a ripe old age by Burmese standards."

I calculated. "Between the ages of twenty and fifty you did nothing but look after your mother?"

"It kept me quite busy."

"I'm not saying you were lazing around. I, I . . . going to college in England. You would have had every opportunity in the world."

Now it was he who could not understand me.

"You could have done research as a physicist. With a bit of luck you could have landed a job in America." Why was I so wound up?

"I am well satisfied with my life, Julia. Though my wife, whom I loved dearly, died too young. Still, that could have happened to me anywhere in the world."

We weren't finding any common ground. Did he really not know what I meant? Each of my questions left us further apart. I was getting furious while he was keeping cool. As if I were the one who had misspent a life.

"Have you never regretted coming back to Kalaw?"

"I can only regret a decision made consciously and of my own free will. Do you regret that you write with your left hand? What I did went without saying. Any Burmese in my position would have done the same."

"Why didn't you go back to Rangoon after your mother died? There might still have been a chance to emigrate to England."

"Why? Must one have seen the world? In this village, in every house, in every shack, you will find the entire range of human emotions: love and hate, fear and jealousy, envy and joy. You needn't go looking for them."

I looked at him and was moved by the sight: a little man, dressed in rags, with stumps for teeth, who with a bit of luck might just as easily have been a professor with a luxurious apartment in Manhattan or a house in some London suburb. Which of us had lost perspective? Was it me with my demands or him with his modesty? I was not sure what I felt for him. It wasn't pity. It was a curious kind of affection. I wanted to shelter him even while I knew very well that he had no need of my protection. At the same time, I felt secure—cozy, almost—in his company. As if he were shielding me from something. I trusted him. Until then I had thought you needed to know a person in order to like him or feel close to him.

# Chapter 8

MY FATHER AND I are standing on the Brooklyn Bridge in New York. I'm eight or nine years old. An autumn day with a crisp wind that already hints at the cold of winter. I'm dressed too lightly, and I'm freezing. My father puts his jacket around my shoulders. The sleeves are much too long. I'm drowning in it, but it warms me. Through the cracks in the boards at my feet I see sunbeams dancing on the surface of the East River far below. Would my father be able to save me if the bridge were to collapse right now? I size up the distance to the bank. He's a good swimmer, and I have no doubt. I don't know how many times we stood there like that. Often without a word.

My father loved those parts of New York that are really of interest only to tourists. The Circle Line ferries that loop around Manhattan. The Empire State Building. The Statue of Liberty, the bridges. As if he were only passing through.

Most of all he was drawn to the Staten Island Ferry. Sometimes after a full day's work he would walk down to the pier just to take the boat ride out and back. I remember one time when we stood at the ferry's railing, just above the cars, and he said that he couldn't fathom how much the harbor and the skyline of the city had changed. When he closed his eyes he could still see the same image as on that bitter cold morning in January 1942, when the wind was so icy that hardly anyone besides him could stand to be on deck.

At the time I couldn't understand what he saw in the very places most New Yorkers avoided except when they had uninitiated visitors. Later I found it boring. As a teenager it got embarrassing, and I wouldn't go with him anymore. Now I think it was among tourists that he found the distance he needed between himself and the city to which he never really belonged. I suspect these places were his vanishing points when he was beside himself with longing. Is that where he felt closest to Mi Mi? Did he see himself leaving New York by ship or plane? Was he dreaming of it?

U Ba and I walked up the ox trail to the summit. The afternoon was getting on now. The first fires were burning in front of the huts, and the wind wafted the smoke across the yards. By now I had grown accustomed to the scent of burning wood in the evening.

I didn't know where we were going. U Ba had said there was only one place he could finish his story. He had stood up, packed his thermos and mug into his bag, returned the bench, and gestured for me to follow him. He looked at his watch and eased his pace. As if we were early for an appointment.

I was nervous.

"There's not much more I can tell you," said U Ba, pausing for a moment in his tracks. "You know more than I do about his time in America."

There it was again, the question I had suppressed for the past two days: What did I really know?

I had memories, many beautiful and tender memories for which I was very thankful, but what good were they when it came to understanding my father? It was the world through a child's eyes. They couldn't answer the questions running through my mind. Why didn't my father return to Kalaw after the war?

Why did he marry my mother? Did he love her? Was he unfaithful to her with Mi Mi or to Mi Mi with her?

"U Ba, why did my father stay in New York after finishing law school?" I was startled by my tone. It was my mother's tone when she was trying to contain her fury.

"What do you suppose, Julia?"

I did not want to suppose anything. I wanted answers. The truth. "I don't know."

"Did your father have a choice? If he had returned to Burma, he would have had to bow to his uncle's wishes. He was indebted to him. U Saw had assumed the role of the father, and a son does not defy his father's will. It was not Mi Mi that awaited him in Rangoon, but an arranged life. A young bride. A big company. New York was his only chance to avoid that." He looked at me as if he could read in my eyes whether or not he had persuaded me. "It was fifty years ago. We are a conservative country, now as then."

I thought of U Ba's decision to care for his mother instead of going to college. Maybe it was wrong for me to judge him or my father according to my own standards. Was it my place to pass sentence? Had I come here to find my father, to understand him, or to try him?

"He might have come back after U Saw's death." It was a suggestion, an implicit question, no longer an accusation.

"U Saw died in May 1958."

Three months before the birth of my brother.

"Why did he marry my mother? Why didn't he just wait for U Saw to die and then go back to Mi Mi?"

"I'm afraid I cannot answer that question for you."

It was the first time I detected any irritation in U Ba's voice. He was more perplexed than angry. I remembered what my mother had told me before my departure. My father had refused to marry her for a long time. He had warned her about their marriage. Why did he finally relent? Was he lonesome after all those years on his own in New York? Was he looking for solace? Had he hoped she would help him forget Mi Mi? Given everything I now knew, it seemed highly unlikely. Did he love her? It didn't seem so. Not from my mother's perspective. Did he hope he would eventually come to love her? Was the desire for a family of his own finally so great that he faltered?

Maybe he loved her, only she couldn't see it, couldn't believe it, because it was not her style of love.

My poor mother. I saw her hard, embittered face. I heard her cool, cutting voice when my father came home late because, once again, he had taken the ferry to Staten Island. I recalled the days she spent at regular intervals in her darkened room. Chained to her bed by some mysterious illness whose name we children never learned. No one besides the family physician was allowed to see her, not even my father. Now I know that she was suffering from depression. Each of my parents would have been better off without the other.

I felt sorry for both of them. Whatever my father felt for my mother, however much he enjoyed certain hours with us, his children, he was not where he belonged. He was not with Mi Mi.

Was he to blame for having succumbed to my mother's coaxing? Or was she in the wrong for wanting something from him that he could never give her?


We walked on in silence. The path descended gently and took a sharp turn in front of a wildly overgrown hedge. We continued straight ahead, forcing our way through the brush, crossing the train tracks, hiking across a meadow and then turning onto a path that brought us to a rather isolated corner of Kalaw. U Ba led me past several yards in which children played. We stopped in front of a garden gate. The property was well maintained. Someone had swept it recently. There was fresh chicken feed in a trough. Under the porch was a stack of firewood and a pile of kindling. The house, though not large, was in very good condition. On the porch I saw tin pots and tableware. We sat down at the top of the stairs and waited.

I looked across the yard. A eucalyptus tree marked the border with the neighboring property. In front of the hen house was a wooden plank for sitting. In front of that a stone mortar. I looked at the broad stanchions of the porch railing—a child might easily have pulled herself up on them. It took a few moments before the pieces fell into place. I knew where we were. I jumped up and spun around.

I heard my father's breath in the house. I heard Mi Mi crawling across the floor. I heard them whispering. Their voices. I had caught up to them.

U Ba resumed his tale.

# Chapter 9

IT WAS QUIET in the teahouse when Tin Win finished telling his story. You could hear the candles guttering and the patrons breathing evenly. No one moved. Even the flies, sitting motionless on their sticky sugar pastries, had ceased to buzz.

Tin Win had said all there was to say. Now his voice failed. His lips formed words, but they were no longer audible. Would he ever say anything again? He rose, took a sip of cold tea, stretched briefly, and made for the door. It was high time. He turned around once more and bid farewell. A smile was the last they saw of him.

On the street was a truck full of soldiers. Children in green uniforms. The people seemed not to notice them, but still everyone gave the vehicle a wide berth. It had gotten late.

Tin Win tightened his longyi and strode slowly down the main thoroughfare. On his right was the monastery. Boards had broken out of the walls in several places, and the rusted, corrugated tin roof did not look as if it offered much protection from the rain. Only the little bells of the pagoda tinkled as they once had. Coming toward him was a pair of young monks in bare feet. The dust had turned their red-brown robes to gray. He smiled at them. They smiled back.

He walked past the empty marketplace, and at the little train station he crossed the tracks and walked slowly up the hill to where her property lay. He was certain she still lived in her parents' house. He stopped often to look around. He was in no hurry. Not after fifty years. He was not even anxious. The moment his Thai Air Boeing 737 landed in Rangoon all his nervousness had ebbed away, and now he allowed himself instead the luxury of joy. A joy beyond all measure, no longer tinged with fear or caution, expanding by the hour. He had abandoned himself to it, and already it was so vast that he could hardly keep back the tears. Half a century had passed. There he was.

The sight of Kalaw fascinated him. At once strange and familiar. He remembered the aromas. He knew how the town smelled in winter and in summer, on market days and feast days, when the fragrance of the incense filled the houses and alleyways. And he knew how the place sounded. His Kalaw groaned and wheezed. It squeaked and rattled. It could sing and weep. But he did not know how it looked.

He had seen it last as a child, and even then only through clouded eyes. He came to the English Club, in whose empty swimming pool saplings grew. Beyond it he saw the tennis courts, above them the Kalaw Hotel in Tudor style with its red roof. Just as Mi Mi had described it. Somewhere behind the next rise he must have lived with Su Kyi.

He stood at a fork in the road, not knowing which way to turn. Straight ahead or to the left, the steeper climb? For four years he had carried Mi Mi up this path without ever having seen it himself. He closed his eyes. They would be of no use to him now. His legs would have to remember, his nose, his ears. Something drew him straight ahead. Eyes closed, on he went. He smelled ripe mangoes and jasmine. Tin Win recognized the fragrance. This must be where the flat rock lay on which they had sometimes rested. He found it easily.

He heard children playing in the yards, laughing and shrieking. These were no longer the voices of his youth, but their quality had not changed. He was amazed how confidently he moved with closed eyes. When he had tried it in New York he had run into pedestrians, bumped into streetlamps and trees. One time a taxi had nearly run him down.

Here he did not stumble once.

He stopped in front of a garden gate.

The scent of the eucalyptus. How often he had thought of this tree. How many hours he had lain awake at night in New York imagining this fragrance in his nose.

He opened the gate. How often he had envisioned this moment.

He stepped in. Two dogs scampered about his feet. The chickens were in the coop.

Tin Win heard voices in the house. He took off his sandals. His feet remembered this earth. This soft, warm soil that tickled between his toes. He felt his way to the stairs, reached for the railing. His hands remembered the wood. Nothing had changed.

He climbed the stairs, step by step. He was in no hurry. Not after fifty years.

He walked along the porch. The voices were muted now. When he stood in the doorway they fell silent.

He heard people slipping out past him and disappearing. Even the moths that had lately circled the lightbulb flew through the window out into the twilight. The beetles and cockroaches scurried hurriedly into cracks in the wood.

All was still.

He walked over to her without opening his eyes. He did not need them anymore.

Someone had built a bed for her.

Tin Win knelt before it. Her voice. Her whispers. His ears remembered.

Her hands on his face. His skin remembered.

His mouth remembered, and his lips. His fingers remembered, and his nose. How long he had craved this scent. How had he managed without her? Where had he found the strength to get through a single day without her?

There was room enough for two in the bed.

How light she had become.

Her hair in his face. Her tears.

So much to share, so much to give, so little time.

By morning their strength was spent. Mi Mi fell asleep in his arms.

The sun would be coming up soon, Tin Win knew from the song of the birds. He laid his head on her breast. He had not been mistaken. Her heart sounded weak and weary. It was ready to stop.

He had come in time. Just.

# Chapter 10

A RELATIVE FOUND them toward midday. He had already been there once that morning and thought they were sleeping.

Tin Win's head lay on her breast. Her arms were draped around his neck. When he returned a few hours later they were pale and cold.

The man hurried down to town to fetch the physician from the hospital.

The doctor was not surprised. Mi Mi had not left her property for more than two years. She had lain in bed for the past twelve months. He had been expecting her death any day. The sounds he heard through his stethoscope had not been encouraging. He couldn't understand how she could go on living in spite of her weak heart and inflamed lungs. He had offered several times to bring her to the capital. The medical care there, while also miserable, was at any rate better than here. But she had refused to go. When he asked her how on earth she managed to stay alive in spite of her several afflictions, she just smiled. Only a few days ago he had visited her and brought some medication. He had been amazed to see how vibrant she seemed. Better than in the previous months. She was sitting upright in bed, humming to herself with a yellow blossom in her hair. As if she was expecting company.

He did not recognize the dead man next to her. He was Mi Mi's age, presumably of Burmese descent, though he could never have been from Kalaw or the vicinity. In spite of his advanced age, his teeth were flawless. And the doctor had never seen feet so well maintained. They were not the feet of a man who had spent much of his life walking barefoot. His hands were not a farmer's hands. He was wearing contact lenses. Maybe he was from Rangoon.

He appeared to have been in good health, and the doctor could only speculate on the cause of his death.

"Heart failure," he wrote on a piece of paper.

News of Mi Mi's passing spread throughout the region as quickly as the rumor of Tin Win's return had the evening before. The first townspeople were standing in the yard that afternoon with little wreaths of fresh jasmine and bouquets of orchids, freesias, gladiolas, and geraniums. They laid them on the porch and—when there was no room there—arranged them on the steps, in front of the house, and in the yard. Others brought mangoes and papayas, bananas and apples up the hill as offerings and constructed little pyramids of fruit. Mi Mi and her beloved ought not to lack for anything. Sticks of incense were lit and stuck into the ground or into vases filled with sand.

Farmers came from their fields, monks from their cloisters, parents with their children, and anyone too weak or too old to climb the mountain was carried by neighbors or friends. By evening the yard was full of people, flowers, and fruit. It was a clear, mild night, and by the time the moonlight fell across the mountains, the road and the adjacent properties were overflowing with mourners. They had brought candles, flashlights, and gas lanterns, and whoever stood on Mi Mi's porch looked out across a sea of lights. No one spoke above a whisper. Anyone unacquainted with the story of Tin Win and Mi Mi heard it now in hushed tones from a neighbor. A few of the oldest residents even asserted that they had known Tin Win and had never doubted he would eventually return.

The following morning the schools, the teahouses, and even the monastery were empty, and there was no one in Kalaw who did not know what had transpired. The procession that followed the deceased to the cemetery resounded with weeping and song, with dancing and laughter. In consultation with the military, the abbot, and other local dignitaries, the mayor had granted permission to confer in death one of Kalaw's greatest honors on Mi Mi and Tin Win: that their bodies might be cremated at the cemetery.

Since the first light of day a dozen young men had been gathering kindling, twigs, and branches and piling them in two heaps. It took nearly three hours for the funeral parade to make its way from Mi Mi's house to the cemetery on the other side of town.

There were no ceremonies and no speeches. The people needed no consolation.

The wood was dry, the flames greedy. The bodies were alight within minutes.

It was a windless day. The columns of smoke were white like jasmine blossoms. They rose straight up into the blue sky.

# Chapter 11

U BA'S STORY of my father's death caught me off guard. Why? I had had ample time. But what in life can prepare us for the loss of a parent?

Every hour I had listened to him, my confidence had increased. His story had brought my father more vividly to life than my memories ever could. In the end he was so close that I could no longer imagine his death. He was alive. I would never see him again. I sat beside U Ba on the steps, certain they were in the house. I heard their whispering. Their voices.

The end of the story. I wanted to stand up and go inside. I wanted to greet them and put my arms around my father again. Seconds passed before I understood what U Ba had said. As if I had taken no notice at all of this final chapter of his tale. We did not go into the house. I did not want to see it from inside. Not yet.

U Ba took me back to his place, where I fell asleep exhausted on his couch.

I spent the next two days in an armchair in his library, watching him restore his books. We didn't talk much. He sat bent over his desk, engrossed in his work. Examining pages. Dipping bits of paper in the glue. Copying *A*'s and *O*'s. Flouting every principle of efficiency.

The equanimity with which he pursued this routine calmed me. He asked no questions and demanded nothing. Now and then he would look at me over the rim of his glasses and smile. I felt safe and secure in his company, even without many words.

On the morning of the third day we went together to the market. I had offered to cook for him. As I did for friends in Manhattan. He seemed surprised but happy. We bought rice, vegetables, herbs, and spices. I wanted to make a vegetarian curry that I sometimes cooked with an Indian girlfriend in New York. I asked him for his potato peeler. He had no idea what I was talking about. He had one knife. It was dull.

I had never cooked over an open fire. I scorched the rice. The vegetables boiled over, dousing the fire. He patiently kindled another.

Still, he thought it was good. So he said.

We sat cross-legged on his couch and ate. The cooking had distracted me. Now my grief returned.

"Did you think you would see him again?" he asked.

I nodded. "It hurts."

U Ba said nothing.

"Is your father still alive?" I asked after a pause.

"No. He died a few years back."

"Was he sick?"

"My parents were old, especially by Burmese standards."

"Did their deaths change your life?"

U Ba considered. "I used to spend a lot of time with my mother so I am alone more often now. Otherwise not much has changed."

"How long did it take you to get over it?"

"Over it? I'm not sure I would put it that way. When we get over something, we move on, we put it behind us. Do we leave the dead behind or do we take them with us? I think we take them with us. They accompany us. They remain with us, if in another form. We have to learn to live with them and their deaths. In my case that process took a couple of days."

"Only a couple of days?"

"Once I understood that I had not lost them I recovered quickly. I think of them every day. I wonder what they would say at a given moment. I ask them for advice, even today, at my age, when it will soon be time to be thinking of my own death." He took a bit more rice and continued: "I had no need to grieve for my parents. They were old and tired and ready to die. They had lived full lives. Dying caused them no anguish. They suffered no pain. I am convinced that at the moment their hearts stopped beating, they were happy. Is there a more beautiful death?"

"Maybe you need to be fifty-five in order to see things that way."

"Perhaps. It's more difficult when one is young. It was a long time before I could accept my wife's death. She was not old, not even thirty. We had just built this house and were very happy together."

"What did she die of?"

U Ba thought for a long time. "We do not allow ourselves that question because we would so seldom get an answer. You see the poverty we live in. Death is part of everyday life for us. I suspect that people in my country die younger than in yours. Last week a neighbor's eight-year-old son came down with a high fever overnight. Two days later he was dead. We lack medications to treat even the simplest of diseases. The question why, the search for a cause of death, is too great a luxury under such circumstances. My wife died in the night. I woke up in the morning and found her dead next to me. That's all I know."

"I'm sorry."

Neither of us spoke for a long time. I was considering whether I had ever lost anyone I knew well besides my father. My mother's parents were still alive. A girlfriend's brother had drowned in the Atlantic last year. We had sometimes gone with him to Sag Harbor and Southampton on the weekend. I liked him, but we weren't especially close. I hadn't attended his funeral. It conflicted with an appointment in Washington. My tennis partner's mother had recently died of cancer. I had taken piano lessons with her as a child. She had suffered a long time, and I had put off my promised visit to the hospital until it was too late. Apparently death was not ubiquitous for me. There was the world of the sick and dying and the world of the hale. The healthy and hale did not want to know anything about the sick and dying. As if they had nothing to do with one another. As if one false step on thin ice, one forgotten candle, were not enough to pluck you from the one world and land you in the other. An X-ray with a white nodule in the breast.

U Ba took the plates into the kitchen. He blew several times vigorously into the fire, added a log, and put on some water.

"No tea for me, thanks," I called, and stood up, turning toward the door. "Will you come with me?"

"Of course," said U Ba through the wooden wall. "Where to?"


We slackened our pace. I was out of breath, but it wasn't the hill. The incline was gentle enough. We were on the way to the last stop on my quest. I had stood in front of the house where my father died. I had eaten in the garden where he spent his childhood and youth. Now I wanted to know where his journey ended.

"There is no grave and no memorial stone. The wind scattered his ashes in all directions," U Ba had warned me.

I was afraid of the sight of the cemetery. As if I would be admitting that my own journey also had an end.

The scantily paved street gradually gave way to sand, then turned into a rough, muddy track. Soon I could make out the first graves hidden among bushes and dried grass. Concrete slabs, grayish brown, many of them ornate and furnished with Burmese inscriptions, though others lay unadorned and uninscribed in the dust, like rubble from a long-abandoned construction site. Grass was growing out of the cracks in some of the stones. Others were overgrown with briars. There were no fresh flowers to be seen. None of the graves had been tended.

We climbed to the top of the hill and sat down. A desolate place. The only signs of human activity were the footpaths that ran like ant trails through the mountains. It was quiet. Not even the wind was rustling.

I thought of our walks. Of the Brooklyn Bridge and the Staten Island Ferry, of our house and the scent of warm cinnamon rolls in the morning.

I could not have been farther from Manhattan. Yet I didn't miss it. Instead, I felt an almost eerie peace. I thought of those evenings when he would tell me fairy tales. The opera productions in Central Park. Folding chairs and a much-too-heavy picnic basket. My father would not tolerate plastic cutlery or paper cups. He wore a black suit as if he were at the Met. A warm summer night. Candlelight. I fell asleep on his lap every time. I thought of his soft voice and his laugh, his glance and the powerful hands that would toss me into the air and catch me.

I knew why he had stayed with us and why he had returned to Mi Mi after fifty years. It was more than a sense of duty that had kept him in New York. I was certain he had loved his family, my mother, my brother, and me, each in our own way. And he loved Mi Mi. He remained faithful to both loves, and I was grateful to him for that. "There is one more detail that might interest you," said U Ba.

I looked at him inquiringly.

"Mi Mi's pyre stood there," he pointed to a round circle a few steps away, "and your father's over there, about twenty yards farther down. The fires were ignited simultaneously. The wood was dry, and the flames devoured the branches. The air was very calm that day. The columns of smoke rose straight into the sky."

He had told me as much already, and I wondered where this was leading. "And?"

"Then it became quiet," he said, and smiled.

"Quiet?"

"Completely. In spite of all the people. No one said a word. Even the fires ceased to crackle, burning on in silence."

There was my father again, sitting on the edge of my bed. A light pink room. Bees striped black and yellow hanging from the ceiling. "And the animals began to sing?" I asked.

U Ba nodded. "Several mourners reported later that they had heard the animals singing."

"And suddenly—no one knew why—the two columns of smoke began to move?"

"I can personally attest to it."

"Although there was no wind, they drew toward each other until . . . ?"

"Not all truths are explicable, Julia," he said. "And not all explicable things are true."

I looked at the places where the piles of wood and the bodies had been and then into the sky. It was blue. Blue and cloudless.

# Chapter 12

I AWOKE IN darkness. I lay in my hotel bed. A dream had roused me. I was twelve or thirteen years old. It was the middle of the night at our place in New York. I'd heard sounds from my father's bedroom. My brother's and mother's voices. My father was gasping, a loud, terrifying, inhuman sound that filled the whole house. In my white nightshirt I got up and walked across the hall. The wood was cold on my bare feet. There was a light in my father's room. My mother knelt beside his bed. She was weeping. "No," she stammered. "For God's sake, no. No, no, no."

My brother shook my father. "Wake up, Dad, wake up." He was kneeling over him and massaging his chest, giving him mouth-to-mouth resuscitation. My father was swinging his arms. His eyes were popping out of his head. His hair was soaked with sweat. He clenched his fingers. He struggled. He did not want to go.

Again he groaned out loud. His arms moved more slowly. They twitched and went slack. Moments later they hung motionless out of the bed.

The dream had woken me, and I appreciated how merciful reality had been.

I closed my eyes and tried to imagine my father's final hours with Mi Mi. I couldn't do it. I had to admit that this was a part of him I did not know. Yet the more I thought about it the better I understood that I had no reason to mourn. I felt a closeness to my father that I could neither explain nor describe. It was the intimacy of a child, natural and unconditional. His death was no calamity, neither for me nor for him. He had not resisted it. He had taken his leave. He had died at the time and place of his choosing. In the company of his choosing. That it was not me sitting by his side was of no consequence. It in no way diminished his love for me. I fell back asleep a few minutes later.

It was late morning by the time I woke again. It was hot in my room, and the cold shower felt refreshing.

The waiter was dozing in a corner of the dining room. He'd probably been there since seven. Scrambled or fried. Tea or coffee.

I heard the woman from the front desk shuffling across the dining hall. She came straight toward me and, with a perfunctory curtsy, laid a brown envelope on my table. U Ba had brought it early that morning, she said. It was too thick to be a letter. I opened it. It contained five old, hand-colored photographs that reminded me of postcards from the twenties. The dates were marked in pencil on the back. The first was from 1949. A young woman sitting in lotus position in front of a light wall. She was wearing a red jacket and longyi, her black hair up in a bun with a yellow blossom in it. A ghost of a smile. It had to be Mi Mi. U Ba had not been exaggerating. She commanded a grace and beauty that impressed me deeply, and there was a calm in her features that moved me in an odd way. Her gaze was quite intense, as if she were looking at me and only me. Beside her sat an eight-, maybe nine-year-old boy in a white shirt. The son of a brother? He was gazing with earnest mien into the camera.

The pictures, taken at ten-year intervals, always featured Mi Mi in the same pose. In the second one she seemed hardly to have aged. Behind her stood a young man, his hands on her shoulders. Both were smiling in the same open and friendly way, but with a clear trace of melancholy.

In the next picture the years had begun to tell on her, though it did not detract at all from her radiance. On the contrary, I found the older Mi Mi even more beautiful. I didn't know a single woman back home who had not resorted to cosmetics or surgery in a vain attempt to stave off—or at least mask—any signs of aging. Mi Mi looked as if she was growing old with dignity.

Again there was a man in the picture.

The last picture had been taken in 1989, two years before my father's return. Mi Mi had lost weight. She looked weary and sickly. Beside her sat U Ba. I recognized him only at second glance. He appeared younger than now. I spread the photos out in front of me and reexamined each one closely.

My heart was first to sense the resemblance. All at once it pounded so fiercely that it hurt. It took my brain a few seconds to formulate the preposterous thought and put it into words. My eyes flew from one picture to the next. The man in the picture from 1969 was likewise U Ba. The one ten years earlier presumably as well, and the resemblance to the child beside Mi Mi was undeniable. I calculated. I pictured U Ba in front of me. His strong nose. His laugh. His soft voice. The way he scratched his head. I knew who he reminded me of. Why had he not said anything?

I wanted to see U Ba at once. He was not at home. A neighbor said he had gone into town. It was already late afternoon. I walked up and down the main street inquiring after him. No one had seen him.

He had already been to the teahouse. He generally stopped in twice a day, the waiter explained, recognizing me. Today, though, he would certainly not be coming back. Today was the fifteenth. Tin Win and Mi Mi died on the fifteenth, you know, and for more than four years, on the fifteenth of every month, the people of Kalaw held an evening memorial for the lovers. U Ba would be on his way to Mi Mi's house by now. I needed only to cross the tracks and follow the crowd.

There was no missing it. As soon as I got to the train station I could see the procession winding up the hill. Women balanced bowls and baskets of bananas, mangoes, and papayas on their heads. Men carried candles, incense, and flowers. The red, blue, and green of their longyis, the fresh white of their shirts and jackets shone in the evening sun. Halfway there I caught the sound of children's voices. Accompanied by bells tinkling in the wind, they were singing the same melody that had rolled down from the monastery in the mountains a few days earlier.

I would not have recognized Mi Mi's house. It was decorated with colorful pennants. Below the eaves hung a chain of little bells. The yard and the porch teemed with people who greeted me with smiles. I made my way carefully through the throng. Beside the porch the children sat singing, and many of the adults were humming along quietly. Again and again people climbed the steps and disappeared into the house while others came back into the yard. Where was U Ba?

I pushed my way forward, moving with the current up onto the porch.

The house consisted of a single large room, unfurnished save for a bed. The shutters were closed. Dozens of candles, spread out across the floor, bathed the room in a warm reddish-yellow glow. On a shelf near the ceiling stood a large Buddha. Flowers, plates of fruit, tea leaves, cheroots, and rice were piled on the bed, which was entirely covered in gold leaf—the posts, the foot- and headboards, even the slats that had once supported the mattress. It sparkled in the flickering candlelight. Vases stuck full of incense and additional basins and bowls with offerings stood on the floor. It smelled of incense and cheroots. The women exchanged fresh fruit for old, took wilted flowers from the bed and put fresh arrangements in their place.

They bowed before the Buddha, then stepped up to the bed, closed their eyes, raised their hands, and brushed their fingers across the wood. As if they might thus awaken the virus. The virus lurking in all of us.

"Death," U Ba had said, "is not the end of life, but a stage thereof." He would not have had to explain himself to a single person there.

I hung back, motionless, in one corner. Darkness had settled over the yard. Through a crack in the wall I could see that the whole place was now illuminated by candles.

Suddenly U Ba was standing next to me. He smiled as if nothing had happened. I wanted to say something, but he put his finger to his lips, signaling me to keep silent.

# Author's Acknowledgments

I wish to thank my friends in Burma, especially Winston and Tommy, for their generous and tireless assistance with research in Kalaw and Rangoon.

I am especially grateful to my wife, Anna, without whose advice, patience, and love this book would never have come to be.

Jan-Philipp Sendker, born in Hamburg in 1960, was the American correspondent for *Stern* from 1990 to 1995, and its Asian correspondent from 1995 to 1999. In 2000 he published *Cracks in the Great Wall*, a nonfiction book about China. He has since written three novels; *The Art of Hearing Heartbeats* marks his English-language debut. He lives in Berlin with his family.